"A D...
by ...

Their passion for poetry was matched only by their hatred for each other. But what will it take to bring their simmering rivalry to the boiling point?

"Just in Case"
by Sarah Shankman

She always kept a gun on a nearby shelf and a watchful eye on the door. She was always expecting trouble. Then, one day, it finally came.

"www.deadbitch.com"
by Steven Womack

At first, their fights were just about money. Then she went on-line. And now there's only one thing for a hounded husband to do. . . .

"The Perfect Man"
by Dean James

He tried to fulfill her incessant demands; he tried to resist her incestuous advances. No one ever said being a mama's boy was easy.

A CONFEDERACY OF CRIME

NEW STORIES OF SOUTHERN-STYLE MYSTERY

Edited by

Sarah Shankman

A SIGNET BOOK

SIGNET
Published by New American Library, a division of
Penguin Putnam Inc., 375 Hudson Street,
New York, New York 10014, U.S.A.
Penguin Books Ltd, 27 Wrights Lane,
London W8 5TZ, England
Penguin Books Australia Ltd, Ringwood,
Victoria, Australia
Penguin Books Canada Ltd, 10 Alcorn Avenue,
Toronto, Ontario, Canada M4V 3B2
Penguin Books (N.Z.) Ltd, 182–190 Wairau Road,
Auckland 10, New Zealand

Penguin Books Ltd, Registered Offices:
Harmondsworth, Middlesex, England

First published by Signet, an imprint of New American Library,
a division of Penguin Putnam Inc.

First Signet Printing, January 2001
10 9 8 7 6 5 4 3 2 1

Contents

v

CONTENTS

Introduction

Write me a story about the South, your South, any story at all, as long as there's a crime in it.

Such was the assignment for this even dozen of contributors, some of the finest voices in American literature today, Southern or otherwise.

I'm ever so proud to present the results.

Once upon a time Peg Conroy, the mother of Pat Conroy, that loquacious Son of Dixie, said, "All Southern literature can be summed up in these words: On the night the hogs ate Willie, Mama died when she heard what Daddy did to Sister."

And though there's no death-by-livestock within these stories, in fact, only a couple of kitties in the whole bunch, there is incest. Certainly plenty of white trash and tacky behavior. And a gracious plenty of preoccupation with caste and class, which has led more than one Southerner down the road to ruin, if not homicide.

There's also the Southern obsession with history, and the writing and rewriting thereof. You can depend on that from the folks who lost the Civil War, which some even yet refer to as "The Recent Unpleasantness."

Humor, it goes without saying, enlivens these tales, some of which are also knee-deep in morbidity and darkness.

You'll read wonderful language, both colloquial and literary. Southerner writers, of course, have an unfair advantage in that arena, growing up with the words of the King James Bible and the rhythms of Southern preachers drummed into their young ears, not to mention the elaborately brocaded euphemisms necessitated by Southern decorum. God forbid a Southerner should ever say something as simple as "No, I don't want to" or "Give me the money." If they could, their lives would probably be less complicated, less streaked with gunfire, but also far less interesting. Nor would they provide nearly as much fodder for those who record, and embroider, their exploits.

Now there *is* the thought that all Southerners not only sound alike but *are* alike. You'll hear the voices of many different kinds of Southerners herein. Not only is the Mississippi accent different from that of North Carolina or Atlanta, just as folks from northern Louisiana sound nothing like those from New Orleans, but also ex-cons, retired schoolteachers, judges, detectives, bartenders, businesswomen, and reporters all speak in different tongues.

Yet for all the differences in these stories, it's worth noting how many have a strong Southern woman at the center, how many "Steel Magnolias" blossomed herein, regardless of the writer's gender. Whether she overcomes adversity or just plain gets her way with guile or intelligence or flirtatiousness, with arsenic or melatonin, with wheedling or bitchery or honeyed endearments, the "Iron Fist in the Velvet Glove" remains an implacable force. Scarlett O'Hara is alive and well in Dixie, in a ball gown, a shirtwaist, a negligee, or a miniskirt.

All said, this is a truly wonderful collection, which I'm honored to have shepherded and which I know y'all are going to enjoy. it gives me great pleasure to present *A Confederacy of Crime*.

—Sarah Shankman
January 2001

Thomas H. Cook

Thomas H. Cook is a Southern expatriate, having lived in New York City for many years. "I've come to believe," he writes, "that there are such things as geographical transsexuals, people who are simply born in the wrong place the way people can be born in the wrong body."

His Southern roots, however, inform much of Mr. Cook's work, fifteen novels and two works of nonfiction. But it was coastal Massachusetts, where he now lives part-time, that was the setting for his *The Chatham School Affair*, which garnered the Edgar for Best Novel of 1996.

Though J.R. Ballard of "Conviction" is a purely fictional character, the Leo Frank case is a real and unfortunate one. In 1913 Frank was convicted of murdering thirteen-year-old Mary Phagan, even after his housekeeper testified that Frank was at home, having lunch, at the time of the crime, and despite serious inconsistencies in janitor Jim Conley's damning testimony. After Frank's death sentence was commuted to life imprisonment by Georgia's governor, anti-Jewish sentiment ran high in Atlanta, and many

Jewish families fled town. Soon after, a mob stormed the prison hospital where Frank was being held, removed him to Mary Phagan's hometown, and lynched him from a tree.

Conviction

The phone rang at six in the morning.

J.R. Ballard grabbed the receiver squeezed it like a chicken neck.

"Ballard, here."

He'd thought that maybe, just maybe, it being the morning after Confederate Memorial Day, the bigwigs downtown might have considered a slow start. But that illusion died on the back of Eddie McCorkindale's boyishly excited voice.

"Got something Chief Langford wants you to see, J.R."

He meant Newport Langford, Chief of Detectives, Atlanta Police, a polite, well-mannered man, almost courtly, who had, over the years, come to trust Ballard more than anyone else in Homicide.

"And what might that be?" Ballard asked.

"A girl."

Ballard languidly stroked his substantial jowls. "A girl not altogether well, I take it?"

"Dead," McCorkindale said. "White. Thirteen–fourteen. Something like that."

"What happened to her?"

"Beat-up, looks like. Strangled, too. Been dead about a twelve hours or so, we guess."

The "we," as J.R. surmised, was probably McCorkindale and a few other layabouts who, despite their rank stupidity, held to the dream, more of a fantasy, that they might one day be competent homicide detectives. The guess was no doubt precisely that, with nothing to back it up but the thoroughly unjustified self-confidence of those who'd made it.

"In a basement," McCorkindale added. "On Forsyth Street."

"Whereabouts?"

"Over next to the coal chute."

"I don't mean whereabouts in the basement, Eddie," Ballard said crisply, though not without trying to keep the tone of condescension from his voice. "I mean whereabouts on Forsyth Street."

"Oh. National Pencil Company. You know it?"

Of course he knew it, but J.R. let it go.

"We're trying to locate the guy who runs the place."

"I wouldn't even bother with that, Eddie," J.R. said.

"You wouldn't? How come?"

"Because there is a likely suspect," J.R. said. "A colored man who works at the building. He's been in a good deal of trouble before now."

"Colored man? Would that be Newt Lee?"

"No, that would not be Newt Lee," J.R. said, no

longer able to keep the snappishness from his voice. "Newt Lee is a family man. A fine man, by all accounts. I'm talking about the roustabout. Jim Conley." He drew in a soft, weary breath. "Follow me here, Eddie. You have a dead girl in the pencil factory, and you have a colored man of very low reputation like Conley working there. Does the logic strike you?"

"Well, the thing is, nobody's seen another one. Just Newt."

"Well, you ask Newt where Conley is, and then you go get him," J.R. said in a measured, though still not impolite tone.

"Yeah, but what . . ."

'Eddie, please," Ballard said. "Just do it."

"Okay," Eddie said. "The name's Conley, you say?"

J.R. knew he was writing it down, misspelling it, trying again, *Conly, Conlee, Konley.*

"That's right," J.R. said softly. "Jim Conley. C-O-N-L-E-Y."

"Got it, J.R."

"Good," J.R. said. He dropped the receiver back into its cradle, the murder already playing out in his mind, Conley stumbling backward, dragging a girl along the floor, out of breath and sweaty by the time he reached the coal chute, reaching for his battered thermos, munching a banana sandwich. Case closed, he thought.

*   *   *

Confederate Memorial Day had been a cold, drizzling affair, and as he drove down Peachtree Street, J.R. surveyed its sodden aftermath. Drenched battle flags hung limply, dripping water from their tips. Blue and gray bunting whipped about the streets or hung in ragged clumps from trees and bushes. Some of it slumped, wet and soggy, from over doors and fence railings. It gave the whole city a miserable, defeated look, just the opposite of its original intent. The only Lost Cause it brought to J.R.'s mind was the one of finally cleaning it all up.

The National Pencil Company had once been the Granite Hotel, complete with its own theater, the Venable, and J.R. knew that its conversion into a clanging, dusty factory had irritated more than a few of Atlanta's old guard, another symbol of the "Yankeefication" of their city. But most of that sort of talk had died away over the years, replaced by the sort of sentiment J.R. saw on a large red and white poster as he wheeled onto Five Points, "Watch Atlanta Grow."

The National Pencil Factory was part of that growth, and J.R. was perfectly happy with it. He'd been born into a family of hardscrabble tenant farmers in South Georgia, lost his father in the Battle of Lookout Mountain, and had no love for the moonlight and magnolia crowd who ran Atlanta, always "stirring up the ashes," as he'd once put it, of a world their own arrogance had burned down. Thus freed from a poor boy's idolatry for his "betters,"

5

he'd struggled to acquire a certain refinement in dress and comportment, adopted an arch manner of speech he associated with the highly educated, and even secretly come to admire the sophisticated Northerners his rude associates in the Police Department still insisted upon calling carpetbaggers.

Luke Withers was standing in front of the factory as J.R. pulled up.

"Good morning, J.R.," he said.

"Not particularly good for one of our female citizens, I hear," J.R. said. "Have you established her identity yet?"

Rogers plucked the cigarette from the corner of his mouth. "Phagan. Mary Phagan. Worked here at the factory. Mama said she came down yesterday morning to get her pay."

J.R. lumbered toward the door, overweight to the point of being embarrassed by it. To her dying day, his mother had always described him as pleasantly plump, a lie that had signaled a world of liars in J.R.'s mind. After that, police work could not have come more naturally to him.

"Did the mother have any other pertinent information?" he asked.

"Nope."

"And the father?"

"He's a lint head."

"His occupation is irrelevant," J.R. said. "Was he of help regarding the murder?"

Rogers shook his head, opened the door as J.R.

strode toward it. "The Great J.R. Ballard is now on the scene," he announced with a broad grin.

A wall of men in rumpled suits blocked J.R.'s view of the body. John Black and S.J. Starnes, both detectives, along with Craig Britt, a whiskey-soaked police reporter for the Atlanta *Constitution* whose own activities, J.R. thought, were only a notch above the criminals he covered.

As J.R. approached, the wall broke up, and he saw the girl lying on a slag heap, the left profile of her face scratched and torn, dotted here and there with splinters, smudged with coal dust.

Dragged across the floor, J.R. surmised, killed somewhere else.

The other men grumbled greetings as J.R. joined their circle, looking more closely now, carefully observing the white throat, a cord knotted around it, along with a piece of cloth, as J.R. noted immediately, torn from her petticoat. He glanced about the room, surveyed the factory's dark innards, boilers, furnaces, a coal chute, boxes of pencils scattered throughout, some open, spilling out their contents, some tied with—yes, J.R. thought—the same cord that had been used to strangle Mary Phagan.

"So, what do you think, J.R.?" Starnes asked. "Think it's the same one?"

Starnes was referring to the fact that over the last few months thirteen colored women had been murdered in Atlanta.

"Think he's jumped from the quarters to the house?"

Meaning, as J.R,. knew, from black to white.

He returned his eyes to the dead girl, the few parts of her that were visible among the lavender heap of her dress and the soiled swirl of her petticoat. Her tongue protruded from her mouth. One eye was black, swollen. The real wound was at the back of her head, her scalp split open, blood in a dark, sticky wash down her back. The cord around her throat had been wrung so tightly it had bitten into her flesh, leaving a raw, red circle around her neck.

Jim Conley swam into J.R.'s mind, pop-eyed and vicious, a liar and a thief. "Could be," he said.

Rogers laughed. "Newt was shaking like a leaf when we got here," he said. "I had to practically hold him up on the way to the basement."

"Newt had nothing to do with this," J.R. said assuredly.

"What do you make of these, then?" Rogers asked. "Craig found them beside the girl." He handed J.R. two scraps of paper, one white, one brown, then shined his flashlight on them, revealing a crude scrawl. The first read, "he said he wood love me and land down play like night witch did it but that long tall black negro did buy his self."

"What do you think?" Britt asked, pencil at the ready, looking for a quote.

J.R. didn't answer, went on to the second: "mam, that negro hire doun here did this I went to make

8

water and he push me doun that hole a long tall negro black that hoo it was long sleam tall negro I wright while play with me."

"I don't have to tell you, J.R.," Rogers said. "Newt's one tall, skinny nigger."

"He's the night watchman, too," Craig said. "Get it? In the note, I mean. Night witch. Night watch."

J.R. handed the notes back to Rogers. "Newt Lee had nothing to do with this."

Starnes nodded. "J.R.'s right. Newt wouldn't have the balls for something like this."

Britt grinned. "How 'bout the inclination? If that's strong enough, a man can grow the balls."

J.R.'s eyes slid over to Britt, then back to the girl. "Have you located Jim Conley yet?" he asked no one in particular.

"McCorkindale told us what you said about him," Starnes answered. "We're out looking for him."

"Try the rail yard," J.R. said. "Bus depot. He's probably long gone by now, but try them."

"You really think he did it, do you, J.R.?" Starnes asked.

J.R. looked at him directly. "I'm dead sure of it," he said.

Suddenly Eddie McCorkindale burst through the circle. "They found the factory manager."

Starnes laughed. "Why, was he lost?"

"Well, let's go get him," Rogers said.

J.R. didn't move.

"You don't want to come along, J.R.?" Rogers asked him.

J.R. waved his hand dismissively, then returned his gaze to the dead girl.

"Name's Frank, the factory manager," Rogers said, glancing at his notes as he and the other men headed for the door. "Leo Frank."

J.R. was having a cigar, sitting massively behind his small wooden desk in the detective bull pen when Rogers and the others appeared again, Leo Frank in tow, but barely visible as they bustled him among the empty desks toward Newport Langford's office. Watching, J.R. saw only an oily flash of black hair, a glint of spectacles, the gold wink of a cuff link, the rest obscured by a flowing curtain of wrinkled suits.

He blew a column of smoke into the air, leaned back, sniffed, planned his method of approach when they finally dragged Jim Conley into the bull pen. He was still lining up the questions, planning how he'd lurch forward from time to time, plant his huge face directly in front of Conley's, close enough, as he imagined it, for a little spit to hit him in the eye with each question, when the door to Langford's office swung open. It was a crude persona he'd adopted before in such cases, often to hilarious, but always telling, effect.

"J.R." Rogers called. "Chief Langford wants you in on this."

J.R. rose ponderously, put his enormous frame in motion, fat like congealed air around him, forever walking, as it seemed to him, through a thick, invisible gelatin.

The room was hot, crowded, rancid with tobacco smoke. Frank sat in a plain wooden chair, facing Newport Langford. He was dressed in a black suit, freshly starched white shirt, with gold cuff links, a small, skinny man, so short his feet dangled a good half inch above the floor. He didn't smoke, and from time to time he lifted his hand and waved away the curls of smoke that swirled around his nose and eyes. The lenses of his glasses occasionally glinted in the light that fell over him from the high window behind Langford's desk. He cleared his throat every few minutes and sometimes coughed softly into a tiny, loosely clenched fist.

To J.R. the idea that such a man might have anything to do with the murder of a teenage girl was, to use the phrase he intended to use should such a possibility be offered, "patently absurd."

"How many girls do you have working there at the factory, Mr. Frank?" Langford asked.

"About a hundred."

"And you handle the payroll?"

"Actually, Mr. Shiff pays the girls."

"Well, you were paying them on Saturday, weren't you?" Starnes asked, a sudden, accusatory note in his voice.

"Yes."

"What do you pay them, by the way?" Rogers asked.

"The girls make twelve cents an hour," Frank answered.

Black smiled. "What do you make, Mr. Frank?" he asked. He glanced at the other detectives. "In case I ever got interested in managing a pencil factory, I mean."

The men laughed. Frank didn't.

"My salary is sixty dollars a week," he said.

"And you say you've got a hundred girls working for you, Mr. Frank?" Langford asked.

"About a hundred, yes."

"That's a lot of girls," Starnes said. "All young, right?"

Frank gave a quick, jerky nod. "Most of them are young, yes."

"You like them that way?" Rogers asked. "Young?"

Frank looked at him silently.

"As employees, he means, Mr. Frank," Langford added softly.

Frank glanced about nervously. "I don't have any preference, really. As to age. It just happens that most of the girls are young. I think that you would find that in any factory of this kind, that most of the girls are. . . ."

"What about Mary Phagan?" Starnes interrupted. "When we went to your house, you said you didn't know who she was."

Frank tugged gently at his right cuff link. "At first, I didn't recognize the name."

"So you don't know the names of the people who work for you?" Rogers asked.

Frank allowed himself a quick, jittery laugh. "Well, there are so many . . ."

"A hundred, yes," Black said sharply. "A hundred girls."

Frank's eyes darted away, settled briefly on J.R.'s, then fled back to Newport Langford. "Once I saw her . . . Mary . . . I knew who she was. I mean, I recognized her." He adjusted the cuffs of his shirt unnecessarily, twisted his cuff links. "That it was Miss Phagan."

"And you remembered paying her on Saturday, is that right?" Rogers asked.

"Yes, she came to my office."

"On the second floor," Starnes said.

"That's right."

The men stared at him silently.

"She asked for her pay," Frank added. "I looked it up. The amount, I mean. How much I owed her. Then I gave her what she was due."

"And she left?" Starnes asked.

"Yes."

"And you stayed put," Black said.

"At my desk."

"For how long?" Rogers asked.

"At least two hours."

The questions and answers continued, J.R. listening

idly, glancing out into the bull pen from time to time, hoping to see McCorkindale or some other uniform escort Jim Conley into the room. He'd learned by then that Newt Lee was denying everything, claiming that the murder was being "put off" on him. He thought of the notes Craig Britt had found beside the body, the low, subliterate writing scrawled on them.

"Let's get back to Mary for a moment, Mr. Frank," Langford said.

Frank fingered a gold cuff link.

"Had she ever been in your office before?"

"Not that I recall."

"What about the other girls?" Starnes asked. "Were they in the habit of coming up to the second floor?"

Frank looked at Langford quizzically, then turned back to Starnes. "In the habit?"

"Did you bring these girls up to your office on a regular basis?" Black snapped.

"I never brought them up," Frank said.

"Well, they been seen up there," Rogers told him.

"To get their pay," Frank replied.

"Do they ever come up there just to see you?" Starnes asked.

"Me?"

"Pay a call, you might say."

"No."

"No girl ever comes up there alone?" Black asked doubtfully.

"To get her pay, she might," Frank said.

14

"Never for anything else?" Starnes asked.

Frank shook his head.

"How about Mary Phagan," Langford said. "Had Mary ever been in your office before yesterday afternoon, Mr. Frank?"

Frank's right hand moved from his lap to his left cuff link. "Not that I recall. No."

"Well, you would recall it, wouldn't you?" Starnes asked. "If she'd come up there before?"

"Not necessarily," Frank answered. "I mean, I have . . ."

"A hundred girls, yeah, we know," Black said sharply. He looked knowingly at the other men. "We've heard all about it."

Frank lowered his eyes, and for a moment J.R. tried to read the gesture. Embarrassment? Fear? Something else? The notes returned to him. He tried to imagine Conley writing them in the shadowy corner of the basement, hunched, apelike, over Mary Phagan's dead body, dabbing the tip of the pencil on his thick red tongue, eyes rolling toward the ceiling as he tried to figure out exactly what he should "wright."

"You're not from around here, are you, Mr. Frank?"

It was Starnes going at him again.

"I was born in Texas," Frank said.

"Texas?" Black asked. "You don't sound like you're from Texas."

"My family moved to Brooklyn when I was a baby," Frank said. He offered a quick, nervous smile.

"My wife was born here in Atlanta, though. A native. Her father is head of the B'nai B'rith."

"What's that?" Starnes asked.

Frank's smile vanished. "An association."

"Of what?"

Frank grabbed his knees, squeezed. "Of Jews," he said, glancing about. "Of Jewish people."

Langford nodded softly. "How long did you live in Brooklyn, Mr. Frank?"

"Until I graduated from college."

"What did you study, may I ask?"

"Mechanical engineering."

J.R. felt something shift in his mind. Could the notes have been planted by someone else? Someone a lot smarter than Conley? Able to figure out a double insinuation, put the murder on an inferior being, Conley, by making it seem that he, Conley, had tried to implicate a second inferior being. Newt. Knowing all the time that Newt would never fit the bill, but that Conley would. He smiled at the idea of such a scheme. Clever, he thought.

"Normally, you wouldn't have been at the factory on a Saturday, is that right, Mr. Frank?"

It was Langford asking, softly, politely, always adding, "Mr. Frank" at the end of it.

"No," Frank said. "I wouldn't have been there at all if it hadn't been raining."

"Why's that?" Rogers asked.

"I'd planned to go to a baseball game with my brother-in-law."

16

Starnes smiled. "Baseball? You like baseball?"

Frank looked at him. "Why does that surprise you?"

Starnes' face turned grim. "Who was playing?"

Frank shifted slightly. "Well, the Atlanta team, I believe."

"The Crackers," Black said.

"Yes."

"Who were they playing?" Starnes asked. "Who were the Crackers playing yesterday?"

Frank was silent for a moment, then shook his head. "I don't . . ."

Starnes smiled thinly. "Birmingham," he said. "The Birmingham Barons."

Frank shrugged. "I . . ."

Langford leaned forward, his eyes boring into Frank now. "Mr. Frank, one thing bothers me. Why did you call Newt Lee down at the factory on Saturday afternoon?"

Before he could answer, Starnes leaned forward. "After you'd left. Two hours after you'd left."

"I wanted to make sure everything was all right at the factory."

"Why wouldn't it be?" Rogers asked.

"Well, Newt is new at the factory, and so . . ."

"He was even newer last Saturday," Starnes said. "But you didn't call him then."

Frank shrugged. "I just wanted to check on things."

"On Mary Phagan?" Black asked.

Frank stared at him quizzically, one hand drifting toward the left cuff, tugging at the cuff link. "Mary Phagan? Why would I . . ."

"Maybe you wanted to find out if anybody had found her yet," Rogers asked starkly. "Is that why you called Newt?"

Frank shook his head. "Of course not," he said, then went on, sputtering. "I had no idea that anything had . . . that-that Miss Phagan was . . . no idea."

J.R. eased his weight from the wall, watching Frank's hands, something he'd noticed, the way his slender, delicate fingers toyed with the gold cuff links each time he heard Mary Phagan's name. He thought of the notes again, how cleverly they'd been constructed, pointing at guilt by pointing away from guilt, which pointed back to guilt again. He wondered if Conley could ever have hatched such a scheme. He was smart, but was he that smart? He considered the nature and scope of Conley's intelligence, both his shrewdness and its limits. His shrewdness would inform him of his limits. Which meant, J.R. reasoned, that since Conley was smart, he'd know better than to get himself mixed up in a contest of mind with a mechanical engineer. He would know that he could never outsmart so superior a person. This, J.R. reasoned, was an argument that worked both ways. For just as surely, Leo Frank would know that he could outsmart Conley. This logic applied with telling force, J.R. mused, on the notes Britt had found on the factory floor. For although Conley would know that he could never hope to write like Leo Frank, Frank would no less clearly perceive that he, Frank, could quite easily imitate the crude sublanguage of such a brute as Jim Conley.

"You must admit, Mr. Frank, that that call is somewhat of a problem," Langford said.

Frank stared at him silently.

"It seems out of character, you see," Langford explained politely.

Frank's eyes took on a strange, animal agitation. "Out of character? In what way?"

"In that a man like you, Mr. Frank," Langford said, "if you'll permit my saying so"—he tapped the side of his head—"a man like you has a reason for everything he does."

Frank started to answer, but the door to Langford's office swung open suddenly, and Luther Rosser strode in.

"I'm Mr. Frank's lawyer," he declared. "There will be no more questioning of my client without my being present."

Langford stood up slowly, shook hands with Rosser, then let his gaze drift down to where Frank sat, completely still, in his chair. "You may go, Mr. Frank," he said. He smiled at Rosser. "I'll walk you to your car, Luther," he added brightly.

The detectives shifted about, muttering, then drifted away from Frank, giving him room to straighten himself, watching silently as he buttoned his coat, adjusted his tie. Then Frank turned and headed for the door, J.R. standing massively in his path, so that he slowed suddenly, as if a great stone had suddenly rolled into his path.

J.R. stood in place for only the briefest moment, then shifted to the right, cleared the way. "Thank you for coming in, Mr. Frank," he said.

Frank read something in his gaze. "I didn't kill Mary Phagan."

J.R. smiled. "Better straighten your cuff links," he said.

For an instant their eyes locked. Then Rosser took Frank's arm, urged him forward. "Let's go, Leo," he told him.

J.R. watched as the three men, Langford somewhat in the lead, made their way across the empty bull pen to the stairs. Once they'd gone through the double doors, become mere blurs behind its frosted glass, he stepped over to the window and looked out. A black car rested at the curb, its chrome fenders shimmering even in the gray light. Briefly, the three men stood in a tight circle, talking amicably. Then the conversation ended, and Rosser opened the car's back door to let Frank in.

The other detectives had joined J.R. at the window by then. "What do you think, J.R.?" Rogers asked.

J.R. turned from the window just as McCorkindale walked into the bull pen, Jim Conley at his side. He watched as McCorkindale led Conley to a chair, cuffed him to it, then walked away, leaving Conley alone, staring about. J.R. peered at him closely, noted the thick neck, the small, curled ears and popped brown eyes, the way, when he caught J.R. watching him, he offered up a wide, gap-toothed grin.

Very low, J.R. thought, as he turned back to the window, his gaze now on Leo Frank once again.

"Langford will ask you first," Starnes said. "It's probably up to you, J.R. If you say he's clear, he's clear."

Below, Frank stood for a moment in the clear, clean air, gazing about, as if in melancholy appreciation, like someone saying good-bye to something he'd never noticed before, but held precious now.

"Well," Black asked. "Did Frank do it?"

Gold cuff links winked in the sunlight.

"What do you think, J.R.?"

Truth dawned as it always did in J.R.'s mind, clean and bracing, fresh as a bright new day.

"Dead sure," he said.

Jeffery Deaver

The internationally bestselling author of thirteen suspense novels, Jeffery Deaver has been nominated for three Edgar awards and is a two-time recipient of the Ellery Queen Reader's Award for Best Short Story of the Year. His book *A Maiden's Grave* was made into an HBO movie, and *The Bone Collector* is a feature release from Universal Pictures. His latest novel, *The Empty Chair*, is a Lincoln Rhyme thriller set in North Carolina.

It was only five years ago that Mr. Deaver cast his eyes southward. Born outside of Chicago, a resident of Manhattan for twenty years (on the southern part of the island, for what it's worth) he moved to Virginia five years ago to research a book and decided to stay. The Commonwealth of Virginia is pleased to claim the eloquent Mr. Deaver as an adopted Son of the South who, as "The Widow of Pine Creek" will evidence, has learned the nuances of the behavior of a particular breed of Southern belle very well, thank you kindly.

The Widow of Pine Creek

"Sometimes help just appears from the sky."

This was an expression of her mother's, and it didn't mean angels or spirits or any of that New Age stuff, which the old lady never had any patience for, but meant "from thin air"—when you were least expecting it.

Okay, Mama, let's hope. 'Cause I can use some help now. Can use it bad.

Sandra May DuMont leaned back in a black leather office chair and let papers in her hand drop onto the old desk that dominated her husband's office. As she looked out the window, she wondered if she was looking at that help right now.

Not exactly appearing from the sky—but walking up the cement walk to the factory, slowly through the dank Georgia spring air.

She turned away and caught sight of herself in the antique mirror she'd bought for her husband ten years ago, on their fifth anniversary. Today, she had only a brief memory of that happier day; what she concentrated on now was her image: a large woman, though not fat. Quick green eyes. She was wearing an off-white dress, imprinted with blue cornflowers. Sleeveless—this *was* Georgia in Mid-May—revealing sturdy upper arms. Her long hair was dark blond and was pulled back and fixed with a matter-of-fact tortoiseshell barrette. Just a touch of makeup. No perfume. She was thirty-eight but, funny thing, she'd come to realize, her weight made her look younger.

By rights she should be feeling calm and self-assured. But she wasn't. Her eyes went to the papers in front of her again.

No, she wasn't feeling that way at all.

She needed help.

From the sky.

Or from anywhere.

The intercom buzzed, startling her though she was expecting the sound. It was an old-fashioned model, brown plastic, with a dozen buttons. It had taken her some time to figure out how it worked. She pushed a button. "Yes?"

"Mrs. DuMont, there's a Mr. Rawl here."

"Good. Send him in, Loretta."

The door opened and a man stepped inside. He said, "Hi, there."

"Hey," Sandra May responded as she stood automatically, recalling that in the rural South women rarely stood to greet men. And thinking too: How my life has changed in the last six months.

She noticed, as she had when she'd met him last weekend, that Bill Rawl wasn't really a handsome man. His face was angular, his black hair unruly, and though he was thin he didn't seem to be in particularly good shape.

And that accent! Last Sunday, as they'd stood on the deck of what passed for a country club in Pine

Creek, he'd grinned and said, "How's it going? I'm Bill Rawl. I'm from New York."

As if the nasal tone in his voice hadn't told her already.

And 'how's it going?' Well, that was hardly the sort of greeting you heard from the locals (the "Pine Creekers," Sandra May called them, though only to herself).

"Come on in," she said to him now. She walked over to the couch, gestured with an upturned palm for him to sit across from her. As she walked, Sandra May kept her eyes in the mirror, focused on his, and she observed that he never once glanced at her body. That was good, she thought. He passed the first test. He sat down and examined the office and the pictures on the wall, most of them of Jim on hunting and fishing trips.

She thought again of that day just before Halloween, the state trooper's voice on the other end of the phone, echoing with a sorrowful hollowness.

"Mrs. DuMont . . . I'm very sorry to tell you this. It's about your husband. . . ."

No, don't think about that now. Concentrate. You're in bad trouble, girl, and this might be the only person in the world who can help you.

Sandra May's first impulse was to get Rawl coffee or tea. But then she stopped herself. She was now president of the company, and she had employees for that sort of thing. Old traditions die hard—more

26

words from Sandra May's mother, who was proof incarnate of the adage.

"Would you like something? Iced tea?"

He laughed. "You folks sure drink a lot of iced tea down here."

"That's the South for you."

"Sure. Love some."

She called Loretta, Jim's longtime secretary and the office manager.

The pretty woman—who, it seemed, must spend two hours putting on her makeup every morning—stuck her head in the door. "Yes, Mrs. DuMont?"

"Could you bring us some iced tea, please?"

"Be happy to."

"Thank you, Loretta."

The woman disappeared, leaving a cloud of flowery perfume behind her. Rawl was smiling. "Everybody's sure polite in Pine Creek. Takes a while for a New Yorker to get used to it."

"I'll tell you, Mr. Rawl—"

"Bill, please."

"Bill . . . It's second nature down here. Being polite. My mother said a person should put on their manners every morning the way they put on their clothes."

He smiled at the homily.

And speaking of clothes. . . . Sandra May didn't know what to think of his. Bill Rawl was dressed . . . well, *Northern*. That was the only way to describe it. Black suit and a dark shirt. No tie. Just the opposite of Jim—who wore brown slacks, a powder-blue shirt and a tan sports coat as if the outfit were a mandatory uniform.

"That's your husband?" he asked, looking at the pictures on the wall.

"That's Jim, yes," she said softly.

"Nice-looking man. Can I ask what happened?"

She hesitated for a minute and Rawl picked up on it immediately.

"I'm sorry," he said, "I shouldn't've asked. It's—"

But she interrupted. "No, it's all right. I don't mind talking about it. A fishing accident last fall. At Billings Lake. He fell in, hit his head and drowned."

"Man, that's terrible. Were you there when it happened?"

Laughing hollowly, she said, "I wish I had been. I probably could've saved his life. But, no, I only went with him once or twice. But fishing's so . . . messy. You hook the poor thing, you hit it over the head with a club, you cut it up. . . . Besides, I guess you don't know the Southern protocol. Wives don't fish." She gazed up at some of the pictures. Said reflectively, "Jim was only forty-seven. I guess when you're married to someone and you think about them dying, you think it'll be when they're old. My mother died when she was eighty. And my father passed away when he was eighty-one. They were together for fifty-eight years."

"That's wonderful."

"Happy, faithful, devoted," she said wistfully.

Loretta brought the tea and vanished again with the demure exit of a discreet servant.

"So," he said, pouring sugar into his tea, "I'm delighted the attractive woman I picked up so suavely actually gave me a call."

"You Northern boys are pretty straightforward, aren't you?"

"You betcha," he said.

"Well, I hope it's not going to be a blow to your ego when I tell you that I asked you here for a purpose."

"Depends on what that purpose is."

"Business," Sandra May said.

"Business is a good start," he said. Then he nodded for her to continue.

"I inherited all the stock in the company when Jim died, and I became president. I've been trying to run things the best I can, but the way I see it"—she nodded to where the accountant's reports sat on the desk—"unless things improve pretty damn fast, we'll be bankrupt within the year. I got a bit of insurance money when Jim died, so I'm not going to starve, but I refuse to let something my husband built up from scratch go under."

"Why do you think I can help you?" The smile was still there but it had less flirt than it had a few minutes ago—and a lot less than last Sunday.

"My mother had this saying. 'A Southern woman has to be a notch stronger than her man.' Well, I am *that*, I promise you."

"I can see," Rawl said.

"She also said, 'She has to be a notch more resourceful too.' Now, before I married Jim, I had three and a half years of college. I was planning on a career of my own. But I'm in over my head here. I need somebody to help me. Somebody who knows about business. After what you were telling me on Sunday, at the club, I think you'd be just the man for that."

When they'd met—well, Rawl *had* tried to pick her up at the Pine Creek Club—he'd explained that he was a banker and broker. He'd buy small, troubled businesses, turn them around and sell them for a profit. He'd been in Atlanta on business, and somebody had recommended he look into real estate in northeast Georgia, here in the mountains, where you could still get good bargains on investment and vacation property.

"Tell me about the company," he said to her now.

She explained that DuMont Products, with sixteen full-time employees and a gaggle of high school boys in the summer, bought crude turpentine from local foresters who tapped longleaf and slash pine trees for the substance.

"Turpentine . . . That's what I smelled driving up here."

After Jim started the company some years ago, Sandra May would lie in bed next to his sleeping form, smelling the oily resin—even if he'd showered. It never seemed to leave him. Finally she'd gotten used to it. She sometimes wondered exactly when she'd stopped noticing the scent.

She continued, telling Rawl, "Then we distill the raw turpentine into a couple different products. Mostly for the medical market."

"Medical?" he asked, surprised. He took his jacket off and draped it carefully on the chair next to him. Drank more iced tea. He really seemed to enjoy it. She thought New Yorkers only drank wine and bottled water.

"People think it's just a paint thinner. But doctors use it a lot. It's a stimulant and antispasmodic."

"Didn't realize that," he said. She noticed that he'd started to take notes. And that the flirtatious smile was gone completely.

"Jim sells . . ." Her voice faded. "He *sold* the refined turpentine to a couple of jobbers. They handle all the distribution. We don't get into that. Our sales seems to be the same as ever. Our costs haven't gone up. But we don't have as much money as we ought to. I don't know where it's gone and I have payroll taxes and unemployment insurance due next month."

She walked to the desk and handed him several accounting statements. Even though they were a mystery to her he pored over them knowingly, nodding. Once or twice he lifted his eyebrow in surprise. She suppressed an urge to ask a troubled, "What?"

Sandra May found herself studying him closely. Without the smile—and with this businesslike concentration on his face—he was much more attractive. Involuntarily she glanced at her wedding picture on the credenza. Then her eyes fled back to the documents in front of them.

Finally he sat back, finished his iced tea. "There's something funny," he said. "I don't understand it. There've been some transfers of cash out of the main accounts, but there's no record of where the money went. Did your husband mention anything to you about it?"

"He didn't tell me very much about the company. Jim didn't mix business and his home life."

"How about your accountant?"

"Jim did most of the books himself. . . . This money? Can you track it down? Find out what happened? I'll pay whatever your standard fee is."

"I might be able to."

She heard a hesitancy in his voice. She glanced up. He said, "Let me ask you a question first."

"Go ahead."

"Are you sure you *want* me to go digging?"

"How do you mean?" she asked.

His sharp eyes scanned the accounting sheets as if they were battlefield maps. "You know you could hire somebody to run the company. A professional businessman or woman. It'd be a hell of a lot less hassle for you. Let him or her turn the company around."

She kept her eyes on him. "But you're not asking me about hassles, are you?"

After a moment he said, "No, I'm not. I'm asking if you're sure you want to know anything more about your husband and his company than you do right now."

"But it's *my* company now," she said. "And I want to know everything. Now, all the company's books are over there." She pointed to a large, walnut credenza. It was the piece of furniture atop which sat their wedding picture.

Do you promise to love, honor, cherish and obey . . .

As he turned to see where she was pointing, Rawl's knee brushed hers. Sandra May felt a brief electrical jolt. He seemed to freeze for a moment. Then he turned back.

"I'll start tomorrow," he said.

With the evening orchestra of crickets and cicadas around her, Sandra May sat on the porch of their house. No, *her* house. It was so strange to think of it that way. No longer *their* cars, *their* furniture, *their* china. Hers alone now.

Her desk, her company.

She rocked back and forth in the swing, which she'd installed a year ago, screwing the heavy hooks into the ceiling joists herself. She looked out over the acres of trim grass, boarded by loblolly and hemlock. Pine Creek, population sixteen hundred, had trailers and bungalows, a few shotgun apartment buildings and a couple of modest subdivisions, but only a dozen or so houses like this—modern, glassy, huge.

If the Georgia-Pacific had run through town, then the pristine development where Jim and Sandra May DuMont had settled would have defined which was the right side of the tracks.

She sipped her iced tea and smoothed her denim jumper. Watched the yellow flares from a half dozen early fireflies.

I think he's the one can help us, Mama, she thought.

Appearing from the sky. . . .

Bill Rawl had been coming to the company for the past three days. He'd thrown himself into the job of saving DuMont Products Inc. When she'd left the office tonight at six he'd been working since early morning, reading through the company's records and Jim's correspondence and diary. He'd called her at home a half hour ago, telling her he'd found something she ought to know about.

"Come on over," she'd told him.

"Your house, you mean?"

"Sure." She'd laughed.

"Be right there."

Now, as he parked in front of the house, she noticed shadows appear in the bay windows of houses across the street. Her neighbors, Beth and Sally, checking out the activity.

So, the widow's got a man friend come a-calling . . .

She heard the crunching of the gravel before she could see Rawl approach through the dusk.

34

"Hey," she said.

"You all really do say that," he said. "Hey."

"You bet. Only it's 'y'all.' Not 'you all.'"

"Stand corrected, ma'am."

"You Yankees."

Rawl sat down on the swing. He'd Southernized himself a bit. Tonight he wore jeans and a dark shirt. And, my Lord, boots. He looked like one of the boys at a roadside tap, escaping from the wife for the night to drink beer with his buddies and to flirt with girls pretty and playful as Loretta.

"Brought some wine," he said.

"Well. How 'bout that."

"I love your accent," he said.

"Hold on—*you're* the one with an accent."

In a thick Mafioso drawl: "You, forgeddaboutit. I don't got no accent." They laughed. He pointed to the horizon. "Hey, look at that moon."

"No cities around here, no lights. You can see the stars clear as your conscience."

He poured some wine. He'd brought paper cups and a corkscrew.

"Oh, hey, slow up there." Sandra May held up a hand. "I haven't had much to drink since . . . Well, after the accident I decided it'd be better if I kept a pretty tight rein on things."

"Just drink what you want," he assured her. "We'll water the geranium with the rest."

"That's a bougainvillea."

"Oh. I'm a city boy, remember." He tapped her

35

cup with his. Drank some wine. In a soft voice he said, "It must've been really rough. About Jim, I mean."

She nodded, said nothing.

"Here's to better times."

"Better times," she said. They toasted and drank some more.

"Okay, I better tell you what I've found."

Sandra May took a deep breath then another sip of wine. "Go ahead."

"You're husband was intentionally hiding money. And he did a damn good job of it. It looks like he was taking some of the profits from the company for the last couple of years and bought shares in some foreign corporations. . . . He never mentioned it to you?"

"No. I'm sure not. I wouldn't have approved. Foreign companies? I don't even hold much with the U.S. stock market. I think people ought to keep their money in the bank. Or better yet under the bed. That was my mother's philosophy. She called it the First National Bank of Posturepedic."

He laughed. Sandra May finished her wine. Rawl poured her some more.

"How much money was there?" she asked him.

"Two hundred thousand and some change."

"Lord, I sure could use it. And soon. Is there any way to trace it?"

"I think so. But he was real cagey, your husband."

"Cagey?" she drew the word out.

"He wanted to hide those assets bad. It'd be a lot easier to find if I knew why he did it."

'I don't have a clue." She lifted her hand and let it fall onto her solid thigh. "Maybe it's retirement money."

But Rawl was smiling.

"I say something silly?"

"A four-oh-one K is where you put retirement money. The Cayman Islands isn't."

"Is it illegal, what Jim did?"

"Not necessarily. But it might be." He emptied his cup. "You want me to keep going?"

"Yes," Sandra May said firmly. "Whatever it takes, whatever you find. I have to get that cash."

"Then, I'll do it."

Sandra May took the barrette out of her hair, let the blond strands fall free. She leaned her head back, looking up at the sky, the stars, the captivating moon, which was nearly full. She realized that she wasn't resting against the back of the porch swing at all but against Rawl's shoulder. She didn't move away.

Then the stars and the moon were gone, replaced by the darkness of his silhouette, and he was kissing her, his hand cradling the back of her head, then her neck, then sliding around to the front of her jumper and undoing the buttons that held the shoulder straps. She kissed him back, hard. His hand moved up to her throat and undid the top button of her blouse, which she wore fastened—the way, her mother told her, proper ladies should always do.

* * *

She lay in bed that night alone—Bill Rawl had left some hours before—and stared up at the ceiling.

The anxiety was back. The fear of losing everything.

Oh, Jim, what's going to happen? she thought to her husband, lying deep in the red clay of Pine Creek Memorial Gardens.

She thought back on her life—how it just hadn't turned out the way she planned. How she'd dropped out of Georgia State six months before she graduated to be with him. Thinking about how she gave up her own hopes of working in sales. About how they fell into a routine: Jim running the company while she entertained clients and volunteered at the hospital and the Women's Club and ran the household. Which was supposed to be a household full of children—that was what she'd hoped for anyway. But it never happened. Jim was always so busy, always on the road, always coming home late, falling into bed, asleep before his head hit the pillow, rarely touching her, rarely rolling over onto her side of the bed. ("Honey, if a girl's not getting pregnant, most of the time there's no mystery," her mother had told her. "It's like baking. If you don't add the ingredients, you don't get the cake.")

And now Sandra May Foote DuMont was just a childless widow. . . .

That was how the people in Pine Creek looked at her. The town widow. They knew that the company would fail, that she'd move into one of those dreadful apartments on Sullivan Street and would just melt away, become part of the wallpaper of small-town Southern life. They thought no better of her than that.

But that wasn't going to happen to her.

No, ma'am. . . . She could still meet someone and have a family. She was young. She could go to a different place, a big city maybe—Atlanta, Charleston . . . Hell, why not New York itself?

A Southern woman's got to be a notch stronger than her man. And a notch more resourceful too.

She *would* get out of this mess.

Rawl could help her get out of it. She knew she'd done the right thing picking him.

When she woke up the next morning, Sandra May found her wrists were cramping; she'd fallen asleep with her hands clenched into fists.

It was two hours later, when she arrived in the office, that Loretta pulled her aside, gazed at her boss with frantic, black-mascaraed eyes and whispered, "I don't know how to tell you this, Mrs. DuMont, but I think he's going to rob you. Mr. Rawl, I mean."

"Tell me."

Sandra May sat slowly in the high-backed leather chair. Looked again out the window.

"All right, see, what happened . . . What happened . . ."

"Calm down, Loretta."

"See, after you left last night, I started to bring

some papers into your office and I heard him on the phone."

"Who was he talking to?"

"I don't know. But I looked inside and saw that he was using his cell phone, not the office phone, like he usually does. I figured he used that phone so we wouldn't have a record of who he called."

"Let's not jump to conclusions. What did he say?" Sandra May asked.

"He said he was pretty close to finding the money, but it was going to be a problem to get away with it."

" 'Get away with it'?"

"That's what he said. Right, right, right. Then he said some stock or something was all held by the company, not by you personally. And that could be a problem."

"Then what?"

"Oh, then I kind of bumped into the door and he heard and hung up real quick."

"That doesn't mean he's going to rob us," Sandra May said. " 'Get away with it.' Maybe that just means get the money out of the foreign companies."

"Sure, maybe it does, Mrs. DuMont. But he was acting like a spooked squirrel when I came into the room." Then Loretta brushed one of her long purple nails across her chin. "How well do you know him?"

"Not well. Are you thinking that he somehow arranged this whole thing?" Sandra May shook her head. "Couldn't be. I called *him* to help us out."

"But how did you find him?"

Sandra May grew quiet. Then she said, "He met me . . . Well, he picked me up. At the Pine Creek Club."

"And he told you he was in business."

She nodded.

"So," Loretta pointed out, "he might've heard that you'd inherited the company and went there on purpose to meet you. Or maybe he was one of the people Mr. DuMont was in business with—doing something that wasn't quite right. What you were telling me— about those foreign companies."

"I don't believe it," Sandra May protested. "No, I can't believe it."

She looked into the assistant's face, which was pretty and demure, yes, but also very savvy. Loretta said, "Maybe he looks for people who're having trouble running businesses and moves in and, bang, cleans 'em out."

Sandra May shook her head.

"I'm not saying for sure, Mrs. DuMont. I just worry about you. I don't want anybody to take advantage of you. And we all here . . . well, we can't hardly afford to lose our jobs."

Sandra May's eyes scanned the office again, the pictures of her husband with the fish and game he'd bagged, the pictures of the company in the early days, the groundbreaking for the new factory, Jim at the Rotary club, Jim and Sandra May on the company float at the county fair.

Their wedding picture . . .

Honey, don't you worry your pretty little head about anything I'll take care of it everything'll be fine don't worry don't worry don't worry . . .

The words her husband had said to her a thousand times echoed in her head. Sandra May sat down in the office chair once more.

The next day Sandra May found Bill Rawl in the office, hunched over an accounting book.

She set a piece of paper in front of him.

He lifted it and read, frowning.

"What's this?"

"It's a power of attorney. It gives you the right to vote all my shares in the company however you want. I talked to my lawyer, and he said if the company has money hidden anywhere only the majority shareholder can get it back. This gives you the power to do that."

He kept reading, said to her, "But why give it to me? I can just give you my recommendations about the money, and you could vote yourself."

"Because it's important for me to trust you."

"Trust me?"

"I had some doubts about you. Before Jim's accident I would've run to him with a problem. And before Jim I would've run to my mother. I wouldn't've made any decisions. But I'm on my own now, and I have to make my own choices. One of those choices was hiring you and trusting you." She nodded at the paper. "This is something I'm doing

42

for *me*. Now, use that and find the money and get it back."

He read the power of attorney carefully once more, noted the signature. "It's irrevocable."

"The lawyer said a revocable one is useless."

"Good." He folded up the paper and put it in his pocket. He gave her a smile . . . but it was different from earlier. There was a coldness to his expression. And even a sneer of triumph—like you'd see on the face of a red-neck Pine Creek High tackle. "I'll tell you, Sandy, I thought it'd take months to get control of the company."

"Get control?" She stared at him. "Of the company?"

"It could've been a nightmare—and the worst part was I'd have to stay in this hellhole of a town for a month or two . . . Pine Creek . . ." He put on a hillbilly accent as he said, sarcastically, "Lord above, how do *y'all* keep from going stark, raving mad here?"

"What are you talking about," she whispered.

"Sandy, the whole point of this was to get your company." He tapped the power of attorney. "I'll vote myself in as president, pay myself a nice, big salary and bonus, then sell the place. You'll make some money—don't worry. You're still the owner of the stock. Oh, and don't worry about that hidden money. It wasn't hidden at all. Your husband put some company money into overseas investments, like a million other businessmen last year. He got hurt a little when the market dipped. No big deal. It'll come back. You were never even close to bankruptcy."

"You bastard! This's fraud!"

"Not if you executed the power of attorney willingly. There wasn't any coercion or undue influence. It was *your* idea."

Rawl shook his head sadly then he paused, frowning. He noticed that the rage on Sandra May's face had turned to amusement. Then she started laughing.

"What?" he asked uncertainly.

She stepped toward him. Rawl eased back uneasily.

"Oh, relax, I'm not going to slap you upside the head—even though I ought to." Sandra May leaned past him and pushed the intercom button.

"Yes?" came the woman's voice.

"Loretta, could you come in here, please?"

"Sure, Mrs. DuMont."

Loretta appeared in the doorway. Sandra May's eyes were still on Rawl's. She said, "That power of attorney gives you the right to vote all my shares. Right?"

He glanced at his jacket pocket, where the document rested. He nodded.

Sandra May continued, speaking to Loretta. "How many shares in the company do I own?"

"None, Mrs. DuMont."

"What?" Rawl asked.

Sandra May continued. "We thought you were trying to pull something. So we had to test you. I talked

44

to my lawyer. He said I could transfer my shares to somebody I trusted so that I didn't hold any of them. Then I'd sign the power of attorney, give it to you and see what you did. And I sure learned that fast enough—you planned to rob me blind."

"You transferred the shares? To somebody you trusted?"

She nodded to Loretta. "I don't own a bit. The power of attorney is useless. She owns a hundred percent of DuMont Products."

Her voice faded. Now Rawl was the one smiling.

"Actually, Sandy," Loretta said, "Bill *and* I own a hundred percent of the company. Sorry, honey." And she walked forward and put her arm around Rawl. "I don't think we mentioned it, but Bill's my brother."

"You were in it together!" Sandra May whispered. "The two of you."

"Jim died and didn't leave me a penny!" Loretta snapped. "You *owe* me that money."

"Why would Jim leave *you* anything?" Sandra May asked uncertainly. "Why would . . ." But her voice faded as she looked at the knowing smile on the thin woman's face.

"You and my husband?" Sandra May gasped. "You were seeing each other?"

"For the last three years, honey. You never noticed that we were out of town at the same time? That we'd both work late the same nights? Jim was putting that money away for me!" Loretta spat out. "He just never had a chance to give it to me before he died."

Sandra May stumbled backward, collapsed onto the couch. "The stock . . . Why, I trusted you," she muttered. "The lawyer asked who could I trust and you were the first person I thought of!"

"Just like I trusted Jim," Loretta snapped back. "He kept saying he'd give it to me, he'd open an account for me, I could travel, he'd get me a nice house. . . . But then he died and didn't leave me a penny. I waited a few months then called Bill up in New York. I told him all about you and the company. I knew you were going to Pine Creek Club on Sunday. We figured he should come on down and introduce himself to the poor widow."

"But your last name, it's different," she said to Rawl, picking up one of his business cards and glancing at Loretta.

"Hey, not that hard to figure out," he said, lifting his palms. "It's fake." He laughed. As if this were too obvious to even mention.

"When we sell the company, honey, you'll get *something*," Loretta said. "Don't you worry yourself about that. In recognition of your last six months as president. Now, why don't you just head on home? Oh, hey, you don't mind if I don't call you Mrs. DuMont anymore, do you, Sandy? I really hated—"

The office door swung open.

"Sandra May . . . you all right?"

46

A large man stood in the doorway. Beau Ogden, the county sheriff. His hand was on his pistol.

"I'm fine," she told him.

He eyed Rawl and Loretta, who stared at him uneasily. "These them?"

"That's right."

"I come as soon as I got your call."

Rawl glanced at the phone. "What call?"

Ogden warned, "Just keep your hands where I can see them."

"What the hell're you talking about?" Rawl asked.

"I'd ask you to keep a respectful voice, sir. You don't want to go making your problems any worse than they already are."

"Officer," Loretta said, sounding completely calm, "we've been doing some business dealings here and that's all. Everything's on the up and up. We got contracts and papers and everything. Mrs. DuMont sold me the company for ten dollars 'cause it's in debt and she thought I could turn it around. Me knowing the company as good as I do, since I worked for her husband for so many years. Her own lawyer did the deal. We're going to pay her a settlement as a former employee."

"Yeah, whatever," Ogden said absently; his attention was on a young, crew-cut deputy, entering the office. "It matches," he told his sheriff, and Ogden nodded toward Loretta and Rawl. "Cuff 'em both."

"You bet, Beau."

"Cuff us! We haven't done anything!"

Ogden sat on the couch beside Sandra May. He said solemnly, "We found it. Wasn't in the woods, though. Was under Lorreta's back porch."

Sandra May shook her head sadly. Snagged a Kleenex and wiped her eyes.

"Found what?" Rawl snapped.

"May as well 'fess up, both of you. We know the whole story."

"What story?" Loretta barked at Sandra May.

She took a deep breath. Finally she struggled to answer, "I knew something wasn't right. I figured out you two were trying to cheat me—"

"And her, a poor widow," Ogden muttered. "Shameful."

"So I called Beau before I got to work this morning. Told him what I suspected."

"Sheriff," Loretta continued patiently, "you're making a big mistake. She voluntarily transferred the stock to me. There was no fraud, there was no—"

The sheriff held up an impatient hand. "Loretta, you're being arrested for what you did to Jim, not for fraud or some such."

"Did to Jim?" Rawl looked at his sister, who shook her head, and asked, "What's going on here?"

"You're under arrest for the murder of Jim DuMont."

"I didn't murder anybody!" Rawl spat out.

"No, but she did." Ogden nodded at Loretta. "And that makes you an accomplice and probably guilty of conspiracy too."

"No!" Loretta screamed. "I didn't."

"A fella owns a cabin on Lake Billings come forward a couple weeks ago and says he saw a woman with Mr. DuMont around Halloween. He couldn't see too clear, but he said it looked like she was holding this club or branch. This fella didn't think nothing of it and left town for a spell. Soon's he comes back—last month—he hears about Jim dying and gives me a call. I checked with the coroner, and he said that Mr. DuMont might not've hit his head when he fell. Maybe he was hit by somebody and shoved in the water. So I reopened the case as a murder investigation. We've been checking witnesses and forensics for the past month and decided it definitely looks like murder but we can't find the weapon. Then Mrs. DuMont calls me this morning about you two and this scam and everything. Seemed like a good motive to murder somebody. I got the magistrate to issue a search warrant. That's what we found under your porch, Loretta: the billy club Mr. DuMont used to kill fish with. It had his blood and hairs on it. Oh, and I found the gloves you'd worn when you hit him. Ladies' gloves. Right stylish too."

"No! I didn't do it! I swear."

"Read 'em their rights, Mike. Do a good job of it too. Don't want no loopholes. And get 'em outa here."

Rawl shouted, "I didn't do it!"

As the deputy led them out, Sheriff Ogden said to Sandra May, "Funny how they all say that. Broken record. Now I'm truly sorry about all this, Sandra May. Tough enough being newly widowed, but to have to go through all this nonsense too."

"That's okay, Beau," Sandra May said, wiping her eyes with a demure Kleenex.

"We'll be wanting to take a statement, but there's no hurry on that."

"Anytime you say, Sheriff," she said firmly. "I want those people to go away for a long, long time."

"We'll make sure that happens. Good day to you now."

When the sheriff had left, Sandra May stood by herself for a long moment, looking at the photo of her husband taken a few years earlier. He was holding up a large bass he'd caught—probably in Billings Lake. Then she walked into the outer office, opened the mini refrigerator and poured herself a glass of iced tea.

Returning to Jim's, no, *her* office, she sat down in the leather chair and spun slowly, listening to the now-familiar squeak of the mechanism.

Thinking: Well, Sheriff, you were almost right.

There was only one little variation in the story.

Which was that Sandra May had known all along about Jim's affair with Loretta. She'd gotten used to the smell of turpentine on her husband's skin but never used to the stink of the woman's trailer-trash perfume, which hung like a cloud of bug spray around him as he climbed into bed two or three times a week, supposedly too tired to even kiss her.

(How could she *not* know about the affair. As her mother told her too: "There's one thing that men always need and if they don't want it at home, that means they've found it someplace else.")

And so when Jim DuMont drove off to Billings Lake last October, Sandra May followed and confronted him about Loretta. And when he admitted it she said, "Thank you for not lying," took the billy club and crushed his skull with a single blow, then kicked him into the frigid water.

She'd thought that would be the end of it. The death was ruled accidental and everybody forgot about the case—until that man at Billings Lake had come forward and reported seeing a woman with Jim just before he'd died. Sandra May knew it was only a matter of time until they tracked her down for the murder.

The threat of a life sentence—not the condition of the company—was the terrible predicament she'd found herself in, the predicament for which she was praying for help "from the sky." (As for the company? Who cared? The "bit of insurance money" she'd mentioned totaled nearly a million dollars. To get away with that she would've gladly watched Du-Mont Products go bankrupt and given up the money Jim had socked away for his scrawny slut.) How could she save herself? But then Rawl gave her the answer when he'd picked her up. He was too slick. She'd sensed a scam and guessed that he knew Loretta. She figured they were planning some way to get the company away from her.

And so she'd come up with a plan of her own.

Sandra May now opened the bottom drawer of the desk and took out a bottle of small-batch Kentucky bourbon and poured a good three fingers' worth into the iced tea. She sat back in her husband's former chair, now hers exclusively, and gazed out the window at a stand of tall, dark pine trees bending in the wind as a spring storm moved in.

Thinking to Rawl and Loretta: Never did tell you the rest of Mama's expression, did I?

"Honey," the old woman had told her daughter, "a Southern woman has to be a notch stronger than her man. And she's got to be a notch more resourceful too. And, just between you and me, a notch more conniving. Whatever you do, don't forget that part."

Sandra May DuMont took a long drink of iced tea and picked up the phone to call a travel agent.

Mickey Friedman

Mickey Friedman's first published novel, the marvelously atmospheric *Hurricane Season*, was set in the fictional Palmetto, a twin for Port St. Joe, Florida, the small coastal Panhandle town where she grew up. Since then she has lived in Tallahassee, northern Ohio, the San Francisco Bay Area, Paris, and for the last fifteen years, New York City. She's worked as a freelance journalist and as a reporter and book columnist for the San Francisco *Examiner*. She is the author of seven highly acclaimed mystery novels and many short stories.

In all of the places she's lived, Ms. Friedman has sought out Southerners, or children of Southerners, as friends since "they have nice manners and don't tell me my accent 'isn't so bad.'" She adores the South with the passion of an exile and truly believes she would love nothing better than to return to Port St. Joe and live in a house on the beach.

Cape St. Sebastian, the setting for "A Day at the Saltworks," bears more than a passing resemblance to Port St. Joe/Palmetto and stars the indomitable Marva Trout, retired schoolteacher, and a force of near-hurricane proportions.

A Day at the Saltworks

Marva Trout glared across the lobby. She had reached her limit.

Marva's most recent enemy, Angeline Aylesworth, was holding court near the windows, surrounded by fawning acolytes. Murmurs of "wonderful," "so expressive," and "nearly cried" reached Marva's steaming ears.

Lying on Marva's substantial lap was a hot-off-the-presses copy of *Peavy Topics*, the monthly newsletter of the Estelle Peavy Residence for Women. On page two, in a place of honor, was a poem: "St. Sebastian Bay at Dawn," by one Angeline P. Aylesworth. This puerile piece of pap was not worthy of being printed in the weekly shopping throwaway, much less *Peavy Topics*. "St. Sebastian Bay at Dawn," indeed! What did Angeline Aylesworth, a Northerner who had arrived at the Peavy Residence less than a month ago, know about St. Sebastian Bay? St. Sebastian Bay was Marva Trout's territory, and so was the town of Cape St. Sebastian. So was the Estelle Peavy Residence, where Marva had lived and reigned since her retirement from schoolteaching. And so, for that matter, was northwest Florida, the area commonly known as the Panhandle. There was room for only one poet in Marva Trout's vicinity, and that poet had been and would be Marva Trout herself.

The Estelle Peavy Residence, formerly the Hacienda Hotel, was a respectable lodging for women of slender means, an oasis of shabby gentility in the Marvelous Mile section of Cape St. Sebastian Beach. Outside its stucco walls, the diversions of the Redneck Riviera—instant photo booths, boutiques selling seashell jewelry, carnival rides, nightclubs featuring country and western music—crowded near. Beyond these attractions lay the beach itself, where scantily clad visitors flocked to paddle in the lukewarm waves or stretch out on the sand to roast themselves to a carcinogenic crisp. Outside, tackiness and disorder reigned. Not so within the Peavy Residence. Not, at least, while Marva had anything to do with it.

Angeline Aylesworth and her party were rising from their seats. Marva quickly folded *Peavy Topics* and opened her notebook to conceal it. She clicked her ballpoint pen and let the point hover over a blank page. By the time Angeline swept by, Marva was, or appeared to be, in the throes of literary composition.

In truth, inspiration was slow to come. Marva's epic historical poem, "Legend and Legacy: The Saga of Cape St. Sebastian," had not progressed in weeks. The muse had flown, now that Marva thought of it, about the same time Angeline Aylesworth arrived, with her platinum-dyed hair, willowy figure, and superior attitude. Although Angeline claimed to be in town to research her ancestors, Marva would swear she was a Yankee through and through. Angeline, to the amazement of all, drank her iced tea unsweetened. She confounded the kitchen staff by insisting on having her seafood broiled instead of deep-fried and served, not with tartar sauce as God intended, but with a wedge of lemon. Most egregiously, on a morning soon after her arrival she had plopped herself down in the lobby on the very sofa that had always been the personal roosting place of Marva Trout and her friend Lilith Gervase. When Marva gently apprised Angeline of her trespass, Angeline had replied pertly that she didn't see a "reserved" sign anywhere and proceeded to remain there a good two hours, perusing the *Reader's Digest*.

Forget Angeline, Marva instructed herself. She tried to concentrate on Canto III of "Legend and Legacy." Canto III was crucial, treating the role of Cape St. Sebastian in the Civil War. Even Marva, an avid local historian and Cape St. Sebastian booster, had to admit the town, which had barely existed in that era, hadn't played much of a role in the Civil War at all. The only local conflicts of note had been over the clandestine production of salt from seawater on the many hidden inlets of St. Sebastian Bay.

As a warming-up exercise, Marva searched her mind for words that rhymed with "salt." After twenty minutes, she had come up with "halt," "gestalt," and "basalt." She sighed and clicked her pen closed.

"Good morning, Marva," a cheerful voice said.

From her depths of frustration, Marva looked up to see her buddy and sidekick, Lilith Gervase. Lilith and Marva were both widowed, both retired school-teachers of a certain age, but the resemblances ended there. Marva clothed her solid frame in shirtwaist dresses and kept her steel-gray hair cut sensibly short, while Lilith decked herself in brightly printed shifts and caftans and let her faded ginger-colored locks fly freely around her shoulders. Marva was, or considered herself to be, a person with her feet planted firmly on the ground. Lilith was a flighty artist. She sketched constantly, rendering quick por-traits of anyone who came near the Peavy Residence. When she wasn't sketching, she was painting small watercolor depictions of seagulls and sand dunes.

Marva pulled out her copy of *Peavy Topics*. Turning to the page with Angeline's poem, she said, "Did you see this?"

Lilith sat and read, while Marva studied her face for reaction. Eventually, Lilith put down the newslet-ter and said, "Why, it's quite lovely, isn't it? Who would've imagined that Angeline Aylesworth could—"

Marva couldn't stand it. Shaking her head, she cov-ered her eyes with her hand. "Never mind," she said. "Just never mind."

Marva simmered all day. That evening after dinner, matters came to a head. Marva entered the television lounge intent on tuning in her favorite program, "The Prime Minister's Question Time," broadcast from the British Parliament on C-Span. In the lounge, she discovered Angeline and several of her cohorts slouched on the best chairs, watching *Wuthering Heights*, with Laurence Olivier and Merle Oberon. When they refused to abandon the Romance Channel for C-Span, Marva was overtaken by cold fury. Before stalking out, she said, in an ominous tone, "Angeline, you're going to regret this. You're going to be very, very sorry."

Angeline's thinly plucked eyebrows climbed to bisect her forehead. "Good heavens! Get hold of yourself, Marva!" she said.

As Marva left, she muttered to Lilith, trailing in her wake, "She can't come in here and take over. She has to be stopped."

The next morning, Marva woke up determined to go to the saltworks.

Marva wanted to destroy Angeline Aylesworth completely, devastate her with a poem that, by comparison, would show "St. Sebastian Bay at Dawn" to be the sentimental trash it was. Marva had to write Canto III, and to write it she had to have inspiration. She would court the muse at the very site where the gallant Confederate sympathizers doggedly boiled seawater and made salt in the face of constant Union raids. The Union soldiers broke up boilers, destroyed wagons, killed mules, but the salt makers kept on producing salt to preserve the food that nourished the South.

Marva's blood surged. Angeline Aylesworth personified the heartless invading Yankees; Marva herself represented the persistent and courageous salt makers. All Marva needed to get herself going was a day at the saltworks.

The old saltworks site, aptly named Saltworks Cove, was located not far outside the city limits. Lilith had to come along on the outing, because Lilith had a car and Marva didn't. By mid-morning, they had left the Marvelous Mile behind and were chugging past the automobile dealerships and fast-food outlets of the town borders in Lilith's ancient Chevy. As they went along, Marva gave Lilith chapter and verse about the history of Confederate salt production in the Florida panhandle. Lilith, who was driving, responded with comments like, "What an interesting cloud formation that is up there!"

They reached the turnoff to Saltworks Cove, cruising down a pine-shadowed road with considerably less traffic. Soon, they passed another landmark for Marva to lecture about. Set back on a rise, surrounded by glossy-leaved camellia bushes, was a graceful two-story frame house with wide verandas. Marva waved a hand at it. "Japonica Hall," she announced. "Built in 1875 by Hector Peavy, the lumber baron."

"Did you see that flash of blue? Was that a jay?" Lilith said.

"Japonica Hall was the ancestral home of the Peavys, the same family that endowed the Peavy Residence years later," Marva droned on.

"It must've been a blue jay."

"The house was sold to the Cape St. Sebastian Historical Society after a terrible family feud." Marva craned her neck to gaze behind her at the disappearing mansion. "It's a museum now."

"Look at the way the sun dapples the road. Isn't that lovely?"

They reached the rusting historic marker, giving a brief history of Confederate salt making, and parked the car. The Cove was a marshy finger of St. Sebastian Bay, the shore overgrown with saw grass and clumps of palmetto, punctuated every so often with hammocks of live oak. The sky was cloudless, the weather oppressively hot. There was a pervasive smell of dead fish. Insects buzzed loudly among the reeds, fiddler crabs swarmed to and fro on the strand, clouds of gnats hovered in the air. Perhaps not surprisingly, they had the place to themselves.

Prepared for a day of intense writing, Marva had brought: her notebook, a selection of pens, a straw hat, a folding lawn chair, insect repellent, sunscreen, and a cooler bag containing ham sandwiches, Cokes, and Snickers bars. Lilith had brought her sketchbook, and a pencil, which she had tucked behind her ear.

Picking her way across the soggy ground, Marva set up her chair on a stretch of dank yellow sand at the water's edge. She put her straw hat on, applied insect repellent and sunscreen, and opened her note-book. Lilith, in the meantime, had wandered away to sketch on her own. Marva breathed the fishy air and stared out over the sun-burnished bay. She imagined the shore ringed with the fires of the salt makers. On a day like this, it must've been hot work. Miserably hot work. Seawater boiling in huge kettles, smoke pouring out. The thought of it made her weary. Seawater kettles boiling, mules and wagons hauling the salt. Tiring work. Her eyelids were heavy. Very, very tiring work.

"I'm back, Marva!"

Roused from profound and prolonged slumber, Marva squinted at Lilith, silhouetted by the lowering sun. "I've had a wonderful time!" Lilith fluted on. "I sketched until my fingers hurt. Did you get a lot of writing done?"

Lilith was quite sunburned, Marva noticed, with red blotches on her arms that looked like mosquito bites. Marva checked her notebook, just to be sure she hadn't jotted down a few heroic couplets before drowsing off. The pages were bare. "I didn't expect to do a lot of writing here," she said. "This trip was strictly for inspiration."

"And did you get inspired?"

"That remains to be seen," Marva growled. She stood and folded her chair, and they started for home.

*   *   *

The next morning after breakfast, Marva and Lilith were sitting on their sofa in the lobby. Marva was staring morosely into space, while Lilith perused the front page of the local daily paper. Suddenly Lilith said, with indignation, "My goodness! The sketch I did was much better than this one!"

Marva glanced over Lilith's shoulder. On the front page was a drawing of a sinister-looking man. Underneath was the caption: *Have you seen the man who stole a Winslow Homer watercolor from Japonica Hall yesterday?*

"They haven't got him right at all," Lilith went on as Marva lifted the paper from her hands. While Lilith complained, Marva read: "Police are searching for the man who tied up a guard and stole a small watercolor painting, recently identified as a Winslow Homer, from the Japonica Hall historic house museum yesterday afternoon. The daring daylight theft was carried out—"

"Let me show you!" Lilith was leafing furiously through her sketchbook.

Marva ignored her and continue reading. The watercolor, a depiction of palm trees on the bank of a river, had been hanging in Japonica Hall for years, but was always assumed to have been rendered by one of the maiden daughters of Hector Peavy. Only when an expert in nineteenth-century American art wandered through the museum during a recent vacation was it correctly attributed. The great American artist Winslow Homer probably painted the work during one of his several visits to Florida, possibly in 1904. How it came into the possession of the Peavy family was not known. The painting had been removed from display and placed in the office safe, but the thief had known where it was and forced the guard at gunpoint to open the safe. The museum trustees had offered a reward of one thousand dollars for the return of the painting.

"See?" Lilith thrust her sketchbook under Marva's nose.

Marva refocused and studied the rough pencil sketch. It showed a sinister-looking man who bore, it was true, a significant resemblance to the man depicted on the front page of the newspaper. There were the same pudgy cheeks, the same crooked nose, the same small eyes, the same ragged eyebrows. Marva said, "Lilith, what are you telling me?"

"I saw him! Yesterday at the saltworks! There were two of them burying something!"

Even in repose, Lilith's voice had a tendency to be shrill. When she was excited, as she was now, the adjective "piercing" was appropriate. The words "reward of one thousand dollars" whirled in Marva's brain. She glanced around. The usual bridge game was going on in the corner, but nothing ever broke the players' concentration on the cards. "Keep your voice down," she said.

Lilith paid no attention. She all but shrieked, "There were two of them!" She leafed through the sketchbook and showed Marva a picture of a spreading live oak tree with two figures bent over shovels beneath it. One was tall and thin, wearing a loose shirt and trousers and a large hat with a floppy brim. The other, the subject of the portrait, was burly and hatless.

"I was in a clump of trees, sitting in the shade, working on a landscape," Lilith said. "I turned around and there they were, digging. They didn't see me at all."

"They were a long way away from you," Marva said. "How did you get close enough to draw this man's face?"

"Well—" Lilith blushed. "He came right over to where I was, just for a minute or two. Long enough for me to get a good look at him. He still didn't see me."

"Came over to you? What for?"

Her color deepened. "Actually, he came over to— to urinate. I was hidden, as I said, and I didn't want to make myself known and embarrass him."

Marva sat back to contemplate these developments. She and Lilith would share the reward. Five hundred dollars each! The fact that it was Lilith alone who had seen the perpetrators and made the sketch did not occur to her.

If, of course, Lilith actually had seen the perpetrators. Lilith tended to be flaky. The whole thing could be a colossal error. To avoid humiliation, they would have to go back to Saltworks Cove and retrieve the painting, if that's really what it was, and take it to the police. Then they could claim the reward. "Do you remember exactly where you saw them digging?" she asked.

As the question left her lips, she saw a sight that filled her with horror. Across the room, protruding just above the back of one of the rattan sofas, was a platinum blonde head that could belong only to Angeline Aylesworth. Angeline, Marva's nemesis, must have heard everything! It would be so typical, so infuriatingly typical, if she got to the saltworks first, retrieved the painting, and claimed the reward herself.

"Of course I remember where I saw them!" Lilith was saying indignantly. "There was a little path through the grass away from the water, and beyond that you came to a—"

"Shut up!" Marva hissed as she pulled herself to her feet, grabbed Lilith by the wrist, and dragged her from the room.

Within minutes, they were once again in the Chevy heading for Saltworks Cove. Marva sat forward, staring through the windshield. If Angeline got there first, if Angeline claimed the reward, Marva would— Marva didn't know what she would do.

Lilith was nattering on: "Gracious, I hope they had it in a watertight container, Marva. A Winslow Homer! The thought makes me feel weak all over."

Marva gritted her teeth. "Drive," she said.

The grassy parking area by the historic marker was empty. Before Lilith could remove the key from the ignition, Marva had jumped from the car and was plowing along the narrow path Lilith had described. She heard Lilith hurrying behind her, gasping, and then Lilith cried out, "Marva!"

Marva whirled to see Lilith bent over her foot. One of her sandals, a Roman-style that laced up around the calf, had come untied and was hanging off. "My shoe!" Lilith cried.

Marva had no time to worry about Roman sandals. "I'm going ahead!" she cried. She turned and pressed forward.

The insects were once again out in force, and the sun was blinding. Today, Marva did not have her hat, sunscreen, or repellent. Perspiration poured down her forehead. Her dress stuck to her back. Up ahead, she caught sight of the spreading live oak, hung with Spanish moss, depicted in Lilith's sketch. She speeded her pace, her breath hot in her throat.

The saw grass was so tall she could not see the base of the tree until she was almost on top of it. Her heart drumming, she burst through the undergrowth into a small, shady clearing. Charging forward, she nearly stumbled over the motionless, prostrate form of Angeline Aylesworth.

Marva gave a low yell, hampered by her lack of breath. Yes, it was Angeline, lying on top of a pile of damp muck beside an empty hole in the ground. There was no evidence of a painting anywhere. So Angeline had indeed overheard, and had rushed to cheat Marva and Lilith out of their reward, only to be savaged by someone else. It seemed likely that the thieves had mounted a guard over their booty. If that was the case, Marva could only be grateful Angeline had arrived first.

Seeing the detested Angeline brought low had not opened wellsprings of pity in Marva's breast. Reluctantly, she approached close enough to bend over and try to determine if her enemy was still breathing. She had reached no conclusion on the point when a full-throated scream behind her paralyzed her in her tracks. *"Marva! What have you done?"* Lilith wailed.

Marva wet her lips, but before she could speak Angeline's eyelids fluttered open and she stared up into Marva's face with a look of horror. "Get away from me! Help! Somebody help me!" she bellowed.

For a while, it went on like that: "Get away from me!" *"What have you done?"* "Somebody help me!" *"Marva! Oh, Marva!"* A group of bird-watchers heard the commotion and dialed 911 on a cellular telephone. Shortly afterward, the police arrived.

By this time, Angeline was hysterical. "She attacked me! Oh, my God, keep her away from me!" she sobbed to everyone within earshot. "She threatened me yesterday! Save me, please save me!" Eventually, she was bundled into an ambulance and driven off with sirens screaming, and a sullen Marva was taken to the sheriff's office for questioning.

At this point, and it was high time, the tide turned in Marva's favor. After she had spent ten minutes stewing alone in an interview room, a spindly black man wearing a suit and tie came in, studying a fist full of paperwork. As he stood at the door, still preoccupied, Marva gave him a long look. She said, "Hello, Travis."

The man's head jerked up, and he focused on Marva for the first time. As he blinked in disbelief, Marva said, "Yes, it's me."

"Mrs. Trout!" Travis Boykins had changed very little since the days when Marva was his eleventh-grade homeroom teacher. As he came to grips with Marva's presence, his face assumed the hangdog look it used to get on the frequent occasions when she caught him in some mischief and sent him to the principal's office. He said, "What are you doing here, Mrs. Trout?"

"That's a very interesting question."

Marva told Travis Boykins, now an investigator for the county sheriff, the story of her trips to the saltworks. Travis listened, frowning and taking an occasional note. When she finished her tale, he said, "This woman, Aylesworth, claims you attacked her. Said you'd threatened her before."

Working on the theory that the best defense is a good offense, Marva shot back, "And what does she say *she* was doing out there?"

"She admits she heard you talking about the painting back at the Peavy Residence and went out there to beat you to it. She knew a shortcut to Saltworks Cove, and parked around the other side where the bird-watchers go. She found the place, and dug up a watertight plastic container. Before she had a chance to open it, somebody hit her. When she came to, your friend was asking why you had done it."

Silently, Marva thanked Lilith for nothing. "So I'm supposed to have attacked her and stolen the painting," she said with heavy irony. She spread her meaty arms wide. "What did I do with the Winslow Homer? Do you want to search me?"

Travis looked appalled at the idea. "No, ma'am, I surely don't," he said. "Not if I don't have to."

In the end, he did the right thing. Marva was released, although cautioned to keep herself available for further interviews. She found Lilith, clutching her sketchbook, waiting in the lobby.

"I waited to drive you home," Lilith said timidly.

Marva gave a noncommittal grunt.

"They were very interested in what I saw yesterday. They made photocopies of my sketches."

Another grunt.

Lilith took a deep breath. "I'm sorry, Marva. It's just that when I saw her lying there, and I remembered what you'd said—"

"Let's forget it, shall we?" said Marva in a tone that indicated she never would. They drove back to the Peavy Residence in silence.

Marva brooded through the evening. Although Angeline Aylesworth had been kept in the hospital overnight for observation, she seemed a constant and unwelcome presence. Angeline had impugned Marva's honor, accusing her of a brutal attack that Marva only wished she had carried out. Angeline had hustled out to Saltworks Cove, taking a shortcut like the sneak she was, in order to do Marva and Lilith out of their thousand dollars. Angeline had dug up the painting and lost it, ruining everything. Angeline, Angeline, Angeline.

It was worse the next morning when Angeline reappeared in the flesh, a gauze wrapping partially obscuring her platinum hair. She tottered in to loud exclamations from her coterie, and proceeded to murmur to them at length in a low voice, while casting meaningful glances across the room at Marva. Obviously, Marva was still the prime suspect in Angeline's mind, and Angeline was determined to poison the entire Residence against her.

Marva was in an intolerable position. In order to regain her rightful place as literary and social arbiter of the Estelle Peavy Residence, she was going to have to clear her name. Arms crossed and bottom lip stuck out, Marva sank deeper into thought and into the sofa cushions. She had to do something. She had to.

The more Marva cudgeled her brain, however, the less brightly it functioned. Marva needed to find the thug who had stolen the picture, run him to earth and retrieve it, make him confess that he, not Marva, had attacked Angeline. Marva seemed as likely to accomplish any of this as she was to become a prima ballerina with the Ballets Russes de Monte Carlo.

In desperation, she decided to go to Japonica Hall. Perhaps she could talk with the guard who had been the victim of the robbery. She would show him Lilith's drawing, which was after all a bit different from the one that had been in the newspaper, and see if it brought out new information. Even if the trip was as futile as seemed likely, at least Marva would be off the premises of the Peavy Residence and out of the immediate vicinity of Angeline Aylesworth. She went to find Lilith.

Lilith was due at yoga class but, still consumed with guilt over the troubles of yesterday, she insisted that Marva take the Chevy and sketchbook and go without her. After spending fifteen minutes in the parking lot trying to start the engine, Marva at last met with success and was on her way. Shortly, she was turning up the shady drive marked with a sign for the Japonica Hall Historic House Museum.

Marva had always loved Japonica Hall. The wide plank floors, threadbare Oriental carpets, displays of fine china and monogrammed silver tea and coffee services, were as much the stuff of local legend as the many ruptures and quarrels that had dogged the wealthy Peavy descendants. It was distressing that the most significant treasure, the Winslow Homer watercolor, had been plucked away so rudely.

Today, the museum looked slightly unkempt, as if the Peavys had been surprised by unexpected guests. The hall carpet showed the tracks of many dusty feet, the information leaflets at the front desk were in disarray, one end of the red velvet rope across the parlor door trailed on the floor.

A harried-looking young woman, chubby and wide-eyed, with frizzy red hair, was behind the front desk. She looked about junior-high-school age, but her name tag identified her as Debbie Ann Sharp, Curator. She rolled her eyes heavenward when Marva asked about recent events at the museum. "Unbelievable!" she said. "The police, the press—not to mention all the people who showed up out of curiosity. We were shorthanded anyway, and now that Jimmy is out indefinitely, I don't know what we're going to do. At least we've had a lull today."

Jimmy, it seemed, was the guard Marva had hoped to meet. "Heaven knows when he'll be back," Debbie Ann Sharp said. "He's at home under sedation. It was a dreadful shock, being held at gunpoint. He feels terribly guilty about opening the safe, but he had no choice."

There went the possibility of showing him Lilith's drawing of the perpetrator. Marva's shoulders slumped. More to prolong her visit than from any real curiosity, she said, "When did you learn the painting really was a Winslow Homer?"

"We had sent it to be authenticated, and it came back one afternoon last week. The staff was so thrilled. There was a big hubbub because everyone wanted to look at it. As if all of us hadn't seen it many times already, hanging outside the kitchen door across from the broom closet."

"It must have been exciting."

"It was!" Debbie Ann's lips curved in a reminiscent smile. "What a day! Besides the furor over the painting, a child from a school group tripped on the stairs and sprained his wrist, and a woman felt faint and had to lie down with a cold cloth on her head. That's more upheaval than we usually have in a year." Debbie Ann shook her head. "A Winslow Homer! Our most important holding, and we lost it."

They stood in thoughtful silence. Marva fingered the cover of Lilith's sketchbook. She said, "You weren't here when the painting was stolen, were you?"

"No. It was after hours. Only Jimmy, the guard, was around."

"Then, there would be no point in showing you my friend's drawing of the thief."

When Marva explained that Lilith had actually seen and drawn a portrait of the perpetrator, Debbie Ann looked amazed. "Let me see!"

Marva opened the sketchbook on the front desk and exhibited Lilith's pictures. Debbie Ann studied them carefully, but shook her head. "I'm afraid I'm drawing a blank."

So that was that. Marva picked up the sketchbook, thanked her, and left.

In the Japonica Hall parking lot, the Chevy once again refused to start. Marva ground away at it, pumping the pedal, until the car filled with the smell of gas and she realized she had flooded the engine. Typical of the way things were going. While she gave the car a rest, she propped Lilith's sketchbook on the steering wheel and leafed through it.

Marva had to admit, even if grudgingly, that Lilith was pretty good. She had truly captured Emily Pye, the stuffy manager at the Peavy Residence, and had done lively studies of the kitchen staff. Various acquaintances from the lobby, television lounge, and dining hall appeared on the pages, sometimes two or three to a sheet. Marva herself was amply represented. Absorbed, Marva turned another page and found herself staring into the eyes of a sketch of Angeline Aylesworth.

Could Marva not escape Angeline no matter where she went? Feeling vaguely betrayed that Lilith had drawn a portrait of Angeline at all, she closed the book and put it aside. She could do without that kind of diversion.

Marva leaned her head back against the car seat. She was weary, weary and discouraged. How had she become involved in these sordid peccadillos, accused of assault, hauled in to answer for herself in front of an investigator? Her eyes stung, as self-pity threatened to overflow.

Suddenly, Marva sat up straight behind the wheel. For several minutes, she stared unseeing at the graceful facade of Japonica Hall. Then she seized the sketchbook, got out of the car, and strode toward the front door. She wasn't quite finished with Debbie Ann Sharp.

*   *   *

There was chicken fried steak and country gravy, Marva's favorite, for dinner at the Peavy Residence that night. Marva had three helpings, and finished with a large dish of banana pudding. Angeline, at her table nearby, sipped bouillon and shot guarded looks at Marva. When Angeline and her friends repaired to the lobby after dinner to play Chinese checkers, Marva waited until the game was under way before entering the room.

A hush fell as Marva, followed by Lilith, approached the checker players. A number of residents, sensing a confrontation, drifted in to watch. As Angeline gave her a cold stare, Marva said, "Angeline, I have something to say to you. I misjudged you, and I regret it deeply."

Angeline drew herself up. "I'm contemplating a lawsuit. Perhaps it would be better if we didn't discuss it further."

"I misjudged you drastically," Marva continued, unperturbed. "You see, I believed you were a stranger, a Northerner—" (she forbore to say "damn Yankee") "—who was unfamiliar with Cape St. Sebastian and didn't understand our ways. Only this afternoon have I learned how wrong I was."

Angeline's face remained frozen in an expression of hauteur, but there were murmurs of approval among bystanders. "That's awfully nice of you, Marva," offered one voice from the crowd.

Marva nodded sagely. "I asked myself, for instance, how an outsider would know a shortcut to

Saltworks Cove," she went on. "How would an outsider find one live oak tree out of many, after hearing a few garbled directions? And that made me start to wonder, Angeline, whether you were an outsider after all."

Angeline put a hand to the gauze wrapping on her head. "I'm feeling rather tired," she said. "I think I'll—"

"You're anything but an outsider in Cape St. Sebastian," Marva said. "You wrote a poem about St. Sebastian Bay. Whatever its literary merits, you unquestionably signed it Angeline P. Aylesworth. I am now in a position to know that your middle initial stands for the name *Peavy*. You are Angeline Peavy Aylesworth, a descendant of our own Estelle Peavy, who did so many good works for Cape St. Sebastian, including endowing this Residence."

The news burst over the group like a rocket. Marva waited impassively for the babble to subside. This afternoon was not the first time she had sneaked a forbidden look at the office registration files. Rules were for other people, people who didn't need to know things as urgently as Marva did. The name had been noted down clearly on the form, and it had been the final bit of confirmation Marva needed.

Angeline shrugged. "I confess. I was born Angeline Peavy. I'm extremely proud of the fact."

"But perhaps not so proud of the fact that your branch of the family was left penniless by summary disinheritance," Marva said. "Not so proud of the

76

fact that you've spent the past thirty years in exile, living in Hackensack, New Jersey."

At the mention of Hackensack Angeline shuddered, as if from a blow. She said, "I never forgot my rightful position. Never!"

"You never forgot," Marva repeated. "The memory of the family fortune ate away at you, didn't it, until you had to return. You came back to Cape St. Sebastian, to lurk around your ancestral home, Japonica Hall, eating your heart out at the loss of your birthright. Isn't that true, Angeline?"

Angeline's eyes had puddled up. "The silver coffee service should have been mine," she whispered. "The sugar bowl and creamer, at the very least."

Marva hovered over Angeline, a looming avenger. "You were at Japonica Hall one recent afternoon. You learned that the watercolor that had hung for years by the kitchen door was painted by Winslow Homer. When you heard that you snapped, didn't you?"

Angeline seemed to gather her strength. "No!" she spat. "I had no idea about the painting! You can't prove that I did!"

"Oh, but I can." Marva turned to Lilith and held out her hand. Lilith passed her the sketchbook. Marva riffled to the page with the sketch of Angeline and displayed it. "Debbie Ann Sharp, a curator at the museum, has assured me that this is a portrait of a woman who fainted, or pretended to faint, on the premises the day the Winslow Homer attribution was confirmed. With a cold cloth on her forehead, this woman lay in an anteroom outside the director's office. She eavesdropped on the conversation of the staff, and she learned about the plans to put the painting in the director's safe. Then she made plans of her own."

Angeline Peavy Aylesworth jumped to her feet. "It's mine!" she cried. "Why should a pokey little museum have my Winslow Homer! It's mine! *Mine!*" She flew at Marva, her long fingers closing around Marva's throat. Marva began to gurgle and flail, as screams of horror rang out from the bystanders.

All at once a male voice, a sound rarely heard inside the Peavy Residence, cried, "Back off! Let her go! Now!" Travis Boykins walked into the lobby, followed by two burly deputies.

"Mine!" Angeline screamed, her face scarlet, as the deputies pried her fingers from Marva's throat. "Mine! Mine!" She was carried out, kicking and writhing.

Marva sat down, rubbing her neck. Travis Boykins shook his head at her. "I told you not to do that, Mrs. Trout," he said. "I asked you to wait until I got here."

"I asked you not to throw spitballs during roll call," Marva retorted. She had rarely in her life felt so well.

Two weeks later, Marva and Lilith were guests at a reception at Japonica Hall, where the Winslow Homer watercolor, flanked by security guards, had been given a temporary place of honor over the mantel in the parlor. After brief display to the public, the watercolor would be sold to raise money for the museum's endowment. Earlier, in a private ceremony, Marva and Lilith had been presented with a check for a thousand dollars by the president of the Japonica Hall board of trustees.

Angeline had broken down quickly and ratted on her accomplice, who turned out to be her nephew, a petty criminal from New Jersey. As well as masterminding the plot, Angeline had driven the getaway car. She had been the person in loose clothing and floppy hat who wielded the second shovel. When she overheard Marva and Lilith's conversation in the lobby, she rushed to the hiding place to retrieve the painting before they could. Her nephew, keeping watch, assumed she was double-crossing him. He bashed her and made off with the watercolor shortly before Marva arrived. Once Angeline turned against him, he was apprehended easily.

Lilith stood in front of the painting with her hands clasped. "Winslow Homer," she murmured, awestruck. "It's magnificent, isn't it, Marva?"

Marva scrutinized the watercolor. It was a pretty little scene, she thought, a pleasant depiction of a riverbank, if that's what your taste ran to. As for herself, she preferred works of art with more heft. Epic poems, perhaps. In her mind, she ran through her list of rhymes for "salt." Any day now, she'd begin Canto III.

Joan Hess

Joan Hess is the author of more than twenty-five mystery novels in the Claire Malloy and Maggody series, as well as innumerable short stories. She has won the American Mystery Award, the Drood Review Reader's Poll, and the Agatha Award.

Though she claims to have no discernible Southern accent, Ms. Hess is a fifth-generation resident of Arkansas.

Ms. Hess's mother's maiden name was Tidwell, and her nickname was Twiddle. Ellen Tidwell, "Twiddle," the heroine of this story, is a card-carrying member of the iron-fist-in-the-velvet-glove school of Southern womanhood.

Miss Tidwell Takes No Prisoners

Ellen Tidwell, referred to by her friends from college days as "Twiddle," knew exactly why Drake had insisted on taking her out for lunch on her eighty-third birthday. Driving up to the inn at dizzying speeds could well have given her a heart attack; the ride back down the mountain would be all the more terrifying. She might keel over from a stroke, and ever-so-devoted nephew Drake would be the beneficiary of her house, her cats, Mama's silver service (custom-made in Atlanta, with a particularly elegant creamer and sugar bowl), Grandpapa's Civil War memorabilia, her collection of rare African violets, and all the money she had accumulated over fifty years of teaching school, living frugally, and investing so wisely that her broker called her for advice. Drake, her sister's boy, was the sole heir of what, she had to admit modestly, was a rather substantial estate.

When her time came, she knew perfectly well that the cats would be dispatched, the violets dumped in a trash bag, and the family treasures and homestead sold. The money, however, would be put to good use, keeping Drake and his whiny, anoretic wife in acceptable standing at the country club. Their equally whiny sons, one skulking about town on probation, the other on the verge of expulsion from the college to which Miss Tidwell discreetly wrote checks twice a year to cover tuition, would don coats, ties, and appropriately mournful expressions for her funeral. And dance on her grave forever after.

Twiddle was not stupid. She was willing to admit she was functionally blind. Resisting a walker, but dependent on a cane. Arthritic, and at the mercy of a regimen of prescription and herbal drugs to keep her fingers from curling into gnarled twigs and her knees from locking permanently. Getting old was a pain in the tush, but the alternative was nothing she looked forward to; the time would come, but she had always envisioned a sigh in her sleep. Until then, she had her kittens, her violets, her portfolio, and her friends who dropped by but were also dropping dead at an alarming rate.

"It was kind of you to come all this way just to take me out to lunch," she said to Drake as she opened the elaborate multipaged menu. "Such a nice place. So expensive and all."

"It's your birthday. I wish we could all get together more often, but the boys are so busy and Alisha spends most of her time at the hospice. There seems to be a crisis every day."

'The terminally ill can be a bother," Twiddle said as she put on her glasses and peered at the menu. "I was thinking I might just have soup and a salad. Do they have a nice house dressing?"

"Alisha intended to come," Drake persisted, "but the fund-raiser is this weekend and someone has to see to the details. She sends her love."

Twiddle took off her glasses. "I'm quite sure she sends something. Whatever it is remains to be seen, but by someone with better eyesight than I."

A figure loomed beside her. "Good afternoon," he said. "My name is Peter and I'll be your server. We have three specials today . . ."

After he'd droned on about orange roughy,

chicken in some sort of soy sauce, and pasta involving sun-dried tomatoes, Twiddle prudently opted for French onion soup and a side salad.

"How are the boys doing?" she asked when the waiter at last drifted away.

"Derek was hoping to spend a year abroad in London, but it's out of the question. Tuition and expenses will run well over twenty thousand dollars. Alisha and I have made it clear that he'll have to finish up at the state college."

"I hope you don't expect me to indulge him," Twiddle said bluntly. 'He's very lucky to be able to attend college without working in the cafeteria as I did. His grades tend to indicate he does not value his education."

"But he does." Drake leaned forward and made a futile attempt to clasp her hand, which she whisked into her lap. "He would have given anything to be here today on your birthday, but his girlfriend has a solo in the concert this afternoon and he feels as though he needs to be there for her. His mother and I have always encouraged that kind of loyalty."

She would have wiped away a tear had there been one. "What instrument does she play?"

He sat back. "Ah, cello, I think, or one of those stringed things. A most talented girl. She's an orphan, as I must have told you. Very sad."

"Three months from now, you'll be telling me that Derek and Hugh are orphans, too, and therefore worthy of my generosity. It may not ring true, Drake.

Are you once again experiencing financial problems?"

"It's not my fault, Auntie. The prime rate's up and buyers are reluctant to take out mortgages. I have four houses on the market and five more under construction. The finance company wants a substantial payment on existing construction loans. It's temporary—I swear it. Six months from now, I can pay you back with whatever interest you want."

"Seventeen percent?"

"That's hardly reasonable, and most likely illegal."

Twiddle touched her linen napkin to her mouth to hide her smile. "Well, then," she said, "you might do better at your bank. If you'll excuse me, I think I'll visit the ladies' room before we have our meal."

She seized her cane and made her way along the hallway wallpapered with dark flock, wondering if her suggestion of seventeen percent interest might prevent Drake from further attempts to borrow money. "Neither a borrower nor a lender be," dear Mr. Franklin had opined so astutely. At times, she felt so old that she might have heard it from him in person.

Not, of course, that he would have come south of the Mason-Dixon line (having been much too busy flying kites in France or whatever). She herself had never been farther north than Richmond, and that only for a week. Brossing County, North Carolina, had offered quite enough excitement for a lifetime. She'd been educated there, taught generations of children to read, write, and recite their multiplication tables, played the organ at her church, and buried her parents in the mossy cemetery. Her semi-cognizant friends still came by to spend pleasant afternoons of bridge, iced tea, and gossip. Her cats were content, and her houseplants flourished as if in a rain forest. Her azaleas were particularly lush, possibly in honor of her birthday.

She'd had a slight pang of regret that she had never traveled to New York City or such exotic destinations as London and Paris, but Miss Tidwell had accepted many years ago that these were not to be among her experiences. Brossing County, for better or worse, had been the entirety of her life.

She struggled down the dark hallway. Having failed to bring her glasses, the etched signs on the doors were incomprehensible. Finally, after a few moments, she decided that she had found the proper facility and went inside.

The room itself was dark, which was to be expected with the gathering clouds and the promise of a thunderstorm before the day was over. There was a rather peculiar sink, but Miss Tidwell had more pressing problems on her agenda. She made her way to a stall, checked to make sure there was adequate tissue available, and took a seat.

And heard the door open—and then, a heart-stopping few seconds later, male voices.

Her first instinct was to screech in outrage. How dare men barge into a ladies' room! She'd powdered

her nose and put on her gloves in every proper ladies' room in the county. As a girl, she'd touched up
her lips, patted on rouge, and straightened her ny-
lons. Over the years, she'd listened to tales of woe,
of broken hearts and schemes to take care of "certain
problems" in clinics in distant cities. She'd offered
many a handkerchief, squeezed many a hand, sworn
confidentiality, and in some cases, slipped a few dollars in a beaded evening bag. Ladies' rooms were
meant to be havens.

At that very moment Miss Tidwell came to the
chilling realization that she herself—herself!— was in
the men's room. She, who had never seriously kissed
a boy, much less done something significant, was in
a room in which grown men were apt to expose
themselves. She had no idea what else they did when
distanced from the ladies. Tell each other crude
jokes? Make disgusting noises involving the full spec-
trum of bodily functions? Brag about sexual con-
quests? Debate anatomy, male or female?

She slid her feet as far away as she could from the
stall door. She would have to suffer through whatever rituals were performed, and then, when they
were gone, slip out to the hallway and never so much
as relive a single second of her embarrassment.

"Nobody's ever gonna know, Peter," hissed one
voice. "Dump this in the soup. I'll give you a thousand dollars now and another thousand when she's
dead."

Peter, the "your server" person, sounded quite a

bit more nervous than when he'd rattled on about roughy and pasta. "What about the cops? An autopsy?"

"She's old, and she has a history of heart problems. No one will think twice."

"I don't know . . ." Peter said with a groan.

Twiddle wished he had used a name, but she had little doubt that Drake had taken advantage of her absence to arrange to have her murdered. A cup of soup enhanced with a dollop of poison, and then a delightfully gooey layer of broiled cheese to hide any odd taste. A fatal heart attack. Her fellow diners would shrink back, then flee, their appetites spoiled by the intrusion of death. The next day would be business as usual.

Her sister had died under similar circumstances. Indeed, no one had thought twice. Drake and Alisha had taken Enid out to a buffet at the Holiday Inn on Easter Sunday. She had next been seen in a coffin, chalky and still for all eternity. They had claimed she had choked on a stalk of celery.

Enid had always disliked celery.

As much as Twiddle wanted to bang open the stall door, she was frozen with panic. Once Drake knew she'd overheard the conversation, he would be all the more determined to murder her before she had a chance to contact her lawyer after the weekend and arrange for her estate to go to the local animal shelter. He could merely hustle her out of the inn, claiming she was traumatized by her misguided foray.

There were many places alongside the road without guardrails; all he'd have to do would be to throw open the passenger's door and give her a hearty shove. She'd tumble like a bag of garbage all the way to the bottom of a ravine.

Could she throw herself on the mercy of the manager, telling him how she'd overheard the conversation while huddled in a stall in the men's room? She tried to imagine herself sobbing with fury while Drake made remarks about her purported mental fragility due to her advanced age, and then apologized as he took her to the car. Any protests she might make would be tainted by the reality that she'd been in the men's room. If anyone had noticed him leave the table, he could say he'd made a call on the pay phone halfway down the hallway. Alisha would confirm it, just as she would the Second Coming—if it enriched her checking account.

Twiddle sucked in a breath as the door opened and closed. They were gone. She was more of a "goner" if she did not take action, but what was she to do? Allow Drake to put her down as he would her cats? Sip her soup and die in what might be a most agonizing way?

"Hell, no," she whispered, surprising even herself. Mama and Papa had never used such language, nor had they allowed their daughters to do so. The Tidwell family had not been wealthy, but decorum had ranked just below piety. Neither she nor Enid had ever missed church services or Saturday afternoons at cotillion classes.

She waited another minute, then scurried out of the stall and made it to the hallway without encountering any gentlemen intent on using the room for legitimate reason—as opposed to plotting murder. Drake was seated at the table, nibbling bread and nodding at acquaintances. Peter was nowhere to be seen.

Her salad had been served, as had Drake's. Twiddle sat down and offered a wan, apologetic smile. "I'm so sorry, but I seem to be experiencing some gastric distress. As much as I appreciate your bringing me, I simply cannot eat a bite. Will you please take me home?"

"Of course, Auntie. Do you mind waiting for a minute while I speak to the waiter?"

"How kind," Twiddle said. "I believe his name is Peter."

"And I believe you're right," Drake said jovially as he stood up and disappeared in the direction of the kitchen.

As she came up with a solution.

She was mulling it over when Peter appeared. "I'm disappointed that madam will not be dining with us," he said. "Our French onion soup has been given four stars, and our orange roughy . . . but, well, if madam is feeling ill . . ."

"Madam does not care to feel more ill than she does at the moment," countered Twiddle, wondering if he might have felt obliged to attend her funeral, or at least serve canapés after the services. Doubtful, in that Alisha would prefer to cut costs. Chips and dip atop the coffin, most likely. "Please do not describe the orange roughy once again. I'm feeling queasy, and I do want to be considerate of the other diners."

"Of course," Peter said, trying to sound the tiniest bit European despite his molasses-tainted accent. "Might a cup of tea help settle your stomach before your drive?"

She did her best not to gasp. "Nothing, thank you. Please let Drake know that I'll be waiting for him in the car."

"Yes, madam," he said as he glided away, no doubt chagrined that he would fail to earn two thousand dollars. Drake was penurious enough to demand back the deposit. Peter might have to settle with minimum wage and tips for the afternoon.

Twiddle wobbled her way out of the dining room and down the walk to Drake's car. Her parents, along with Enid, might have done a few flip-flops in their graves, but she was not inclined to be poisoned so that Derek could attend school in London, Hugh could purchase drugs, and Alisha could donate the flower arrangements to the hospice fund-raiser.

Drake said all the right things as he joined her. At her request, he drove at a civilized speed down the mountain, no doubt pondering his possibilities now that he had witnesses at the inn who could confirm his story of her fluctuating health. Did he think he could turn on a gas jet and leave her to die in her sleep? Did he think a well-placed napkin on the staircase might cause her to fall? He undoubtedly had a vial of some sort of poison in his pocket—a poison that would mimic heart failure.

She had no choice but to strike first. She was entirely too vulnerable, should he make a dedicated attempt to kill her. Once he was gone, she would let it be known to Alisha and the boys that everything she owned would go to the Brossing County Animal Shelter, thereby eliminating any expectations that might lead to future attempts on her life. Alisha might flourish off the proceeds of life insurance, but Twiddle suspected Drake was not the sort to keep up the premium payments.

"I do apologize," she said as they arrived back in town. "At my age, this sort of thing does happen. I should have warned you that I was far from robust yesterday. I was hardly able to sip consommé."

"Let me fix you a cup of tea before I leave," Drake suggested.

Twiddle vehemently shook her head. "I am in no way going to allow myself to be a poor hostess."

As they went inside her house, she scooped up a cat and squeezed it with a heartfelt enthusiasm, celebrating its life, if not her own. "You remember Monty, don't you?" she asked Drake as she sat down on the sofa. "He was such a hellfire in his day. Half the cats in this neighborhood have his yellowish-green glint in their eyes."

"I'm sure they do, Auntie. I'll take this opportunity to browse in the library."

"Feel free, dear; you know where it is. I'll put on the kettle."

Twiddle released the squirming cat and went into the kitchen. There, she sank down at the table and thumbed through her soul as if it were a paperback novel. Her most heinous crime to date, during her eighty-three years, was an anonymous note to the school board suggesting that a certain teacher might have been less than circumspect in areas of personal conduct. Although nothing had come of it, she'd always regretted it. "Live and let live" had become her motto; now it seemed that Drake did not share it.

If he had his way, that was.

She sat for a long while, aware that Drake was appraising first editions and wondering where to sell them. She was among the most helpless—old, easily dismissed, and should the situation arise, casually carted away to a mortuary. No one really listened to her anymore. Her insurance salesman sent a birthday card each year, spotted with saliva and signed by a shaky hand. Her accountant called every now and then, mostly to explain how well he was balancing bonds and treasury notes. The nice young woman across the street, recently licensed to sell real estate, dropped by with cookies and brochures about assisted-living facilities. None of them seemed to hear her determination to remain independent, to feed her cats and water her violets, to sit at the piano playing the sentimental songs of her youth, to relax on the porch where her parents and grandparents had sat, watching the lightning bugs flicker as the twilight darkened and the streetlights came on one by one, like sentinels protecting everything that was good and just in Brossing County.

She knew she did not have many years remaining, but she had some. What's more, the very idea that Drake would discuss her imminent demise in a men's room was so revolting that she felt acid rising in her throat. He and Peter, nearly chortling over the possibility. Giggling, perhaps. Would Drake soon be plotting other scenarios with Alisha, who was likely to be more concerned with a funerary menu than the nuts and bolts of murder?

Eighty-three, yes, but far from the hapless victim. Drake had to be stopped. If he continued to make attempts on her life, he would get lucky, sooner or later.

And thus Twiddle made the ultimate decision to kill her nephew before he killed her. She'd toyed with the idea, but its time had come. He was a direct threat. Alisha would weep copiously, but then align herself with the overly tanned golf pro (there'd been rumors). Derek and Hugh might find reason to dance on their father's grave. She had no other option.

As the tea kettle whistled, she split a dozen melatonin capsules into a teacup, then added boiling water, a tea bag, and several teaspoons of sugar and a splash of milk. Eager to leave (and perhaps plot the next attempt on her life), Drake would gulp it down simply to escape her parchment pallor.

Or so she hoped. She sat down across from him and handed him his cup. "You are going to be so angry with me," she said. "I am old and dithery. I'm afraid I may have left my wallet at the inn. I had no reason to take it out of my purse in the ladies' room, but I wanted to powder my nose and I was digging for my compact."

Drake smiled. "Why don't I call them and ask them to keep it until I can fetch it?"

Twiddle contained herself despite the condescension dripping from his voice. "It's a bit more serious, I'm afraid. I know how much you and Alisha look forward to treasuring Grandpappy's collection, but just this morning I sold a letter to dear old Mr. Sweeny, who's been hounding me for years about it. He insisted in paying me in cash, and I intended to deposit it after the weekend."

"A letter?"

"Well, not just a letter. It was a letter signed by General Robert E. Lee granting my great-great-grandmother safe passage through both Confederate and Union lines in order to be with her daughter during a difficult pregnancy in Pittsburgh. A personal note from General Lee across the bottom margin seems to have made it more valuable."

"How valuable?" Drake asked weakly.

"Sixteen thousand dollars. Mr. Sweeny has coveted it for years, and, well, I've been looking at some investment opportunities."

"You left a wallet containing sixteen thousand dollars at the inn?"

She did her best to look chagrined. "I assure you that it was an oversight. My wallet is no longer in my purse, and I haven't so much as gone to the grocery since Mr. Sweeny bought the document. I objected to a cash transaction, but he insisted, and the banks are closed. What was I to do? I was not comfortable leaving it here."

"Sixteen thousand dollars?" Drake repeated. "You think you left it in the ladies' room? For chrissake, Auntie! If I call, the money will disappear into some employee's pocket. How could you do such a thing!"

"Perhaps no one has found it. It's possible it fell behind the sink."

He stood up. "I'll go back immediately."

"I cannot allow you to leave until you've finished your tea," she said, jutting out her chin. "I deprived you of what would have been a lovely lunch. Would you like to take some cookies with you, or perhaps a tuna salad sandwich?"

"I cannot believe you'd leave sixteen thousand dollars in a ladies' room."

"Drink your tea, dear."

Drake drained the cup, seemingly oblivious to what might have scalded his mouth. "You need to allow someone else to see to your financial dealings," he said coldly. "I'll have a word with your lawyer after the weekend. Living alone like this in a drafty old house, with cats underfoot, and all these steep staircases . . ."

Twiddle frowned as he banged down the cup. "That is from Mama's centennial rosebud set. It may be chipped, but it is of value to me."

"But sixteen thousand dollars isn't?"

"You sound agitated, Drake. Are you sure you're capable of driving in this condition? It's already begun to rain, and the roads can become very slick."

Drake looked as if he had more caustic remarks to offer, but grimly put on his raincoat and left. Monty crawled into her lap and purred appreciatively as she scratched his ears.

The melatonin, her favorite sleep aid, would affect him within twenty minutes. It was possible that drowsiness would overcome him to the point that he pulled over halfway up the mountain, but she suspected the specter of vanishing cash would distort his judgment. He was undoubtedly cursing her flightiness as his foot pressed firmly on the accelerator.

The lack of guardrails was disgraceful. Papa had complained to their state senator on more than one occasion. She made a mental note to write a letter to the quorum court.

When the telephone rang an hour later, Twiddle nudged an indignant Monty aside and rose. Her heart pounding, she went into the foyer and picked up the receiver.

"Auntie Tidwell," said Alisha. "Are y'all okay?"

Twiddle battled off a sense of antipathy and maintained a pleasant voice. "Why, yes. I gather Drake has told you how I was a bit overcome at the inn and—"

"No, I just heard something on the news about how a woman was poisoned at the inn and a waiter was taken into custody. She was elderly, and I suppose . . ."

"I am not the only elderly woman in Brossing County, dear. Have you heard from Drake?"

Alisha sighed, either from relief or disappointment. "I expect him any minute now. We're having a few couples over later this afternoon, and he promised to clean the grill, although I don't see how we can use the patio if this nasty ol' weather lasts. I can't believe that the one afternoon I plan a party, it sounds like a bowling alley out there." She sighed once again. "Is he on the way?"

"He most definitely is on the way somewhere," Twiddle said. "I hope nothing happens to spoil your party."

"Me, too. I had all the carpets cleaned just last week. I don't know what I'll do if all these folks come tromping in with muddy shoes."

Twiddle murmured something and hung up, wondering how the carpets might look after the post-funeral festivities. Perhaps Alisha could rent a room at the country club. She was making herself another cup of tea when the doorbell rang.

She approached the front door with some trepidation. Through the frosted glass, she could see a figure silhouetted by the constant flash of lightning. Thunder rattled the house. Rain streamed off the roof in a gray blanket.

Her hand may have trembled as she reached for the doorknob, but Miss Tidwell had never been one to turn faint at the sight of a mouse or to hesitate to fend off unwanted advances. The prospect of an enraged Drake or even a steely county deputy was more daunting, but she'd gone too far to falter now, especially with Monty and his feline consorts watching from the staircase.

"Goodness gracious," she said as she gestured for her caller to come inside. "You're soaked to the skin, Mr. Sweeny. You should have waited until the storm passed. I realize you're eager to buy that letter from General Lee, but you're liable to catch your death of cold in weather like this. How about a nice cup of tea and a cookie before we settle down to business?"

Mr. Sweeny nodded with his typical shyness.

"I have to admit I'm a wee bit nervous about having all that cash in the house," she murmured from the doorway.

He took out a handkerchief and fastidiously dried his wire-rimmed bifocals. "You shouldn't be, my dear Miss Tidwell. Nobody else knows of this transaction of ours, or even that I planned to come here. It's our little secret."

Even at eighty-three, Twiddle mused as she started toward the kitchen, there was no reason why she could not take up a new career. And she did seem to have a heretofore unexplored talent.

Dean James

Dean James's contributions to the mystery world are myriad. He's the manager of Houston's famed mystery bookstore, Murder by the Book. His *By a Woman's Hand: A Guide to Mystery Fiction by Women*, coauthored with Jean Swanson, was nominated for an Edgar and won the Agatha and Macavity. With Jan Grape, he coedited another volume on women mystery writers, *Deadly Women*, and with Ms. Swanson, *Killer Books: A Reader's Guide to Exploring the Popular World of Mystery and Suspense*. And now he's turned his talented hand to writing stories—and a first novel, *Cruel as the Grave*, set in Jackson, Mississippi.

Mr. James himself is a seventh-generation Mississippian, where he grew up with scads of cousins, none of whom married one another, as far as he knows. Sitting around on porches on hot summer days, listening to the adults tell stories made him want to do the same. "No matter where those stories are set," he says, "something Southern creeps in, because growing up Southern was like living in the middle of every one of Shakespeare's plays all at once. Comedy, drama, tragedy, farce—they're with you every day. All you have to do is choose." Certainly all of those elements are at play in his eerie "The Perfect Man."

The Perfect Man

Sunlight filtered through the gaps in the front steps and in the boards of the verandah overhead. Arthur rolled his favorite toy truck through the dirt, being careful as always not to smudge his clothes. Mother mustn't know where he was, and dirty clothes would betray him. She knew nothing about this haven underneath the verandah. Louise probably did, but Louise was good at keeping his secrets. Arthur was only four, but he knew already that Louise watched out for him.

Mother thought he was in his room, dutifully coloring in the new book she had bought him yesterday at the dime store in Greenville. Arthur did enjoy coloring, sometimes, and his mother insisted that he had an eye for color. She always admired his efforts, kissing and hugging him extravagantly. But Arthur had grown tired of being sent to his room to color or look at his picture books every time one of his mother's gentlemen friends came calling.

The Perfect Man

Arthur carefully wheeled his truck across the hard-packed earth. He would soon grow tired of squatting, but he mustn't sit in the dirt. He imagined he was speeding along the road from King's Mount, their home, all the way into Greenville. There he'd go to the dime store and buy all the toys he wanted, the ones his mother insisted weren't proper for someone of his station.

"Dressing up as a cowboy is not suitable for a member of the King family, Arthur," his mother had tried patiently to explain. Arthur didn't understand, but his mother continued anyway. "Our family were among the first to settle in this part of Mississippi, and there have been Kings at King's Mount for over a hundred years. Cowboy suits are rather common, Arthur, and a King simply cannot be common."

Arthur wasn't really sure what that meant, either, and for the moment, at least, he had given up on being a cowboy when he grew up. He rolled his truck back the other way.

He heard the front door swing open. The screen door squeaked like crazy, but no one ever did anything about it. Arthur crouched very still, pretending he was a mouse hiding from a big, hungry cat.

"Ah, Ginevra, you are a marvel, my dear," a deep, hearty male voice said.

"Such a marvel that you're leaving, and I don't know when I shall ever see you again?" Ginevra's voice had a certain tone, and Arthur with little trouble could see the pouting expression on her face.

"Now, Ginevra, don't kick up about this. I told you how sorry I am, but I just can't come and, er, visit you anymore. Things are just gettin' a bit too complicated in town. You know how it goes."

"What you mean is, your wife has come a little too close to figuring out why you've been taking some long lunch hours recently." Ginevra King's husky voice roughened in anger.

"You knew this wasn't anything permanent," the man said, getting impatient. "You knew it wasn't gonna last that long. I mean, how could it?"

"Yes, how could it?" Ginevra said. "You're nothing but a man, and men have never done anything but disappoint me. Why should you be anything else but a gold-plated jackass like the rest of your sex?"

"Well, I guess I know when enough is enough," the man responded, finally sounding as angry as Arthur's mother. He stomped down the stairs over Arthur's head, and Arthur cringed, seeing the boards bulge downward.

Moments later, a car door slammed. The ignition fired, and wheels spun in gravel before the car sped down the driveway toward the road nearly half a mile away.

Arthur waited patiently, hoping his mother would go back inside the house. Then he'd be able to sneak through the wild growth of plants and shrubbery surrounding the verandah, around the side of the house to the back door and up the back stairs to his room before she realized he hadn't been there all along.

The screen door opened again, and he heard Louise's voice. "Miss Ginevra, everything all right out here?"

"What do you think, Louise?" Ginevra said in resignation. "He's gone, and he's not coming back."

"I'm shore sorry, Miss Ginevra," Louis said softly. "But maybe it be all for the best anyway. That Mistuh Putney, he just ain't the kind of folks you oughta be keeping company with."

"Now, Louise, don't you start with me! I've heard enough on the subject. Mr. Putney might have been a mistake, I'll admit that, but I thought he had possibilities."

"Maybe the right man gonna come along. Any day now, Miss Ginevra. The Good Lord will provide. You need to have more faith in Him."

"Please, Louise, the Good Lord never has concerned Himself very much with me," Ginevra replied. Arthur heard her drop into the swing; it was her favorite seat on the verandah. The creaking of the chains began. Arthur might have to hide under the verandah for quite a while now.

"Miss Ginevra, you oughta not talk about the Good Lord like that. He looks after ever'body. And someday He gonna bring you a wonderful man to take care of you and Mist' Arthur."

Ginevra laughed. "I sure would like to see this Mr.

Wonderful you're always going on about. I don't think any such man exists!"

Louise snorted. "Miss Ginevra, you keep waitin' for some kinda Mistuh Perfect to come along, and you know, just like I do, they ain't no Mistuh Perfect. But you can find yo'self a Mistuh Good Enough if'n you put yo' mind to it! That boy needs a daddy!" The screen door slammed.

"What good is a father?" Ginevra asked bitterly. The swing continued to creak. "The perfect man," she muttered. She repeated it several times. Then she laughed.

Arthur got comfortable for what might be a long wait.

"Do I have to?" Arthur said, trying to squirm away.

"Now, Mist' Arthur, you know Miss Ginevra done picked out these clothes special for you. It being the first day of school and all. Hold still, chile!" Louise, normally the most patient of women with children, was tiring of the struggle to get six-year-old Arthur dressed in the bow tie and jacket his mother insisted he wear to school.

Louise was momentarily tempted to let Arthur have his way, since Miss Ginevra was down the hall in her bedroom, heavily sedated. Louise had hated to slip the sleeping pills in her coffee, but Miss Ginevra had cut up something awful, thinking about Arthur going to school, day after day, leaving her alone in the house with just Louise.

Louise had done her best to calm her distraught mistress, but once Ginevra got in one of her moods, nothing much would work. Except maybe a sledgehammer upside the head. Louise sighed. If it weren't for this poor lamb in front of her, Louise would have decamped long before now. Heaven knew her sister could use her help, with all those children and grandchildren living with her.

"Mist' Arthur!" Louise's patience had almost broken.

Arthur stopped wiggling. Louise's wrinkled brown face broke into a big smile as she clipped on the bow tie. She picked up the jacket, and Arthur turned and held his arms back for her to slip it on. He pivoted back to face her, and she smiled again.

"Honey lamb, you do look mighty fine. Yore mamma gone be so proud when she see you come home this afternoon. I jus' cain't hardly believe it's yo' first day of school. You gonna have so much fun today, getting' to know ever'body else in yo' class. You gonna make friends, you jus' wait an' see."

Arthur nodded glumly, unconvinced by Louise's assurances. He moved to his desk and picked up the book satchel Louise had bought for him. He followed Louis down to the kitchen, where she gave him an apple for recess, a nickel for milk, and money to buy his lunch tickets for the week.

"Shore you don't want me to walk down with you

and wait for the bus, Mist' Arthur?'' Louise watched her small charge with concern as they went out onto the verandah. The sun was climbing, and the steamy heat made Louise want to wipe her face with her apron.

"I'll be fine, Louise," Arthur said, his heart beating a bit quickly. "I know where to wait for the bus."

Louise nodded, watching him, small for his age, step carefully through the overgrown grass of the yard and onto the gravel of the driveway. She stood there until he disappeared around a bend in the driveway, then wiped away a couple of tears with the corner of her apron and went back inside to her work.

As soon as he knew he was out of sight of the house, Arthur started looking. About halfway between the bend in the driveway and the road up ahead, there was a dense stand of trees and bushes that would serve his purposes. Approaching it, Arthur set down his satchel, shrugged out of his jacket, and took it into the thicket, being careful to avoid getting scratched. He found a good-sized bush, arranged his jacket with care upon it, then went back to the driveway. He unclipped his bow tie, stuffed it in his satchel, and unfastened the top button of his shirt.

Picking up the book satchel, Arthur marched to the road, ready for the school bus and his first day in first grade.

The Perfect Man

* * *

"Why not, Mother?" Arthur asked reasonably.

Ginevra pouted and released Arthur from her arms. At eight, Arthur was sometimes irritatingly mature for his age. "Darling, do we have to discuss this yet again?"

Arthur simply stared at her, waiting for an answer.

"Arthur, my dearest and only, I've already explained to you why you cannot spend the night— and the weekend, too, I just shudder thinking about it—with that boy and his parents. We don't know them, or anything about them. We certainly don't know whether it's suitable for you to have anything to do with this little Lewis Barnett."

Arthur considered that for a moment. "I think Lewis is very nice, and one day when his mother came to school to pick him up when he was sick, I saw her and she was dressed very nice and she spoke to me and she had a real nice voice, Mother. She sounded like you."

Louise, dusting a table in the corner, chuckled quietly.

Ginevra pretended not to hear. "She may have sounded like me, Arthur, but that doesn't mean she is our kind of people."

Arthur thought some more. "You could always ask that Mr. Pettimore who keeps calling on you. Maybe he knows Lewis's family and can tell you that they're suitable for someone of my station to spend the weekend with."

Ginevra's eyes narrowed as she regarded her son. For a moment she thought he was deliberately mocking her. But, no, she decided, he was too young for that. Thank the Lord!

"I just might do that, Arthur. If I do, and if Mr. Pettimore tells me the Barnetts are unsuitable, will you stop pestering me about this?" She caressed his arm with the back of her hand.

"Yes, Mother," Arthur said, standing very still.

"Very well. Then, you may go up to your room now until Louise calls you for dinner. Mother needs to rest awhile."

"Yes, Mother," Arthur repeated, quickly leaning forward to kiss her cheek before departing.

As Arthur's footsteps receded, Ginevra asked, "I am doing the right thing, aren't I, Louise?" Not pausing to wait for an answer, she continued, "Of course I am. Heaven knows who these people are, and what they really want by inviting my dear little Arthur to spend the weekend at their place. They probably expect me to invite all of them here to King's Mount, where I'd be forced to put up with Heaven-knows-what kind of common behavior."

Arthur, who had climbed out of the window in the next room, paused under the window to hear this last bit of his mother's complaint. Shrugging, he slipped on by to the front of the house, where he pushed his way through the thick foliage into his sanctuary under the verandah. Mother wouldn't miss

110

him for a while, and he could play without interruption.

Mr. Pettimore called on Ginevra the next midday while Arthur was at school, and when Arthur came home in the afternoon, she was on the verandah to greet him.

"Good news, Arthur," she called gaily as she watched him approach the house. She paused for a moment, waiting until he came closer, watching him and thinking how handsome he looked in his jacket and bow tie.

"Yes, Mother?" Arthur asked as he began climbing the stairs up onto the verandah.

"I had a little chat with Mr. Pettimore today," Ginevra said. She swept Arthur into a hug, squeezed him tightly, then released him. Taking Arthur's arm she guided him into the house, toward the kitchen where Louise waited with an afternoon snack of oatmeal raisin cookies and cold milk.

"Mr. Pettimore assured me that the Barnetts are very nice people. He had nothing but praise for both Mr. and Mrs. Barnett and said that they were certainly the kind of people that my son could visit. Aren't you pleased, Arthur?"

Setting his book satchel down on the kitchen table, Arthur said, "Yes, Mother. Thank you very much." He sat down and helped himself to one of Louise's cookies, fresh from the oven.

Ginevra sat down at the table across from him. "I

111

do have one request, darling, and that is, I would at least like to meet one of Lewis's parents before you go for the weekend. Do you think Mr. Barnett could come by on Friday afternoon, after you get home from school, so I could meet him?" She reached out an arm and touched his hand lightly.

Arthur considered. "Tomorrow is Wednesday, so I guess that's enough time to ask Lewis at school and find out from his father if he can do that."

"Good. That's settled, then, darling." She took one of Arthur's cookies and nibbled at it. "I wonder what on earth I'll do all weekend here by myself, without my dear boy here with me."

Louise, taking another batch of cookies out of the oven, snorted. Ginevra deigned not to hear. She chattered brightly while Arthur slowly ate six cookies and drank a glass of milk.

On Friday afternoon, Arthur hopped off the bus and ran down the driveway toward King's Mount. He was so excited he almost forgot to stop and retrieve his jacket and put on his bow tie again. By the time he reached the point where someone at the house could see him, he slowed down to a more sedate pace.

No one was on the verandah, which was odd. Usually Louise, and occasionally his mother, was there waiting for him. He clumped up the steps and into the house.

"Darling, is that you?" his mother called.

"Yes, ma'am." Arthur proceeded down the hall-way toward the kitchen, where he found his mother looking in the refrigerator.

"Where's Louise?" he asked.

Ginevra, shifting things about, said, "She had to go over to Clarksdale to see about one of her sisters who's ill. I'm afraid she's going to be gone until Sunday."

"Oh." Arthur stood very still for a moment.

"Louise packed your bag before she left, darling, so why don't you go on upstairs and change your clothes. Then bring your bag down, and we'll wait for Mr. Barnett out on the verandah." Ginevra closed the refrigerator door. "Now, where did Louise put those preserves?" she muttered to herself.

"Yes, ma'am," Arthur said. As he turned back toward the hall and the direction of the stairs, his mother was dragging one of the kitchen chairs over to the cabinets next to the sink.

Arthur had hung up his jacket and had removed his shirt and bow tie when he heard a loud crash downstairs. He stood irresolute for a moment, then turned and ran down to the kitchen.

Ginevra was sprawled unmoving on the kitchen floor. Arthur knelt beside her. "Mother," he said urgently. "Mother! Are you all right?"

Ginevra stirred and reached blindly for his hand. "Oh, my goodness. Arthur! I fell. I can't believe how stupid I was. Trying to get a new jar of preserves from a cabinet way too high for little bitty me to reach." She lay there for a moment.

Pulling loose his hand, Arthur hopped up and got her a glass of water. Ginevra sat up wincingly and sipped at it. "Thank you, darling." She handed him the glass, which he set on the counter. "Let Mother lean on you while she gets up."

Ginevra pulled herself up, using Arthur heavily as a crutch, and she seemed fine for a moment. But then she cried out, "Oh, that hurts." She hobbled over to the table and sank down into one of the chairs.

"What's wrong, Mother?" Arthur asked.

"I do believe I sprained my ankle," she said. "I can't put my weight on it, and look how it's swelling." She pointed to her right foot, and Arthur peered down at it. Indeed, the ankle was swelling.

Following Ginevra's instructions, Arthur wrapped ice cubes in a clean kitchen towel and knelt on the floor to hold the ice pack against her swelling ankle. "Thank you, darling, that feels so much better." She rubbed his head lovingly.

Next, Ginevra had Arthur retrieve one of his grandfather's canes from the stand in the front hallway, and using it, she was able to make her way slowly into the parlor. "Shall I call the doctor?" Arthur asked worriedly as she sank down on the sofa.

"I'm afraid we probably should," Ginevra said apologetically.

Arthur looked up the number in the phone book and dialed it. He explained what had happened and received assurance that the doctor would come out sometime within the hour. After relaying the message to his mother, he consulted the book again and dialed another number.

"Whom are you calling?" Ginevra asked, a slight smile Arthur couldn't see playing upon her lips.

"Mrs. Barnett," Arthur said. "I'll tell her I can't come this weekend so Mr. Barnett won't drive all the way out here to get me."

"Oh, darling," Ginevra said bravely, "I'll be just fine on my own. I don't want you to miss having fun with your little friend, just for my sake."

"Louise isn't here, so you'll need someone to look after you, Mother," Arthur said reasonably.

Ginevra sighed. "I hate to ask it of you, but I suppose you're right. You're such a responsible young man, darling."

Arthur spoke into the phone and explained to Mrs. Barnett what had happened and expressed his regrets to Lewis. "Maybe," he said finally. "Good-bye, Mrs. Barnett."

"Maybe what?" Ginevra asked.

"Maybe I can come next weekend instead, she said," Arthur responded.

"Of course," Ginevra said. "What a good idea."

Arthur shrugged. He took the now-soggy ice pack back to the kitchen for a dry towel and more ice.

The next weekend Louise was once again called to Clarksdale, and Ginevra cut her hand badly while trying to slice tomatoes for a salad. Arthur regretfully declined Lewis Barnett's invitation and stayed home with his mother.

The next summer, when Arthur turned nine, Ginevra decided that he was old enough for what she termed "deportment lessons," and Arthur spent the summer beginning to learn the manners of a true Southern gentleman. That established the pattern for Arthur's summers. While other children went on vacation with their parents, or went swimming and flying kites and making mud pies, Arthur learned how a gentleman behaved in any situation his mother could devise.

With puberty came various changes. Arthur suddenly shot up and just kept growing. Ginevra could no longer call him her "little man," but now that he was tall enough, towering over her own petite frame, she could teach him how to dance. Arthur had a natural grace and an inborn feel for music, and he easily mastered the various steps his mother taught him. Ginevra insisted on practicing with him almost every night, with Louise quietly persistent in watching over the proceedings.

Now, just beginning high school, Arthur continued to wear his jacket and bow tie down the driveway on his way to the bus, but sometimes he wore them to school. He didn't always stop to leave his jacket hidden away like before. There was a very pretty girl in his algebra class who had been known to say that she truly admired the appearance of a real gentleman. Arthur believed he could attract her attention; certainly his mother had spent enough of his time making him into one. Miss Susan Tucker might as well notice him as anyone else.

There was a dance for freshmen and sophomores at Halloween that year, and Arthur asked Susan Tucker, who gladly accepted. Arthur waited until the day before the dance to inform his mother. Maybe this time there would be no accidents.

"My goodness, Arthur," Ginevra said in a brittle voice, "I had no idea you thought you were old enough to attend a dance. Who is this girl?"

Arthur explained very quickly to his mother who Susan Tucker was, who her parents and grandparents were, and how impeccable her pedigree was. Ginevra's eyes narrowed, but she said only, "And how were you planning to get to this dance in town, darling? You know I don't drive. Do you want Louise to drive you?"

"No, ma'am," Arthur said. "Mr. Tucker will take Susan and me to the dance and bring me home afterward."

"I suppose that's suitable, then," Ginevra responded. "But I'll expect you home no later than ten-thirty. Is that clear?"

"Yes, Mother," Arthur said, bending down to kiss her cheek.

The following afternoon when Arthur arrived home from school, he found that Louise had once again been called away on some family emergency.

He also found his mother unconscious on the floor of the parlor. Furniture was overturned, vases and picture frames were broken, and in general it looked as if a party had gotten way out of hand.

Ginevra revived soon under Arthur's ministrations. He listened calmly to his mother's semi-hysterical explanation of two strange Negro men who had burst in, demanding money. He glanced around the room, noting that several expensive knickknacks were missing, then called, in turn, the doctor and the sheriff. His third and final call was to Susan Tucker, to whom he explained the situation. He expressed his deep and lasting regret that he could not escort her to the dance that evening and hoped she would forgive him, but his mother needed him and he could not desert her at such a time. Susan's assurances—and disappointment—ringing in his ear, Arthur made sure his mother was comfortable, then sat down near her to wait for the doctor and someone from the sheriff's department.

By his seventeenth birthday, the summer before his senior year in high school, Arthur had grown to six feet, with a physique that brought him many an approving eye from young women at his school. Ginevra thought it unsuitable for him to participate in any of the school's athletic activities, particularly since the schools in Mississippi had recently been integrated. Thus Arthur had devised his own exercise program, running through the country roads near King's

Mount and swimming in a small lake nearby. Disapproving at first, Ginevra had eventually conceded that Arthur looked all the better for it.

For his seventeenth birthday celebration, Ginevra had planned a special treat, part of what she called Arthur's continuing education in the proper deportment of a well-bred Southern gentleman. Ginevra's current gentleman caller, a somewhat seedy banker from Clarksdale, indoctrinated Arthur after dinner that evening in the civilized pleasures of cigars and brandy. "Something every Southern man of cultivation enjoys," Ginevra said gaily. "I'll leave you men to it, and you may join me in the parlor afterward."

After an initial bit of coughing, more from the brandy than from the cigar, Arthur enjoyed himself. This latest conquest of his mother's, Caleb Roland, seemed even more captivated than usual by Ginevra, and Arthur hoped that he might even want to marry her. But as the summer wore on, Arthur found himself increasingly enjoying his after-dinner spirits and cigar alone, while his mother chatted with Louise in the parlor or listened to the radio.

With the beginning of his senior year, when his teachers began talking about college, and his classmates were having spirited arguments over the relatively merits of Ole Miss versus Mississippi State, Arthur began pondering his future. He had never given much thought to his past, but suddenly he began to wonder about his father. His mother had rarely spoken about him, other than saying bitterly that he had walked out on her and Arthur for no good reason when Arthur was barely two. Since the subject made his mother so unhappy, Arthur stopped asking her. Louise, usually forthcoming, also had little to say.

But Arthur's long-dormant curiosity about his father awoke, and he felt increasingly compelled to find out something about the man. He would need an ally if he wanted to go to college, and perhaps his father would help him, if only he could find him. If only he was still alive.

Through the fall and into the spring, Arthur snooped around the house when he could, trying to find some evidence of his father's existence. But all his efforts yielded few results, even after he had stooped to searching his mother's room, not once, but on several occasions.

Finally, as the deadline was approaching that spring to submit applications to schools for the fall, Arthur grew desperate. One evening after dinner, fueled by too much brandy and a long session of thought over his postprandial cigar, Arthur asked his mother. Louise had retired to her room with a bad headache, and he thought his mother might be more forthcoming with Louise out of the way.

"Darling, you haven't asked me that since you were about seven years old!" Ginevra's laugh made Arthur's stomach churn. "Why, after all this time, are you bringing up that old business?"

"Because it's only right that I should know who my father is," Arthur stubbornly insisted.

Round and round they went, Arthur doing his best to get his mother to answer, Ginevra trying to cajole him away from the topic.

Suddenly, Arthur couldn't stand it any longer. He stood over his mother, staring down at her, noticing for the first time the signs of aging, though she was only thirty-five. Her indolent lifestyle had not served her well. Arthur noted the small wrinkles around her eyes, the flesh beginning to sag a bit underneath her arms. She was still beautiful, but she was fading. He wanted to grind her head into the back of the sofa.

"God damn you," he said, "tell me now who my father was!" His fists clenched in rage, and Ginevra shrank back from him.

"My God, Arthur, why are you swearing at me?" she whimpered at him. "Why are you doing this to me?"

"Because I have to know, I need to know, and you won't tell me!" By instinct, he held back the most compelling reason, but if she held out much longer he might blurt it out in anger.

"No, I won't tell you!" Ginevra shrieked at him. "You're acting common, Arthur, and I won't tell you anything."

Before he realized what he was doing, Arthur slapped her. Staring, appalled at the red mark on her cheek, Arthur was too numb to apologize.

"You want to know who your father was?" Ginevra asked, her voice all at once cold and completely calm.

Arthur nodded, still dazed by what he had done.

"Look at that portrait over the mantel, then. There's your father!" Then she lost control and screamed, "Does that make you happy?"

Appalled, Arthur stared up at the portrait of his grandfather.

Ginevra brushed past Arthur and went into the dining room; she came back moments later with the brandy decanter and two glasses. Her hands shaking, she poured them both generous portions. Arthur accepted his blindly, brought it to his mouth, and drank it dry. He held the glass out to his mother, his eyes pleading for more. Ginevra filled his glass again and sat back to watch, and wait.

During the night, Arthur moaned in his sleep, troubled by unspeakable dreams. He shifted in the bed. Ginevra wrapped an arm around him, pulling her body against his, feeling the warmth of skin against skin. Her hand traced a path from his right nipple down to the hair of his crotch. "So perfect," she whispered, over and over. "Just what I've been waiting for." She crooned the words like a lullaby, and, soothed, Arthur grew quiet once more.

For the rest of the spring, Arthur worked feverishly to keep his grades at a high level. He graduated first in his class, which made his mother and Louise tremendously proud. But what he didn't tell them was that he had been offered a number of scholarships. Louise, though not sure why he wanted her to, hid all his mail from Ginevra so that Arthur could lay his plans.

During the summer, Arthur spent every day out-of-doors, as much as possible. The nights he tried to blot from his memory, worrying that he was going to make himself an alcoholic from his consumption of brandy. But he had to dull the pain somehow.

Finally, however, the time came. He had sent Louise away, ostensibly to tend to yet another family emergency, and he and Ginevra were alone in the house.

After dinner that evening, Arthur told his mother he had something to talk to her about, and Ginevra motioned for him to join her on the sofa in the parlor.

Wordlessly, Arthur pulled a letter from his jacket pocket and handed it to his mother. "What is this, darling?" she asked.

"Read it," Arthur said.

Too vain to wear the glasses she needed, Ginevra peered at the letter. Her face drained of color as she realized its import.

"You've been admitted to Ole Miss with a full scholarship," she said flatly. "And by the date on this letter, you've known for some time. Why didn't you tell me before now?"

"I wanted it to be a surprise," Arthur said, surprised at his own coolness.

"And just when are you supposed to go?"

"I'm leaving in the morning. Susie Tucker's father is going to take us both up. We can move into our dorms tomorrow and attend an orientation session for freshmen. Classes start on Monday."

"I see. You have it all planned out, don't you?" Ginevra said coldly. 'You're leaving me."

"Yes."

"You ungrateful little bastard," she said, her voice still cold. "Then, I suppose you had better go upstairs and pack."

"Yes, Mother, that's a good idea." Arthur took the letter from her, put it back in his jacket pocket, turned, and walked upstairs.

In his room, he sat on the bed and waited. A few minutes later he heard the crash of something on the kitchen floor and a muffled scream. Slowly he got up from the bed and walked back downstairs.

In the kitchen he found the remains of one of Louise's favorite porcelain serving platters shattered on the floor and his mother sitting at the table, blood spurting out of both wrists. A large shard of porcelain lay on the table, streaked with blood.

Arthur sat down at the other end of the table, away from the blood, and watched.

Ginevra stared at him, her eyes sending a mute appeal as her life ebbed away.

"Not this time, Mother," Arthur said quietly. "Think of it as your graduation gift to me."

"You're not going to leave me," Ginevra said, her

face hardening. "I've made you into the kind of man I've always wanted. You're not going to leave me now." She held up her wrists as the blood continued to flow.

Arthur shook his head. "It won't work this time, Mother. I finally realized, I have to make a choice. Your life or mine."

"You really are your father's son," Ginevra said, slumping back in her chair.

"I wouldn't know," Arthur said. "Grandfather died when I was too young to remember him."

"Jesus, you're as coldhearted as he was!" Once again, but with more of an effort, she held up one wrist. "Call the doctor! Call an ambulance!" Ginevra begged, trying to stand.

"No, Mother," Arthur said. "I can't. And I'm afraid I won't let you go into the parlor, where the phone is."

Ginevra got up and staggered to the counter, looking for something with which she could bind her wounds.

"It won't do any good, Mother. You're going to bleed to death, and nothing will stop it."

Whimpering, Ginevra slumped onto the floor, and Arthur watched until he was sure she was beyond help. He got up from his chair, went back upstairs, and changed into his running clothes. He went out the front door and ran down the driveway.

When he came back an hour later, he called the

sheriff's department, crying so hard he could barely speak.

"I think that's everything," Arthur said, snapping the locks on his trunk. He turned and sat down on top of it, regarding Louise solemnly. "Mr. Tucker will be here soon to pick me up."

"I can't hardly believe my baby's goin' to college," Louise said.

The corners of Arthur's mouth moved slightly. "It doesn't seem real to me, either. Yet."

"You have to get on with your life, Mast' Arthur. Ain't no question about that!" Louise shook her head dolefully. "Yo' poor mama never had a chance. She be better off now. Maybe she finally found peace."

A horn sounded outside. Arthur turned and walked downstairs.

Ten minutes later, Mr. Tucker and Arthur had the trunk safely into the back of his pickup. Arthur gave Louise a quick hug, then joined Susie and Mr. Tucker in the cab of the truck.

As the pickup moved off down the driveway, Arthur looked back one last time, to see Louise sitting in the porch swing, moving gently back and forth. Then he turned to Susie and smiled.

Terry Kay

It would be difficult to find a writer more dedicated to things Southern than Terry Kay, an award-winning novelist and screenwriter who was born on a farm in Hart County, Georgia, the eleventh of twelve children. He has spent a lifetime writing in and about the South as a sportswriter, film and theater critic; he is a spokesperson for Oglethorpe Power, has taught writing at Emory University, and furthered writing as host of a PBS series on *The Southern Voice*.

Mr. Kay's first novel, *The Year the Lights Came On*, about the electrification of the rural South, is a classic coming-of-age story. His *To Dance with the White Dog*, a touching based-in-fact story about his parents, was presented by Hallmark Hall of Fame, which will soon produce his 1997 novel, *The Runaway*.

"I really think I've only written one book that *had* to be set in the South, *The Runaway*, but I've used my Southern heritage and eye and ear to tell all the stories. Seems natural to me. It's where I was born, where I choose to live, what I know best."

It's Mr. Kay's knowledge of the love Southerners have of grandiloquence mated with their fondness for a Katie-bar-the-door, over-the-top, twelve-hankie funeral that he brings to bear in "The Obit Writer."

The Obit Writer

Harley looks good, there in his coffin.

Pale, of course. Even Middy Boswick's clever swipes with a rouge pad cannot replace the blood-coloring of his face.

Yet Harley seems at peace. A smile, or the impression of a smile, rests on the corners of his lips. I have heard whispers from those slow-walking past the coffin: "He's smiling. Isn't that wonderful? He's smiling." There is surprise in their voices. Harley was not a man who smiled discernibly while alive.

Tanner Boswick of Boswick's Funeral Services is handling the funeral only because he won the lottery. Not exactly the lottery. It only seems that way. Before he died, Harley placed the name of every funeral director in Atlanta in an empty gauze box, had a nurse swirl the little strips of paper around, and then he plucked Tanner's name from the lot. I am told that Harley frowned slightly, as though disappointed. It did not matter. He had done the honorable thing. Tanner Boswick would be the handler of his body.

Tanner dressed Harley in one of his dark, faint-stripe tailored suits, a starched white shirt, and a maroon silk tie. I do not know, because the bottom half of the coffin is closed, but I would bet that Tanner also slipped a pair of wing-tip shoes, gleam-shined, on Harley's feet. I cannot imagine Harley without his wing tips.

Tanner does have one nice touch in his presentation of Harley: an umbrella is nestled next to his right arm. Harley was never without his umbrella, the expensive model that opened with a thumb-press and a popping sound not unlike the sound a champagne cork makes when it explodes out of the bottle.

The umbrella was for funerals, for the sun and rain of cemeteries.

Harley went to a lot of funerals. Five or six a week. It was his job, he believed.

"How can I ask for the trust of people in preparing a funeral notice of a loved one if I'm only a voice on the telephone?" he once told me.

Harley Grace was an obit writer. His cubicle was across from mine at the *Atlanta Herald*. We were not exactly friends, but we were friendly. Hello nodding friendly. Occasionally he would comment on one of my stories, and I would do the same regarding one of his obituaries.

It was not a casual swap of compliments on my part. Harley was the best writer we had. He could have been a literary giant, a novelist of renown, or a poet, or a playwright. He was that good.

Yet, he only wanted to write obits. Came out of the school of journalism at the University of Georgia convinced that writing about the deaths of people was noble business. He had a philosophy about it. "Dying is the sum of living," he once suggested to me. "What else is worth writing about?"

To Harley, a funeral was a forum for history, literature, philosophy, religion—those truly civilized regions of man's existence. A funeral was about soul, he contended, and the indisputable fact that a person's soul departing the mire of physical bondage on the occasion of death called for praise, regardless of the absurd reach said praise often required for some people.

"Everyone—*everyone*—has an ounce of good in him, or her," Harley had quietly preached. "And, in the end, that ounce of good outweighs several pounds of flesh."

Kenny Overmeyer, who is the managing editor of the *Herald*, is standing at the foot end of Harley's coffin, and I am stationed at the head. We are like sentries, protecting Harley from the unpredictable actions of the living. We are both uncomfortable, but Tanner has insisted that being where we are was Harley's wish.

"He wanted his service to be dignified," Tanner said in his funeral voice. "And he considered both of you dignified men."

I wondered how a man as astute as Harley could

couple Kenny and dignity in the same thought. I am sure Kenny wondered the same about me.

Earlier, before the church doors were opened, Kenny and I were standing at the coffin, trying not to look at Harley. Kenny asked in a whisper, "What are we supposed to do?"

"Stand here," I suggested. "Look solemn."

"Jesus," Kenny sighed. He turned to gaze reluctantly at Harley. "He was a crazy son of a bitch," he added in a voice that could barely lift the words. "Crazy. But he was damn good at what he did."

And then Kenny shuffled off to the foot of the coffin to take his position. I could hear him mumbling about people on life-support systems sending Christmas gifts to Harley.

It was more than an office joke, the line about the Christmas gifts.

It was true.

If you were anyone worthy of public interest, Harley had your obituary written years in advance, code-locked in the hard drive of his computer, updated as conscientiously as a Monk tending a garden. When it came time for you to cross the great divide, all Harley needed was date and cause of death—a quick lead paragraph—and if you were important enough, the news of your demise and of your late, updated life could scream across the front page of the newspaper before your soul had wiggled completely out of your body.

In short, when the announcement of your death

131

appeared in print, you wanted Harley's name as the byline. His stories were brilliant. Stories of shock and lamentation blossoming into celebration. Stories that members of the radio and television media quoted directly, generously attributing Harley. They couldn't do better and they knew it. Besides, it was likely that each of them had already been word-dressed for death by Harley. No one wanted to offend him. Kenny vowed that he knew of people who moved to Atlanta to die, just for the obituary that Harley would write.

Someone hidden behind a spray of flowers is playing soft, dignified organ music. Bach, I would guess. Tanner has informed me that Harley loved Bach, that a flautist from the Atlanta Symphony Orchestra will play Bach at the grave site, and I know how it will sound—like a lone bird singing over the remains of the Earth on the last day of survival.

Kenny is having trouble with being dignified. His face is red. He looks away to avoid the curious gazes of those in the slow-moving, sway-stepping line to view Harley's body. He seems to be contemplating the ceiling of the church—pretending, I suspect, that he is in harmony with a cloud of saints. It is a pitiful look. Kenny would not know a saint from a fly.

Unlike Kenny, I am a crowd watcher, and it is surprising to me that such a large gathering has wedged its way into the church. Surprising because

Harley was not married, had no siblings, and few known friends.

I hear an occasional sob—suppressed, however. More sigh than sob. Harley would approve. It is more dignified to sigh than to wail.

I also see a number of the staff of the *Herald*, which makes me wonder if Kenny issued a memorandum, ordering attendance. They do not look at Kenny because Kenny does not look at them, and they do not pause long at the coffin. A few of them roll their eyes to me in the language of boredom.

Gaines Whitley, a business writer, leans to whisper, "Too bad he can't see this. He'd love every minute of it."

I watch as the line suddenly stops and a knot of people—mostly men dressed in dark suits and gray shirts with subdued ties—press close to the coffin and bend over to examine Harley like appraisers at an auction. From a door leading to the choir room of the church, Tanner suddenly materializes and briskly walks to the group. There is a lot of hand shaking and head nodding among them. I hear one of the men say, "That's great work, Tanner. Great work." Tanner beams.

"We'll miss him," a woman says quietly. She dabs at her eyes with a dainty handkerchief.

"Yes, we will," agrees Tanner.

For a moment it is a confusing scene, and then it becomes clear. This is a gathering of the city's leading funeral directors, there to pay respect to Harley, probably gossiping among themselves over the possibilities of Harley's replacement. Of course, no one will ever truly replace him, and they know it. Someone will write the obits, but he, or she, will never treat them with awe, as Harley has done.

"Tell Middy she's an artist, simply an artist," another woman says to Tanner.

"I will," Tanner promises. "She'll be delighted to hear it."

"We need to talk about an award in his honor," someone else whispers.

"That's a wonderful idea," the second woman coos. She adds, "Did you hear there's a publishing company coming out with a book of his best obituaries? They're going to call it *Passing Over*."

The group fades away from the coffin, their faces coated with sadness. None of them seem to resent the fact it was Tanner's name that Harley drew from the gauze box when it became necessary to choose a director for his funeral.

Kenny throws a glance my way. He ticks his head toward the line.

And I see him.

Jarvis Hilderbrand.

He has tears in his eyes. His shoulders still slump with the weight of a heavy heart.

Jarvis Hilderbrand.

Former mayor of Atlanta. Insurance executive. Political power broker with strings running deep into the White House. Founder of Arts in Action, a think tank of businessmen dedicated to corporate support of the arts.

Jarvis Hilderbrand.

Widower of Rebecca Hilderbrand, who at the time of her death was a still-sensuous actress, and the most renown woman in Atlanta since Margaret Mitchell. There were people who called her Miss Charity, because if there was a need and a country club party, she would be there, begging checks from the well-to-do.

No woman in America was as loved by the camera as Rebecca Hilderbrand. Even the photographs of her dead body were stunning. I know. I saw them. And she had died in a horrible manner, her throat crushed from a bar containing eighty pounds of weight during an apparent workout in her home gym.

An accident, the coroner ruled.

Odd, the police thought.

I remember the mumblings at the police station, which is my beat.

Too much weight for such a slender and delicate woman.

She was fanatic about exercise. She knew the limits.

I did not know it at the time, but quietly the police made a few inquiries.

Qwen Scribner, the maid who discovered the body, implied that David Oliver, who once had been Rebecca Hilderbrand's personal fitness instructor, was worth investigating.

The two had argued, Qwen reported, and Rebecca had dismissed David. Something about excessive charges for services.

David had an alibi. On the day that Rebecca was discovered, he was in New Orleans participating in a bodybuilding competition. Had been for a week. Placed third.

And then, for a brief time, Qwen Scribner had become a suspect, jealousy being a possible motive. The story I got was that Jarvis Hilderbrand made one phone call and Qwen was never again questioned. For many people, good maids are as desirable as excessive wealth.

"If there's anything to any of it, we'll never know," my detective friend, Marty Dilworth, told me at the time. "They've closed the lid on this one."

I have always believed it was, in part, Harley's story about the death—more appropriately, the life— of Rebecca Hilderbrand that caused the police to retreat from their investigation. It was a spectacular story, written with lighting bolts of energy and passion, with words that seemed to spin magically off the page and seep into the consciousness of readers, mesmerizing them. I remember hearing newspaper veterans sigh in awe. "Jesus," they whispered. "Jesus."

Kenny even observed, "You know, it's almost like he's making love to her."

One week after Rebecca Hilderbrand's funeral, a motion picture company out of Burbank, California, announced that it would produce a movie inspired by Harley's obituary on Rebecca.

Our movie critic, Sarah Saunders, noted in an essay that it may be the first time in history that an obituary was certain to be better than a movie, and it didn't matter who wrote the screenplay, who directed, or who was cast to play Rebecca and Jarvis.

Kenny even mentioned Harley's story this morning.

"It's the finest single piece of writing that's ever appeared in an Atlanta newspaper," Kenny said. "Hell, I should have submitted it for a Pulitzer. Would have, if it hadn't won that obit thing."

The obit thing was officially called the Headstone Award, presented by the National Association for Writers of Obituary Notices, or NAWON. Harley won it for his story on Rebecca Hilderbrand. I saw it the day he returned from the NAWON convention in Philadelphia. A glass tombstone about six inches high, with Harley's name etched into the facing, and an epithet-type line that read: A Man of Dignity.

All of us snickered about it at the time, but in the last two days I have learned that Harley was obsessed with winning the Headstone Award. He prepared for it as arduously as an athlete preparing for the Olympics, twice serving as president of NAWON, and if he wasn't presiding at NAWON meetings, he was volunteering for NAWON projects. Once he chaired a committee to research the impact of including cause of death in funeral notices, a practice he passionately advocated. For Harley, cause of death was more important than cause of life. For the study he wrote, "Everyone is born the same way, from the womb, but not everyone dies the same." His personal research, gained from months of random telephone calls, revealed that 87 percent of the people who read obituaries wanted to know cause of death.

Oddly, the only obituary he wrote that did not include cause of death was for Rebecca Hilderbrand. Those details were handled by news reports.

And I know why. I wish I didn't, but I do.

Jarvis Hilderbrand stands before Harley's coffin for a long time, his sad gray eyes staring at the corpse, as though he is waiting for Harley to rise up and greet him.

"A good man," Jarvis finally says in a voice too loud for the occasion, a voice that has the sound of sudden, exhaled torment. "He was so kind to my wife, so kind."

A handsome young man that I assume is the son of Jarvis and Rebecca Hilderbrand, or maybe the actor who is to play Jarvis in the movie, touches Jarvis's arm, gently tugs him away.

I look at Kenny. He is chewing subconsciously on his lower lip, a habit that telegraphs anxiety. Kenny had rather be in the coffin than standing guard over it. He has said, "When this is over, I don't even want to hear the name of Harley Grace."

He will, though. He will. Later.

And maybe I've been wrong about all of this. Maybe Kenny will fire me.

But, damn it, I didn't ask to be here. It was Harley's doing.

Why Harley selected me to receive the last words he would ever write, I'll never know. Maybe he trusted me. Maybe he didn't like me at all and thought it would be an aggravation to involve me.

Like Harley, this whole thing has been peculiar.

The envelope delivered to me by courier on the morning that he died contained a memorandum that read:

TO: Cary Knight
FROM: Harley Grace
SUBJECT: My Death
When you read this, I will be dead from pancreatic cancer. Please find enclosed on separate sheet the code for accessing my business files. You have my permission to access said files for the purpose of finding a short notice of my own death. It will be necessary to supply the date of death, otherwise all pertinent facts about my life are described. If you feel they need to be edited, please feel free to do so. I request only that you carefully read the follow to my notice. Thank you for your personal and professional courtesies during our many years of acquaintance.

The signature on the memorandum was a shakily scrawled HG.

In the files of his computer, code-locked under *Do Rite*, I found sixty-two prepared obituaries. It was a little like discovering the Dead Sea Scrolls, or at least getting a proper reading on the social registry of Atlanta. My name was not among the sixty-two, thank God. I do not care to read prematurely of my demise, even with date, time and cause of death missing.

I found Harley's obituary in its alphabet order, between that of Abigail Benson Folger and Foster Cameron Greer. Very good company. Abigail Folger was a superior court judge, and Foster Greer was a distinguished professor of religion at the Candler School of Theology. Both of them would be pleased with the way Harley has presented them, obituaries so wonderfully written they sound like letters of introduction to a much higher power.

Not so with Harley's own notice.

It was, in fact, the worse obit that Harley ever wrote. It had no passion, no energy. It was boring. Simply that: boring. I did not edit it; I rewrote it. My first obit. And my last. Not bad, really, but certainly not up to Harley's standard. I lathered up what we all knew, or thought we knew, about Harley's personal life—that he enjoyed the theater, that he was a connoisseur of California wine, and of course, that he had won the Headstone Award. I invented a quote about him from Kenny and received Kenny's disinterested permission to use it. In his quote, Kenny (I) said, "He was the most caring man I have ever known in journalism, working what most journalists regard as a degrading assignment. Harley approached his work with sensitivity and professionalism. He will be missed by everyone."

To Kenny, I was straining to fill space. He had no idea that I didn't write the whole story. I couldn't. God knows, Harley deserved a little respect for all that he had done, a short reprieve for all the remarkable words that had rolled from his fingertips.

Bach is still singing from the pipes of the organ. An almost ethereal sensation, since the organist is hidden. Everyone who wanted to see Harley has seen him, and they are now seated solemnly in church pews, waiting, their hands folded in their laps, their eyes fixed on the coffin. The most peaceful faces belong to the funeral directors. This is their world. They know how to act. I see one glance at his watch. Probably timing Tanner, wondering when Tanner will begin the service.

Tanner must have seen him, also. He appears, nods at Kenny and then at me. It is a nod that dismisses us. Kenny glances at me, confusion riding the frown across his forehead. I start for the assigned pew. Kenny follows. When we sit, Kenny sighs gladly. He whispers, "Almost over."

"Kenny," I whisper back, "it hasn't even begun."

Kenny looks at me quizzically.

It is a very nice service, the kind my mother would have called lovely. My mother had a voice that made words such as *lovely* sound like a benediction.

The Reverend Heard Roberts tells about Harley winning the Headstone Award for his obituary of Rebecca Hilderbrand. He quotes the words etched into the glass—A Man of Dignity—and then he launches into a short sermon about the good works of good men. Harley's gentle regard for the mysterious passing from life to glory was the perfect description of dignity, Reverend Roberts proposes.

And then it is over and Harley's coffin is rolled from the church to a hearse and delivered to the cemetery.

It is a hot, sticky, high-humidity July day, and not everyone has made the trip from church to grave site. I hear someone say something about wanting a beer, and there is a wiseass reply from someone else about having a bottle of Viagra and a keg of Budweiser buried with him. "Well, maybe just the beer," he adds. "I guess I won't have to worry about being stiff."

We put Harley in the ground in record time, with a flautist pushing Bach to the limits.

Ashes to ashes, Georgia red dirt to Georgia red dirt.

And now it is my time.

"Son of a bitch," Kenny grumbles, wiping the perspiration from his face. "You could fry an egg on a magnolia leaf out here." He looks at me and he is irritated. "Now, what the hell is it that you need to see me about?"

"Come on," I say and I lead him to a drab-looking Chevrolet parked under the shade of an oak.

Kenny sees a man sitting inside the car. He says, "Who's that?"

"A friend of mine," I answer. "Get in. It'll be cooler."

I take the front passenger seat. Kenny is in the back. He does not like being so far from the air conditioner.

'This is Marty Dilworth," I tell Kenny. "He's a detective for the city. I asked him to meet us here."

Kenny nods toward Marty.

"And, Marty, you know who Kenny is," I say.

"Sure do," Marty replies casually. He looks at me. "So, what's this about?"

I reach into my inside coat pocket and remove two sheets of folded paper. I hand one sheet to Kenny, one to Marty.

"It's something that Harley left in his computer," I tell them. "But before you read it, I want you to know that I made the decision on my own to hold this back. I liked that man we just put in the ground."

"Well, shit, Cary, we all did," Kenny snaps. He and Marty open the paper they are holding in unison, with the same hand gestures. Mirror motions.

I watch them read, watch their eyes blink in surprise, watch disbelief build in their faces.

Harley's words:

I write this in shame, but I must write it. For the peace of my soul, I must write it. Out of greed,

143

out of the need to achieve the one thing I wanted most in life, I have committed the most grievous of sins: I have taken the life of another human. I am responsible for the death of Rebecca Hilderbrand, whose obituary I consider the highlight of my career. I knew it would win the award that I coveted. Please know that I accept complete responsibility for my actions. Had I not known of my own impending death, I would never have resorted to such desperate tactics. I only hope there are a few people who understand. Rebecca Hilderbrand was the most wonderful person that I had ever met. I had great respect for her, not only as an actress, but as a concerned citizen of our community. On the day of the crime, she had invited me to lunch to discuss a program to establish burial funds for indigent, illegal aliens. She wanted me to serve on the committee. It is my hope that we will meet in another world, and she will understand. Please tell Jarvis Hilderbrand that he has my apology. And please destroy my award. Having it means so little. Earning it meant so much.

Bret Lott

Bret Lott is the author most recently of the literary mystery *The Hunt Club*, as well as the best-selling novel and Oprah's Book Club pick *Jewel*, three other novels, two short-story collections, and the memoir *Fathers, Sons and Brothers*. He is writer-in-residence at the College of Charleston.

Though he was born and raised in Southern California, Mr. Lott grew up there in a Southern enclave of transplanted Mississippians. Life at his grandparents' house in Redondo Beach meant pork chops for breakfast, iced tea at every meal, and the requisite stories of family history at every possible chance. Hence he feels perfectly at home in Charleston, where he's lived with his family for the past thirteen years.

Setting out to write a story for this collection, Mr. Lott was "as daunted by the ghosts of the great Southern writers as I have ever and always been." Finally he decided that the best way to wrestle with these ghosts was to try one on for size. Hence, "Rose," his spin at answering Mr. Faulkner's wonderfully haunting classic Southern gothic story, "A Rose for Emily."

Rose

— —for Mr. Faulkner, with all respect.

Once she was dead, there would be more stories. She knew that, knew how the contemptible commoners of this town thrived on what they could say of her, Miss Emily Grierson. This was a festering town, festered with the grand and luxurious nothingness of small lives that lent them the time, plenty of it, to tell themselves and the dark of humid evenings filled with the stagnant decayed nothingness of their own lives tales of her not true, not true, but true because they would tell them to each other, and believe them.

Of course she had killed him. Someday they would know that. But the truth they would never divine. Given all the years of a base and fallen town's life, they could not know the truth: the depth of her love.

She pulled through her hair the engraved sterling brush, black now with tarnish so that his monogram could no longer be read, just as she had each evening since she had given him the comb, this brush, and the other of his toilet articles. Her gift to him that night.

Each night since that night she had brushed her hair before going to bed, hair iron-gray now with the passing of years, the same iron-gray as her father's when he, too, died so very many years before. Even before she had met the man with whom she had lain, the man she had murdered. Each night, as this night, she brushed her hair by light of the lamp's rose shade as calmly and serenely as she had when, once the man she had lain with was dead, she had risen from the evening summer sheets heavy with the depravity of this life, this town, to find upon the seat of her gown, pure pure white, the small red smudge of red that signaled her the pain she had felt in their sanctification was indeed real. Then she had simply gone to the dressing table and seated herself upon the chair, its rich burgundy velvet that night thick and rare in its feel, now this night the chair worn smooth to a slick dull red from the years she had sat here each night since.

How many nights? she wondered. Was it last night, when she had lain with him and killed him? A week ago, a fortnight? Or years, decades?

Now?

They would tell stories of her because of the man, dead all these years, in the bed behind her. He would be found out, she knew, with her own passing when the townspeople would break into her home to find her. They would find his body in the new nightclothes given to him that night upon which she had killed him, him fused into his nightclothes and the bedclothes that had not been changed since that evening a fortnight, decades, moments ago, his flesh no longer flesh but part of the real of this room, as real as the layer of dust on his suit folded neatly over the cane chair at the foot of the bed, on the dresser his tie, his celluloid collar. As real as flesh and bone and love all fused into the sheets, in just the same way lies were fused into the air about this hungry decrepit peasant town filling now, even as she pulled the brush through her hair as every night, with stories about her.

Let them, she thought. Let them all, in the ugly alchemy of the cracker mind, spawn their bastard lies of her. She knew the truth, knew enough truth to fill the grave, enough to land her in the great bald cold hereafter by dint and force of the truth of love and love and love, love past what any of them could imagine. Then, when each of them met the nothing end of their nothing lives, she would be there on the other side of the muddy disconsolate river of death, and they would see her upon the opposite shore, see she'd crossed pristine and glistening and dressed in pure pure white to the cold bald great hereafter. Then each one of the townspeople, the cretins, who had lived upon lies they would tell about her, Miss Emily Grierson, lies savored like a dog savors a bone gnawed to nothing, these crackers would then cry to her for salvation as they themselves tried to cross the disconsolate river, only to find themselves quickly, surely drawn with the ugly weight of their lies of her to the slick silted bottom of the river, their impotent cries to her for salvation and her requisite silence in answer the last reckoning to the truth they would have before their lungs filled with muddy water of the difference between themselves and her that had stood between them their entire living lives: she was of legitimate blood; they were of empty.

They were dogs, she knew, every townsman save perhaps the Negro, her boy all these years, the boy now an old man who came and had come and would come with the market basket every few evenings, who swept the kitchen, and the pantry, the hall and parlor, as well as the room in which she now slept.

She did not sleep in this room, this room only a place she visited each night, first to lie down beside the dead man for a moment as best to recapture in the fleshless smile he held and fleshless arms drawn to his throat as if in embrace the beginning of love she'd encountered that night, and next to brush her hair at the dressing table as she had the night love had in fact begun.

She did not sleep in this room, but in a room far more significant than any of these crackers would ever know, could ever know. She slept in the room off the hall downstairs, the room in which, she had been told by her father, her mother had died in child-birth. She herself had been all of her years the only proof positive her mother had ever lived, no pictures, no portraits, not even a moment of clothing or smell of a single strand of perhaps iron-gray hair of her mother's own any evidence her mother had ever existed, save for the words given to her by her father: *Your mother passed in childbirth, giving me you,* he had said to her only once, the day of her fifth birthday, when only then it had occurred to her to ask. He spoke of it not again, ever. Not even her name.

She'd had the Negro move her father's articles from his bedroom the day after she had killed the man and into the downstairs room, the birthing room and passing room, the furniture as big and ungainly as the new secret she held inside her bedroom, the Negro, young then, wrestling the mattress and headboard and footboard and night table and dresser along the dark wood walls of the upstairs hall and down the staircase and into the room.

And she had the Negro as well keep her larder full, her pantry filled so that she might eat, and eat, both to hide and to nourish, his trips in with the market basket those days daily pilgrimages, so that even he would not know.

The Negro, she had seen in his eyes when he'd deduced the truth of what had occurred that singular night that would and had and did become every night of her life, was without duty to any but her and her father. A boy born to know his own caste, she knew, born like herself into the life before the War that ended the old life and its way of settling with only the bloodshed of birth who one was upon the face of the earth. The Negro was a boy she could—and this was the horrible miracle, after an entire life lived here in this town rent not with the emancipation of the Negro but a town rent, irreparably torn asunder, by the emancipation of the cracker to become the rulers of this hamlet, the aldermen and mayors and exactors of tax of a generation that did not know its place, that had forgotten the precious gift of a time when order had reigned as it ought to reign, in observance of lineage and standing—the horrible miracle was that now and all these many years it had been only the Negro, unblinking servile Tobe, she could trust.

He had seen things, she knew, and had been trustworthy, had been a good Negro who knew not to let eyes meet and who knew not to question purchases made at the druggist's and who knew not to question as well the smell that had blossomed days after a night that would be the night of all nights in her life.

All nights, save for one. A night even the Negro did not know of, a night beyond reckoning of any sort.

Let the town tell its stories. She had stories of her own.

Of the night four weeks and five days after the purchase of the arsenic from the druggist, writ across the package beneath the skull and crossbones the words "For rats" in the druggist's hand himself. By then the smell from her bedroom was blossoming horrid and full and genuine, Miss Emily seated on the cracked leather of the parlor's furniture mornings and evenings and afternoons while she ate, and while she stared at the crayon portrait of her father upon its tarnished gilt easel before the fireplace, her father with his iron-gray hair, his mouth closed tight, eyes bright with bearing.

The eyes of a vigorous man. The eyes of a man of will and power.

The eyes of a man who had driven away any suitor who might have delivered her from his eyes, and hence the eyes of a man who kept from her the love she so desired. Until the man in the bedroom upstairs had arrived upon her front porch a year after her father's death.

While the smell blossomed from the room upstairs—could it have been this afternoon? A lifetime ago?—she spent those days in the parlor bearing the stench in the same way she had bore the temper of her father who had threatened the horsewhip to men who, of a Sunday evening, had made their intentions evident with their appearance at the door of this house, this same squarish house with its balconies and cupolas and spires, still elegant despite the loss of its white paint in blisters popped and peeling back as the man's flesh blistered and popped, left to rot. But the street that had once been the most select of the entire town had grown indigent with itself for all the bearing these new low-slung spireless sheds could hold, sheds that had crept up on her own poised home like the men who had crept up that midnight four weeks and five days after the purchase of the arsenic from the druggist.

She'd spied the men from her window in this room, where she repaired once the day had been spent before her father's portrait, the lamp no longer lit for the dark in which she wanted to sit with her love growing, the man only newly dead then, the smell inside this room a rank blossom too huge and significant and powerless to keep her from staying here in this dark.

Four weeks and five days after the arsenic purchase, the town believing, she knew, the poison was meant for her, her own suicide a kind of expected gift these dullards wanted as a means to give themselves the self-assured nod, to say among themselves, We knew it. We knew she was crazy after having been jilted by the man.

But neither had he been jilted, nor was she crazy. She knew, of course, he'd meant to jilt her, but she'd allowed instead the arsenic for him, spooned that afternoon into the bottom of the lead crystal glass in which she poured out bourbon for him once their consecration had been made that night. She hadn't even risen from their bed, only leaned to the small table beside her, where she had put the glass and decanter in which her father had kept the bourbon all these years, then watched the man smile at her in the kind of smile that betrayed a man's lust sated and his escape begun.

Then his smile twisted into itself, the arsenic quick and swift and blind in its affections, and she had reached to him, taken the glass from him before he

153

might drop it and spoil these sheets, desecrate them with alcohol when they had been so blessed with the beginning of love only moments before, the two still beneath these sheets as all who have loved with a love as deep as she had begun to know ought still to be. Then his eyes cinched shut with the force and grandeur of a poison meting out its purpose whether for rats or for lovers, and his hands went to his throat, his mouth an O of lovely pain, beautiful and thrilling and exquisite pain, his mouth the same mouth only minutes before she had met with her own lips.

She had watched him die, then brushed her hair.

She watched the men down in her yard that night four weeks and five days after the purchase, watched men look furtively to left and right, each slung over his shoulder a sack as if of seed, each man reaching into the bag like a sower and throwing handfuls to the ground beside her house, at the foundation.

Lime. It was lime they were spreading in the ridiculous belief, she imagined, that somewhere on the premises a rat or dog or some such had died, herself too much the crazy woman to know or care to dispel of the dead animal and its offenses.

Here was a story she could tell of them: they were fools, all of them. The smell had come from here, where she sat watching them work as though they might not be detected. She had seen them here, where love had begun, while they tried as best and stupidly to break down love's fiber and being with a handful of lime thrown along the foundation of this house. As if that might kill love.

She relit the rose-shaded lamp then, and seated herself before the window to signal those who would look up at her; she knew who they were, knew why they were here, knew their place. She knew.

One of the elect down there, his hand inside his bag of lime for another handful of lies to spread, turned slowly to her at this window, in this rose-hued light, and then another man came to the first and just as slowly looked up at her in this light as well. The men then moved away from the house, disappeared into the shadows of the locusts that lined the street, the town's elect vanquished as simply and easily as making her presence known, the smell that had drawn them here in the belief they might end it, that sad gift from the man no longer a man but a vessel, a vessel only for love, still just as horrid and full and powerless as it would ever be.

She had sent the signal: *I know who you are, and you know who I am.*

And you cannot kill the love I know.

She could tell the story of her courtship, so very misunderstood by all, a courtship begun with the negation of all possibility of courtship and hence love, driven away by dint and force of fatherhood.

So that when the contract for the paving of the

town's sidewalks was let a year after the death of her father, and the Yankee foreman had knocked on her door of an afternoon to ask smiling after a glass of lemonade, she knew she'd found the sound and shroudless agency of the love she sought. Though he wore a waistcoat and collar and tie, cuffed starched sleeves and herringbone trousers, a straw boater atop his head—every indication of his affluence and enterprise—still his face and hands were tanned for the overseeing of the Negroes hard at work with pick and shovel on the street beyond the shadow of the locusts, the color of his skin betraying the quality of sun-drenched toil his job entailed; the solid line of his shoulders and the way that line traced its own vigor gave her to believe he might be enough to hold on to in order to find what she needed; and the color of his eyes, a green so very near and yet so very distant from the green of her father's—gilt-green, mordant-green—gave her no choice but to see her father, with his horsewhip and temper, there in this Yankee's eyes.

It was then the man winked at her, in that most impudent and improvident blink of an eye something passing from him into her, a cutting shard of possibility, a dagger of prospect, the notion already taking shape in her mind of the agency of love he was to become.

A Yankee. A glorified day laborer. A man so shameless, so arrant as to seek refreshment from a single woman of her bearing, and to wink. Her father would have already made good on his threats with the horsewhip at so vulgar a gesture.

And her father was dead.

There followed the evening visits after his hours in the sun, his arrival at her front door for all this base and common town to see fodder for more and more stories that would give these dullards life with the telling of them. Sunday afternoons the two rode drenched in the same broad daylight that had perverted his skin to the brown it had become, rode in his yellow-wheeled buggy led by twin bays through the streets of town, her chin high, eyes lighting on no one as they circled the streets, the man's black cigar burning in the glorious and putrid way her own father's had evenings at the dining room table, her food when a child the drenched black and acrid taste of the air as she ate it, a little girl growing and growing toward a resolve to find love that would discover its reward in the man she rode beside, a man with skin too tanned and eyes too near her father's green, that resolve to find love eclipsing the impropriety of their affair, and the impropriety of the man himself.

There followed too his proposal, in secret yet there in the parlor in full view of the portrait of her father on its gilt-easel tarnishing even then, a proposal not for marriage, but for fornication, though he'd used the word *love* upon her, his hands touching her in

A Confederacy of Crime

what she knew was a feigned passion, places she had herself only allowed her own hands to touch.

He did not know what love was, she'd known then and knew it now and knew it all along, his impassioned passionless touch proof enough of his ordination as the one by whom she would find love. He touched her, and though she'd allowed herself small protests at his touching there, and there, and there, she'd found in herself no rising passion at all. Only that resolve: to find love.

Then, as she had known they would, like flitting moths drawn to a flame that would in a moment's touch burn them to ash and air, the town revealed its own ill-bred blood in the impropriety of its admonishment, the town's elect, she had no doubts, sending the Baptist preacher to her door.

The preacher—a dull man, a simple man—let himself in past the Negro one afternoon near a year after she and the Yankee had first been seen together, dispatched no doubt to warn her of indiscretions known to all. She found him seated in the dull afternoon light of the parlor, saw him stand dully as she entered, saw him hold his black hat in both dull hands, his dull eyes daring to meet her own and hold hers, as though the cloth of his vocation were enough to have earned the right to let eyes meet.

She'd held her head high, listened what seemed a lifetime to empty nothings spewed from his mouth like the stagnant decay of evenings in which stories were to be told of her and had been told. She stared at him, head held high, until finally the dull man looked down, his eyes broken by her own.

That was when she turned to the door, drew it open, and made threat to him, on her lips a new-found power, a prayer as old and dangerous and full of horrible promise as the oaths she had heard her father make all her years of possible courtship, oath drawn from the Word and in full ordination of the Christ who oversaw them all—*And when he had made a scourge of small cords, he drove them all out of the temple*, she heard herself say, *and the sheep, and the oxen; and poured out the changers' money, and overthrew the tables* and felt the instantaneous black joy of such words and knowledge and being, a joy she knew her father himself must have known with each driving of a suitor from their door of a Sunday evening.

The preacher, dull eyes open wide, bovine in his look of genuine low birth for its surprise and awe and terror all at once, was at once gone, stumbling down the stairs off the front porch of the house that was now hers, and not her father's.

Yet still the town would not recognize its place: next came her cousins from Arkansas, dispatched, she would learn, by the wife of the preacher to spend with her days and nights filled with these harpies' presence speaking to her of Grierson lineage and birth and bearing, when only she knew how close she was to finding love, to knowing it, to letting it grow into itself as she had dreamed it might from the moment the idea of love had been given her, and given only once, words ever in her ear and heart and mind, words drenched with the black acrid air of his cigars, drenched in the threat of the horsewhip, drenched in the eyes of power and vigor staring down to her from his portrait across the vast abyss of empty days between her father's death and the appearance of the Yankee: *Your mother passed in childbirth*, came her father's words across the broad expanse of all her days until then, *giving me you*.

The cousins had only left once she'd agreed to end the indiscretion of seeing the Yankee.

She could tell the dullards of this town the story of the courtship that had landed her where she had wanted to be, in the arms of a man as near to her father and as distant as the farthest star. But they would not understand, neither the courtship nor the truth behind fact.

They could not understand the depth of her love.

A courtship none of them would understand, ending as arranged with the appearance of the Yankee at her kitchen door three days after the cousins had left, the Negro admitting the Yankee in and then disappearing, leaving the man to find her in the parlor, where she awaited, dressed in an evening gown of pure pure white.

Thus began the night that was to be all the nights of her life.

All nights, save for one.

*　　*　　*

She finished now as she did each night with the brush, and turned it over in her hand, scrutinized with her ancient eyes the sterling silver back for the monogram, the tarnish there a kind of black map to the depth of love she had wanted to begin through him, and had begun.

There was the Yankee's monogram, thin lines curled upon themselves like her own ancient fingers curled upon themselves: *HB*.

Homer Barron, his name had been, Homer Barron, she recalled, and smiled at a name lost each day to the memory of her own life's passing only to be found each night in these same and serpentine black lines in black silver and in the fusion of flesh and bedclothes and nightclothes in the bed behind her, this skeleton and its fleshless grin drawn tight in a new and perfect fleshless smile the same each night, every night.

She stood from the chair, placed his brush upon the dresser, and turned, smiled down in answer to the man, this Yankee, whose name even as she turned was already leaving her, as vague as the outline of her head on the pillow beside his own so ravaged and peaceful with his accomplished decay.

Once she was dead, she knew, there would be stories, even more, and they would make of the outline, and perhaps the iron-gray strands of her hair she knew must lie there upon the pillow something larger than it was. Let them, she thought. Let their belief this man and his wiles and her love scorned be the lie they would tell to each other once she was gone. Let them believe she was crazy.

Because there was another story. There was the truth.

She dimmed the rose-shaded lamp as she did each night, and pulled the bedroom door closed behind her, locked it as she did each night with the key she kept on the white ribbon round her neck, then placed a hand to the dark wood of the hall, the feel of the cold walls as close to the feel of a tomb as she might imagine, and then she was at the stairs, descending them one at a time for the age upon her, and for the love she had bore with such regal ease all these years.

The entire world was of empty blood, she knew, only she of legitimate.

Then she was downstairs, and in the hall, all by no more light than a midnight might allow, and now she was at the door to her room, the one in which she slept. The one in which her mother had birthed, and had passed.

Her own room now.

She turned the knob, admitted herself into the room, and saw in the darkness the white of her bed, the black of the dresser, and the round shape above it that was her lamp, this one rose as well but glass, and she struck a match from the holder beside the lamp, lit it, let the room grow with this rose hue, this warm and reckoning light, then knelt to the bed that had been her father's, the bed in which her mother had birthed her, and in which her mother had died.

A bed of love, she believed, not because of what her father and mother had made her, but because of what her mother had given here, the perfect love she herself had joined her mother in knowing now all these years, the perfect gift she had received upon execution of the covenant she had made with herself, a covenant to find love.

Kneeling, she reached as she did each night beneath the bed, reached and reached, reached as if the loosed board beneath the bed might have of its own accord mended itself, might have made itself whole in a kind of horrible miracle she could not predict but believed might have happened each night she reached for it and could not find it, and then she felt the board's edge, the gap between it and the next, and with one curled finger levered the single board up, all this without seeing it for the rote pilgrimage the search had become all these years. She lifted the board, reached beneath it to touch the corner of the cardboard box, then inched her finger along its side to find the ribbon with which the box had been tied a night so very long ago, a night just last night, a night now upon her.

Her fingers took hold the ribbon and box, slipped it up between the boards, and she pulled it to her until here it was, the square dress box at her knees as mottled and decayed with age as her own hands, the white ribbon the color of parchment, passion finally upon her and rising as new and as ancient as the gift inside she had given herself: love. Here was the only passion worth finding, the only passion worth touching. No other passion existed, save for that rising in her as it rose every night since she had placed the gift here, in the mottled and decayed and beribboned dress box she held.

Slowly, carefully she stood, the box in her hands as though it were the crown of life it was, and lay it on the bed, this bed she and her mother shared in their purpose and design as procreators of the line of legitimate blood. Carefully, gently, she set the dress box on the bed as she set it each night, as every night, even as on the night she herself, Miss Emily Grierson, had bore the child, a night spent alone in this bed and pushing, her body fat with the food she had eaten both to nourish this love and to hide its proof from the Negro, herself the one to remove the bloodied bedclothes and burn them in the cellar furnace, the smoke they might produce evidence further to an ignorant town, a fallen world, that she was crazy for burning the furnace that spring morning, as they would tell one another and believe for the telling of it, her fingernails that self-same night she'd burned the bedclothes digging so deeply into the headboard above her they bled with blood the same red as on the seat of her gown the evening she had made this child with the Yankee who might well have been her father for the mordant, gilt-green of his eyes, her silent and extravagant screams at the relentless pressure below only extravagant in the expanse of her mind as she swallowed them down to nothing in bloodred resolve to find what love is, screams made silent by bearing and heritage and a father with eyes so pitiless and cold she did not know nor want to know what the sound of her own voice in rage and blood-filled resolve might sound like.

It was resolve that mattered, the resolve to find love. Not the luxury and pity of a self-indulgent scream.

Gently, slowly, she untied the ribbon as she did each night, slowly, carefully, she lifted free the lid.

There it had been, would be, and was now: the child she had made, nestled inside the gown that had bore the red smudge of red, that red the firstfruit of the child's birth, her beginning of love, though the gown had become the night she had bore the child brilliant with blood, drenched in it, only to become this night as every night she could recall the powerless and caustic brown of old blood.

A baby, withered into the essence of gristle and bone, brown too with blood, its ribs and arms and legs fused into the gown, collapsed into themselves to become the real of the room itself, its skull with its fleshless grin, empty eyes, teeth not yet teeth waiting to form, all here for her to take in and take up as she had each night, and as she would.

Her child. Love. Love so precious she could not, would not allow its presence felt in so fallen a world as the one she now inhabited, a world rent with emancipation into chaos, a world loosed of its reign of history and order and lineage left to wander dully into the void of all time and eternity.

Here was the depth of love the contemptible commoners of this town could not know: the burden of a family's history in a vulgar world that would shrug history aside, history settled as it was that night and this and those to come always and only with the bloodshed of birth.

She lifted the baby in its once-white nest as she did each night, weightless always in her arms as though history were not the crushing weight it always was, held it close this last moment before she would return the baby to its place hidden from the indigence of this town, her baby's dignity—the whole of her class's history—retained with the secret of its presence kept.

Rose, she whispered now, the name she had given the child the moment after its advent and the moment before its death, that single stranded moment between both when, mouth open in its only inhale and set to scream, the baby ready to hear herself for the first time upon the face of this world, Miss Emily Grierson strangled her, set her free for the great cold bald hereafter ahead of her, so that as the child made her way across the muddy disconsolate river of death she would have a name, and so a history: *Rose*, she whispered again.

Rose. Her mother's name, she believed then and now and on to the end of all belief, the end of all time, the end of a history placed squarely on the backs of those worthy enough to bear it, those with the resolve to bear it.

Rose. Her mother's name, she believed, though she had never heard it spoken, never knew a name existed.

Michael Malone

Eight novels and novellas to his credit, as well as nonfiction books, television plays, screenplays, head writer for ABC's *One Life to Live,* essays, critical articles and reviews, Michael Malone is an amazingly versatile talent. His story "Red Clay" captured the Edgar for Best Short Story in 1997.

Amazon.com describes Mr. Malone's novel *Handling Sin* like this: "Defrocked priest Raleigh Whittier Hayes runs off to New Orleans to save his three-hundred-pound neighbor from the law and is rescued by renegade nuns, confronts the Marines, delivers a child, and has a confrontation with the KKK." Which, taking nothing away from Mr. Malone, sounds about right for a day in the life of New Orleans.

In "Maniac Loose" this North Carolina native takes on Painton, Alabama, which, while not quite as colorful as The Big Easy, has its own claim to magnolia-tinged infamy in Lucy Rhoads and her nemesis, that hussy Amorette Strumlander.

Maniac Loose

Holding a yellow smiley-face coffee mug, Lucy Rhoads sat in her dead husband's bathrobe and looked at two photographs. She had just made a discovery about her recently deceased spouse that surprised her. Prewitt Rhoads—a booster of domestic sanguinity, whose mind was a map of cheerful clichés out of which his thoughts never wandered, whose monogamy she had no more doubted than his optimism—her spouse Prewitt Rhoads (dead three weeks ago of a sudden heart attack) had for years lived a secret life of sexual deceit with a widow two blocks away in the pretty subdivision of Painton, Alabama, where he had insisted on their living for reasons Lucy only now understood. This was the same man who had brought her home Mylar balloons proclaiming, "I Love You," and white cuddly Valentine bears making the same claims, and an endless series of these smiley-face coffee mugs—all from the gifts, cards and party supplies shop he owned in Annie Sullivan Mall and called "The Fun House." This was the same man who had disparaged her slightest criticism of the human condition, who had continually urged her, "Lucy, can't you stop turning over rocks just to look at all the bugs crawling underneath them?"

Well, now Lucy had tripped over a boulder of a

rock, to see in the exposed mud below, her own Prewitt Rhoads scurrying around in lustful circles with their widowed neighbor Amorette Strumlander, Lucy's mediocre Gardenia Club bridge partner for more than fifteen years; Amorette Strumlander who had dated Prewitt long ago at Painton High School, who had never lived anywhere in her life but Painton, Alabama, where perhaps for years she had sat patiently waiting, like the black widow she'd proved herself to be, until Prewitt came back to her. Of course, on his timid travels into the world beyond Painton, Alabama, Amorette's old boyfriend had picked up a wife in Charlotte (Lucy) and two children in Atlanta before returning to his hometown to open The Fun House. But what did Amorette Strumlander care about those encumbrances? Apparently nothing at all.

Lucy poured black coffee into the grimacing cup. Soon Amorette herself would tap her horn in her distinctive pattern, *Honk honk honk* pause *honk honk*, to take Lucy to the Playhouse in nearby Tuscumbia so they could see *The Miracle Worker* together. Lucy was free to go because she had been forced to accept a leave of absence from her job as a town clerk at Painton Municipal Hall in order to recover from her loss. Amorette had insisted on the phone that *The Miracle Worker* would be just the thing to cheer up the grieving Mrs. Rhoads after the sudden loss of her husband to his unexpected heart attack. "I always thought it would be me," said Amorette, who'd boasted of a heart murmur since it had forced her to drop out of Agnes Scott College for Women when she was twenty and kept her from getting a job or doing any housework ever since. Apparently, Lucy noted, the long affair with Prewitt hadn't strained the woman's heart at all.

Lucy wasn't at all interested in seeing *The Miracle Worker*; she had already seen it a number of times, for the Playhouse put it on every summer in Tuscumbia, where the famous blind deaf mute Helen Keller had grown up. The bordering town of Painton had no famous people to boast of in its own long hot languid history, and no exciting events either; not even the Yankees ever came through the hamlet to burn it down, although a contingent of Confederate women (including an ancestor of Amorette's) was waiting to shoot them if they did. A typical little Deep South community, Painton had run off its Indians, brought in its slaves, made its money on cotton, and then after the War between the States, gone to sleep for a hundred years except for a few little irritable spasms of wakefulness over the decades to burn a cross or (on the other side) to send a student to march with Martin Luther King, or to campaign against anything that might destroy the American Way of Life.

In its long history, Painton could claim only three modest celebrities: There was Amorette Strumlander's twice-great-grandmother who'd threatened to shoot the Yankees if they ever showed up; she'd been a maid of honor at Jefferson Davis's wedding and had attended his inauguration as President of the Confederacy in Montgomery. Fifty years later there was a Baptist missionary killed in the Congo either by a hippopotamus or by hepatitis; it was impossible for his relatives to make out his wife's handwriting on the note she'd sent from Africa. And thirty years ago there was a linebacker in an Alabama Rose Bowl victory who'd played an entire quarter with a broken collarbone.

But of course none of these celebrities could hold a candle to Helen Keller, as even Amorette admitted—proud as she was of her ancestral acquaintance of Jefferson Davis. Indeed no one loved the Helen Keller story as told by *The Miracle Worker* more than she. "You can never ever get too much of a good thing, Lucy, especially in your time of need," Mrs. Strumlander had wheedled when she'd called to pester Lucy into going to the play today. *"The Miracle Worker* shows how we can triumph over the dark days even if we're blind, deaf and dumb, poor little thing."

Although at the very moment that her honey-voiced neighbor had phoned, Lucy Rhoads was squeezing in her fist the key to her husband's secret box of adulterous love letters from the deceptive Amorette, she had replied only, "All right, come on over, Amorette, because I'm having a real dark day here today."

Still Lucy wasn't getting ready. She was drinking black coffee in her dead husband's robe, and looking at the photos she'd found in the box. She was listening to the radio tell her to stay off the streets of Painton today because there was a chance that the streets weren't safe. In general, the town of Painton didn't like to admit to problems; the motto on the billboard at the town limits proclaimed in red, white and blue letters, "THERE'S NO PAIN IN PAINTON. THE CHEERFULEST TOWN IN ALABAMA." There was always a patrol car hidden behind this billboard with a radar gun to catch innocent strangers going thirty-six miles an hour and slap huge fines on them. If Deputy Sheriff Hews Puddleston had heard one hapless driver joke, "I thought you said there was no pain in Painton," he'd heard a thousand of them.

The local billboard annoyed Lucy, as did the phrasing of this radio warning; she thought that a town so near the home of Helen Keller had no business suggesting life was "cheerful" or that the streets were ever safe. The reporter on the radio went on to explain rather melodramatically that there was a maniac loose. A young man had gone crazy at Annie Sullivan Mall on the outskirts of Painton and tried to kill his wife. Right now, live on the radio, this man was shooting out the windows of a florist shop in the mall, and the reporter was outside in the atrium hiding behind a cart selling crystals and pewter dwarves. No one was stopping the man because he had a 9mm automatic assault weapon with him, and he had yelled out the window that he had no problem using it. The reporter had shouted at him, "No problem," and urged the police to hurry up. The reporter happened to be there broadcasting live at the mall because it was the Painton Merchants Super Savers Summertime Sale for the Benefit of the Painton Panthers High School football team, 1992 State Semi-Finalists, and he'd been sent to cover it. But a maniac trying to kill his wife was naturally a bigger story, and the reporter was naturally very excited.

Lucy turned on her police scanner as she searched around for an old pack of the cigarettes Prewitt had always been hiding so she wouldn't realize he'd gone back to smoking again despite his high cholesterol. He'd never hidden them very well, not nearly as well as his sexual escapades, and she'd constantly come across crumpled packs that he'd lost track of. Lucy had never smoked herself, and had little patience with the members of the Gardenia Club's endless conversation about when they'd quit, how they'd quit or why they'd quit. But today Lucy decided to start. Why not? Why play by the rules when what did it get you? Lighting the match, she sucked in the smoke deeply; it set her whole body into an unpleasant spasm of coughing and tingling nerves. She liked the sensation; it matched her mood.

On the police scanner she heard the dispatcher rushing patrol cars to the mall. This maniac fascinated her and she went back to the radio, where the reporter was explaining the situation. Apparently the young man had gone to the mall to shoot his wife because she'd left him for another man. According to the maniac's grievance to the reporter, his wife was still using his credit cards and had been in the midst of a shopping spree at the mall before he caught up with her in the Hank Williams Concourse, where they'd fought over her plan to run off with this other man and stick the maniac with the bills. She'd fled down the concourse to the other man, who owned a florist shop at the east end of the concourse. It was here that the maniac caught up with her again, this time with the gun he'd run back to his sports van to collect. He'd shot them both, but in trying to avoid other customers had managed only to hit the florist in the leg and to pulverize one of his wife's shopping bags. Plaster flying from a black swan with a dracaena plant in its back gouged a hole out of his wife's chin. He'd allowed the other customers to run out of the shop but held the lovers hostage.

Lucy could hear the sirens of the approaching patrol cars even on the radio. But by the time the police ran into the atrium with all their new equipment, the florist was hopping out of his shop on one foot, holding on to his bleeding leg and shouting that the husband had run out the back door. The police ran after him while the reporter gave a running commentary as if it were a radio play. As the florist was wheeled into the ambulance, he told the reporter that the maniac had "totally trashed" his shop "terminator time." He sounded amazingly high-spirited about it. The reporter also interviewed the wife as she was brought out in angry hysterics with a bandage on her chin. She said that her husband had lost his mind and had nobody but himself to blame if the police killed him. She was then driven off to the hospital with the florist.

Lucy made herself eat a tuna sandwich, although she never seemed to be hungry anymore. When she finished, the maniac was still on the loose and still in possession of the 9mm gun that he'd bought only a few months earlier at the same mall. News of the failure of the police to capture him was oddly satisfying. Lucy imagined herself running beside this betrayed husband through the streets of Painton, hearing the same hum in their hearts. The radio said that neighbors were taking care of the couple's four-year-old triplets, Greer, Gerry and Griffin, who hadn't been told that their father had turned into a maniac in Annie Sullivan Mall. The couple's neighbors on Fairy Dell Drive were shocked; such a nice man, they said, a good provider and a family man. "I'dah never thought Jimmy'd do something like this in a million years, and you ask anybody else in Painton, they'll tell you the same," protested his sister, who'd driven to the mall to plead with her brother to come out of the florist shop, but who had arrived too late.

The reporter was obliged temporarily to return the station to its Mellow Music program, *Songs of Your Life*, playing Les Brown's Band of Renown doing "Life Is Just a Bowl of Cherries." Lucy twisted the dial to OFF. She did not believe that life was a bowl of cherries, and she never had. In her view life was something more along the lines of a barefoot sprint over broken glass. She felt this strongly, although she herself had lived a life so devoid of horror that she might easily have been tricked into thinking life was the bowl of sweet fruit that her husband Prewitt had always insisted it was. The surprised reaction of the Mall Maniac's neighbors and family annoyed her. Why *hadn't* they suspected? But then, why hadn't she suspected Prewitt and Amorette of betraying her? At least the maniac had noticed what was going on around him—that his wife was stockpiling possessions on his credit cards while planning to run off with the florist. Lucy herself had been such an idiot that when years ago she'd wanted to leave Prewitt and start her life over, he'd talked her out of it with all his pieties about commitment and family values and the children's happiness, when at the exact same time, he'd been secretly sleeping with Amorette Strumlander!

Lucy smashed the smiley mug against the lip of the kitchen counter until it broke and her finger was left squeezed around its yellow handle as if she'd hooked a carousel's brass ring. There, that was the last one. She'd broken all the rest this morning and she still felt like screaming. It occurred to her there was no reason why she shouldn't. She didn't have to worry about disturbing her "family" anymore.

It had been twenty-one days now since the death of the perfidious Prewitt. Last Sunday the Rhoads

son and daughter had finally returned to their separate lives in Atlanta, after rushing home to bury their
father and console their mother. These two young
people, whom Prewitt had named Ronny after
Reagan and Julie after Andrews, took after their father, and they thought life was a bowl of cherries too,
or at least a bowl of margaritas. They were affable at
the funeral, chatting to family friends like Amorette
Strumlander about their new jobs and new condo
clusters. They liked Amorette (and had Lucy not dis-
tinctly recalled giving birth to them, she could have
sworn Amorette was their mother, for like her they
both were slyly jejune). Ronny and Julie were happy
with their lifestyles, which they had mimicked from
trendy magazines. These magazines did not explain
things like how to behave at a father's funeral, and
perhaps as a result Ronny and Julie had acted during
the service and at the reception afterward with that
convivial sardonic tolerance for the older generation
that they had displayed at all other types of family
functions. Amorette later told Lucy she thought "the
kids held up wonderfully."

Lucy was not surprised by her children's lack of
instinct for grief. Their father would have behaved
the same way at his funeral had he not been the one
in the casket. "The kids and I are day people," Prewitt had told his wife whenever she mentioned any
of life's little imperfections like wars and earthquakes
and pogroms and such. "You're stuck in the night,
Lucy. That's your problem." It was true. Maybe she

should have grown up in the North, where skies darkened sooner and the earth froze and the landscape turned black and gray, where there wasn't so much Southern sun and heat and light and daytime. For life, in Lucy's judgment, was no daytime affair. Life was stuck in the night; daytime was just the intermission, the waiting between the acts of the real show. When she listened to police calls on the radio scanner, the reports of domestic violence, highway carnage, fire, poison, electrocution, suffocation, maniacs loose in the vicinity of Annie Sullivan Mall always struck her as what life was really about. It suddenly occurred to her that there must have been a police dispatch for Prewitt after she'd phoned 911. She'd found him by the opened refrigerator on the kitchen floor lying beside a broken bowl of barbecued chicken wings. The scanner must have said: Apparent heart attack victim, male, Caucasian, forty-eight.

Prewitt had died without having much noticed that that's what he was doing, just as her day children had driven off with whatever possessions of Prewitt's they wanted (Ronny took his golf clubs and his yellow and pink cashmere V-necks; Julie took his Toyota) without having really noticed that their father was gone for good. If Prewitt had known he'd be dead within hours, presumably he would have destroyed the evidence of his adultery with Amorette Strumlander, since marriage vows and commitment were so important to him. But apparently Prewitt

Rhoads had persisted in thinking life a bowl of im-
perishable plastic cherries to the very last. Appar
ently he had never seen death coming, the specter
leaping up and grinning right in his face, so he had
died as surprised as he could be, eyes wide open,
baffled, asking Lucy, "What's the matter with me?"

Amorette Strumlander had been equally unpre-
pared when she'd heard about Prewitt's sudden demise from their Gardenia Club president Gloria
Peters the next morning. She had run up the lawn
shrieking at Lucy, "I heard it from Gloria Peters at
the nail salon!" as if getting the bad news that way
had made the news worse. Of course, Lucy hadn't
known then that Prewitt and Amorette had been having their long affair; admittedly that fact must have
made the news harder on Amorette. It must have
been tough hearing about her lover's death from Gloria Peters, who had never once invited Amorette to
her dinner parties, where apparently Martha Stewart
recipes were served by a real maid in a uniform. In
fact, that morning after Prewitt's death when Amorette had come running at her, Lucy had actually apologized for not calling her neighbor sooner. And
Amorette had grabbed her and sobbed, "Now we're
both widows!" Lucy naturally thought Amorette was
referring to her own dead husband Charlie
Strumlander, but maybe she had meant her lover
Prewitt.

Honk honk honk pause *honk honk. Honk honk honk*
pause *honk honk.*

Amazingly it was two in the afternoon, and Lucy was still standing in the middle of the kitchen with the yellow coffee mug handle still dangling from her finger. She quickly shoved the photographs she'd found in the bathrobe pocket as Amorette came tapping and whoohooing through the house without waiting to be invited in. She had never waited for Lucy to open the door.

"Lucy? Lucy, oh, why, oh, good Lord, you're not even ready. What are you doing in a robe at this time? Didn't you hear me honking?" Mrs. Strumlander was a petite woman, fluttery as a hungry bird, as she swirled around the table in a summer coat that matched her shoes and her purse. She patted her heart as she was always doing to remind people that she suffered from a murmur. "I have been scared to death with this maniac on the loose! Did you hear about that on the radio?"

Lucy said that yes she had, and that she felt sorry for the young man.

"Sorry for him?! Well, you are the weirdest thing that ever lived! You come on and go get dressed before we're late to the play. I know when you see that poor little blind deaf-and-dumb girl running around the stage spelling out "water," it's going to put your own troubles in perspective for you, like it always does mine."

"You think?" asked Lucy flatly, and walked back through the house into the bedroom she had shared with Prewitt. She was followed by Amorette, who even went so far as to pull dresses from Lucy's closet and make suggestions about which one she ought to wear.

"Lucy," Amorette advised her as she tossed a dress on the bed, "just because this maniac goes out of his mind at the Annie Sullivan Mall, don't you take it as proof the world's gone all wrong, because believe me most people are leading a normal life. If you keep slipping into this negative notion of yours without poor Prewitt to hold you up, you could just slide I don't know where, way deep. Now, how 'bout this nice mustard silk with the beige jacket?"

Lucy put her hand into her dead husband's bathrobe pocket. She touched the photos and squeezed the key to the secret letters into the fleshy pads of her palm. The key opened a green tin box she'd found in a little square room in the basement, a room with pine paneling and a plaid couch that Prewitt considered his special private place and called his "study." He'd gone there happily in the evenings to fix lamps and listen to vinyl big band albums he'd bought at tag sales, to do his homework for his correspondence course in Internet investing in the stock market. And, apparently, he went there to write love letters to Amorette Strumlander. Lucy had never violated the privacy of Prewitt's space. Over the years as she had sat with her black coffee in the unlit kitchen, watching the night outside, she had occasionally fantasized that Prewitt was secretly down in his study bent over a microscope in a search of the origins of life, or down there composing an opera, or plotting ingenious crimes. But she was not surprised when, the day after her children left for Atlanta, she'd unlocked the "study" door and discovered no mysterious test tubes, no ink-splotched sheets of music, no dynamite to blow up Fort Knox.

What she had found there were toy trains and love letters. Apparently Prewitt had devoted all those nights to building a perfect plastic world for a dozen electric trains to pass through. This world rested on a large board eight feet square. All the tiny houses and stores and trees were laid out on the board on plastic earth and AstroTurf. In front of a little house, a tiny dad and mom and boy and girl stood beside the track to watch the train go by. The tiny woman had blonde hair and wore a pink coat, just like Amorette Strumlander.

Lucy found the love letters in a green tin box in a secret drawer built under the board beneath the train depot. There were dozens of letters written on legal pad, on pink flowered notepaper, on the backs of envelopes, hand-delivered letters from Amorette to Prewitt, and even a few drafts of his own letters to her. They were all about love as Prewitt and Amorette had experienced it. There was nothing to suggest to Lucy that passion had flung these adulterers beyond the limits of their ordinary personalities, nothing to suggest *Anna Karenina* or *The English Patient*. No torment, no suicidal gestures. The letters resembled the Valentines Prewitt sold in his gifts, cards and party supplies shop in downtown Painton. Lacy hearts, fat toddlers hugging, fat doves cooing. Amorette had written: "Dearest dear one. Tell Lucy you have to be at The Fun House doing inventory all Sat morn. Charlie leaves for golf at ten. Kisses on the neck." Prewitt had written: "Sweetheart, You looked so [great, stretched out] beautiful yesterday and you're so sweet to me, I couldn't get through life without my sunshine."

Beneath the letters at the bottom of the box, Lucy had found the two Polaroid pictures she now touched in the bathrobe pocket. One showed Amorette in shortie pajamas on Lucy's bed, rubbing a kitten against her cheek. (Lucy recognized the kitten as Sugar, whom Prewitt had brought home for Julie and who, grown into an obese flatulent tabby, had been run over five years ago by a passing car.) The other photograph showed Amorette seated on the hope chest in her own bedroom, naked from the waist up, one hand provocatively held beneath each untanned breast. After looking at the pictures and reading the letters, Lucy had put them back in the box, then turned on Prewitt's electric trains and sped them up faster and faster until finally they'd slung themselves off their tracks and crashed through the plastic villages and farms and plummeted to the floor in a satisfying smashup.

Now, in the bathroom listening to Amorette outside in the bedroom she clearly knew all too well, still rummaging through the closet, Lucy transferred the key and the photos from the bathrobe pocket to her purse. Returning to the bedroom, she asked Amorette, "Do you miss Prewitt much?"

Mrs. Strumlander was on her knees at the closet looking for shoes to go with the dress she'd picked out for Lucy. "Don't we all?" she replied. "But let time handle it, Lucy. Because of my murmur I have always had to live my life one day at a time as the Good Book says, and that's all any of us can do. Let's just hope this crazy man keeps on shooting people he knows and doesn't start in on strangers!" She laughed at her little joke and crawled backward out of the closet with beige pumps in her hand. "Because there are sick individuals just opening fire whenever and wherever they feel like it, and I'd hate for something like that to happen to us in the middle of *The Miracle Worker* tonight. Here, put that dress on."

Lucy put on the dress. "Have you ever been down in Prewitt's study, Amorette?"

"Ummum." The dainty woman shook her head ambiguously, patting her carefully styled blonde hair.

"Would you like to see it now?" Lucy asked her.

Amorette gave her a curious look. "We don't have time to look at Prewitt's study now, honey. We are waaay late already. Not that jacket, it doesn't go at all. Sometimes, Lucy . . . This one. Oh, you look so pretty when you want to."

Lucy followed her dead husband's mistress out to her car. Amorette called to her to come along: "Hop in now, and if you see that mall shooter, duck!" She merrily laughed.

As they drove toward the interstate to Tuscumbia through Painton's flower-edged, unsafe streets, Lucy leaned back in the green velour seat of her neighbor's Toyota (had Amorette and Prewitt gotten a special deal for buying two at once?) and closed her eyes. Amorette babbled on about how someone with no handicaps at all had used the handicapped-parking space at the Winn-Dixie and how this fact as well as the Mall Maniac proved that the South might as well be the North these days. Amorette had taken to locking her doors with dead bolts and might drop dead herself one night from the shock of the strange noises she was hearing after dark and suspected might be burglars or rapists. It was then that Lucy said, "Amorette, when did you and Prewitt start sleeping together?"

The little sedan lurched forward with a jolt. Then it slowed and slowed, almost to a stop. Pink splotched Amorette's cheeks, until they matched the color of her coat, but her nose turned as white as a sheet. "Who told you that?" she finally whispered, her hand on her heart. "Was it Gloria Peters?"

Lucy shrugged. "What difference does it make?"

"It was, wasn't it! It was Gloria Peters. She hates me."

Lucy took one of Prewitt's left-behind hidden cigarettes out of her purse and lit up. "Oh, calm down, nobody told me. I found things."

"What things? Lucy, what are you talking about? You've gotten all mixed up about something—"

Blowing out smoke, Lucy reached in her purse. She thrust in front of the driver the Polaroid picture of her younger self, flash-eyed, cupping her breasts.

Now the car bumped up on the curb, hit a mailbox and stopped.

The two widows sat in the car on a residential avenue where oleander blossoms banked the sidewalks and honeysuckle made the air as sweet as syrup. There was no one around, except a bored teenage girl in a bathing suit who roller bladed back and forth and looked blatantly in the car window each time she passed it.

Lucy kept smoking. "I found all your love letters down in Prewitt's study," she added. "Didn't you two worry that I might?"

With little heaves Amorette shook herself into tears. She pushed her face against the steering wheel, crying and talking at the same time. "Oh, Lucy this is just the worst possible thing. Prewitt was a wonderful man, now, don't start thinking he wasn't. We never meant to hurt you. He knew how much I needed a little bit of attention because Charlie was too wrapped up in the law office to know if I had two eyes or three, much less be sympathetic to my murmur when I couldn't do the things he wanted me to."

"Amorette, I don't care to hear this," said Lucy.

But Amorette went on anyhow. "Prewitt and I

were both so unhappy, and we just needed a little chance to laugh. And then it all just happened without us ever meaning it to. Won't you believe me that we really didn't want you to get yourself hurt."

Lucy, dragging smoke through the cigarette, thought this over. "I just want to know how long?"

"Wuh, what, what?" sobbed her neighbor.

"How long were you screwing my husband? Five years, ten years, till the day Prewitt died?"

"Oh, Lucy, no!" Amorette had sobbed herself into gasping hiccups that made the sound *"eeuck."* "No! *Eeuck. Eeuck.* We never . . . after Charlie died. I just didn't think that would be fair. *Eeuck. Eeuck.*"

"Charlie died a year ago. We've been in Painton fifteen." Lucy squashed her cigarette butt in the unused ashtray. She flashed to an image of the maniac smashing the glass storefronts that looked out on the concourse of the shopping mall. "So, Amorette, I guess I don't know what the goddamn shit 'fair' means to you." She lit another cigarette.

Amorette shrank away, shocked and breathing hard. "Don't you talk that way to me, Lucy Rhoads! I won't listen to that kind of language in my car." Back on moral ground, she flapped her hand frantically at the thick smoke. "And put out that cigarette. You don't smoke."

Lucy stared at her. "I do smoke. I am smoking. Just like you were screwing my husband. You and Prewitt were a couple of lying shits."

Amorette rolled down her window and tried to gulp in air. "All right, if you're going to judge us—"

Lucy snorted with laughter that hurt her throat. "Of course I'm going to judge you."

"Well, then, the truth is . . ." Amorette was now nodding at her like a toy dog with its head on a spring. "The truth is, Lucy, your negativity and being so down on the world the way you are just got to Prewitt sometimes. Sometimes Prewitt just needed somebody to look on the bright side with."

Lucy snorted again. "A shoulder to laugh on."

"I think you're being mean on purpose," whimpered Amorette. "My doctor says I can't afford to get upset like this."

Lucy looked hard into the round brown candy eyes of her old bridge partner. Could the woman indeed be this obtuse? Was she as banal of brain as the tiny plastic mom down on the board waving at Prewitt's electric train? So imbecilic that any action she took would have to be excused? That any action Lucy took would be unforgivable? But as Lucy kept staring at Amorette Strumlander, she saw deep down in the pupils of her neighbor's eyes the tiniest flash of self-satisfaction, a flicker that was quickly hidden behind a tearful blink. It was a smugness as bland and be-nighted as Painton, Alabama's, history.

Lucy suddenly felt a strong desire to do something, and as the feeling surged through her, she imagined the maniac from the mall bounding down this residential street and tossing his gun to her through the car window. It felt as if the butt of the gun hit her stomach with a terrible pain. She wanted to pick up the gun and shoot into the eye of Amorette's smugness. But she didn't have a gun. Besides, what good did the gun do the maniac, who had probably by now been caught by the police? Words popped out of Lucy's mouth before she could stop them. She said, "Amorette, did you know that Prewitt was sleeping with Gloria Peters at the same time he was sleeping with you, and he kept on with her after you two ended things?"

"What?"

"Did you know there were pictures, naked pictures of Gloria Peters locked up in Prewitt's letter box too?"

Mrs. Strumlander turned green, actually apple green, just as Prewitt had turned blue on the ambulance stretcher after his coronary. Amorette had also stopped breathing; when she started up again, she started with a horrible-sounding gasp. "Oh, my God, don't do this, tell me the truth," she wheezed.

Lucy shook her head sadly. "I am telling the truth. You didn't know about Gloria? Well, he tricked us both. And there were some very ugly pictures I found down in the study too, things he'd bought, about pretty sick things being done to naked women. Prewitt had all sorts of magazines and videos down in that study of his. I don't think you even want to hear about what was in those videos." (There were no other pictures, of course, any more than there had been an affair with Gloria Peters. The Polaroid shot of Amorette's cupped breasts was doubtless as decadent an image as Prewitt could conceive. Every sentiment the man ever had could have been taken from one of his Mylar balloons or greeting cards.)

"Please tell me you're lying about Gloria!" begged Amorette. She was green as grass.

Instead Lucy opened the car door and stepped out. "Prewitt said my problem was I couldn't *stop* telling the truth. And this is the truth. I saw naked pictures of Gloria posing just like you'd done and laughing because she was copying your pose. That's what she said in a letter; that he'd shown her the picture of you and she was mimicking it."

"Lucy, stop. I feel sick. Something's wrong. Hand me my purse off the backseat."

Lucy ignored the request. "Actually I read lots of letters Gloria wrote Prewitt making fun of you, Amorette. You know how witty she can be. The two of them really got a laugh out of you."

Unable to breathe, Amorette shrank back deep into the seat of her car, and whispered for Lucy please to call her doctor for her because she felt like something very scary was happening.

"Well, just take it one day at a time," Lucy advised her neighbor. "And look on the bright side."

"Lucy, Lucy, don't leave me!"

But Lucy slammed the door, and began to walk rapidly along beside the oleander hedge. She was pulling off fistfuls of oleander petals as she went, throwing them down on the sidewalk ahead of her. The teenage girl on roller blades came zipping close, eyes and mouth big as her skates carried her within inches of Lucy's red face. She shot by the car quickly and didn't notice that Amorette Strumlander had slumped over onto the front seat.

Lucy walked on, block after block, until the oleander stopped and lawns spread flat to the doorsteps of brick ranch houses with little white columns. A heel on her beige pump came loose and she kicked both shoes off. Then she threw off her jacket. She could feel the maniac on the loose right beside her as she jerked at her dress until she broke the buttons off. She flung the dress to the curb. Seeing her do it, a man ran his power mower over his marigold beds, whirring out pieces of red and orange. Lucy unsnapped her bra and tossed it on the man's close-cropped emerald green grass. She didn't look at him, but she saw him. A boy driving a pizza van swerved toward her, yelling a war whoop out his window. Lucy didn't so much as turn her head but she took off her panty hose and threw it in his direction.

Naked in her panties, carrying her purse, she walked on until the sun had finished with its daytime tricks and night was back. She walked all the way to the outskirts of Helen Keller's hometown.

When the police car pulled up beside her, she could hear the familiar voice of the scanner dispatcher on the radio inside, then a flashlight was shining in her eyes and then Deputy Sheriff Hews

Puddleston was covering her with his jacket. He knew Lucy Rhoads from the Painton Town Hall, where she clerked. "Hey, now," he said. "You can't walk around like this in public, Mrs. Rhoads." He looked at her carefully. "You all right?"

"Not really," Lucy admitted.

"You had something to drink? Some kind of pill maybe?"

"No, Mr. Puddleston, I'm sorry, I've just been so upset about Prewitt, I just, I just . . ."

"Shhh. It's okay," he promised her.

At the police station back in Painton, they were handcuffing a youngish bald man to the orange plastic seats. Lucy shook loose of her escort and went up to him. "Are you the one from the shopping mall?"

The handcuffed man said, "What?"

"Are you the one who shot his wife? Because I know how you feel."

The man tugged with his handcuffed arms at the two cops beside him. "She crazy?" he wanted to know.

"She's just upset. She lost her husband," the desk sergeant explained.

Prewitt's lawyer had Lucy released within an hour. An hour later Amorette Strumlander died in the hospital of the heart defect that Gloria Peters had always sarcastically claimed was only Amorette's trick to get out of cleaning her house.

Three months afterward, Lucy had her hearing for creating a public disturbance by walking naked through the streets of Painton, the cheerfulest town in America. It was in the courtroom across the hall from the trial of the Mall Maniac, so she did finally get to see the young man. He was younger than she'd thought he'd be, ordinary-looking, with sad, puzzled eyes. She smiled at him and he smiled back at her, just for a second, then his head turned to his wife, who by now had filed for divorce. His wife still had the scar on her chin from where the plaster piece of the swan had hit her in the florist shop. The florist sat beside her, holding her hand.

Testifying over his lawyer's protest that he'd tried to kill his wife and her lover but had "just messed it up," the maniac pleaded guilty. So did Lucy. She admitted she was creating as much of a public disturbance as she could. But unlike the maniac's, her sentence was suspended, and afterward the whole charge was erased from the record. Prewitt's lawyer made a convincing case to a judge (who also knew Lucy) that grief at her husband's death, aggravated by the shock of the car accident from which her best friend was to suffer a coronary, had sent poor Mrs. Rhoads wandering down the sidewalk in "a temporarily irrational state of mind." He suggested that she might even have struck her head on the dashboard, that she might not even have been aware of what she was doing when she "disrobed in public." After all, Lucy Rhoads was an upright citizen, a city employee, and a decent woman and if she'd gone momentarily berserk and exposed herself in a nice neighborhood, she'd done it in a state of emotional and physical shock. Prewitt's lawyer promised she'd never do it again. She never did.

A few months later, Lucy went to visit the maniac at the state penitentiary. She brought him a huge box of presents from the going-out-of-business sale at The Fun House. They talked for a while, but conversation wasn't easy, despite the fact that Lucy not only felt they had a great deal in common, but that she could have taught him a lot about getting away with murder.

Margaret Maron

Margaret Maron is the author of sixteen mystery novels and a collection of short stories. Her Deborah Knott series, set in North Carolina, Ms. Maron's home state, has won the Edgar, Anthony, Agatha, and Macavity.

Ms. Maron lives on the family farm where she grew up, near Raleigh. In fact, she says, she lives on the home place, which means she has all the trees and bushes the women of her family planted: her grandmother's gardenia bushes and antique roses, her great-aunt's crepe myrtles, her aunt's lilacs and daffodils.

As for further claims to Southern, Ms. Maron bakes a mean biscuit and never saw a pecan pie she didn't like. She is bemused that her books have been translated into seven languages and wonders what Croatians must make of Deborah Knott's colloquialisms and her down-home family. One such colloquialism, "between a rock and a hard place," describes most aptly the position of the district attorney in Ms. Maron's "The Third Element." Just as gardening, one of her passions, provides an important clue.

The Third Element

"It's all Douglas Woodall's fault," Miss Eula declared as she waved away the plate of homemade cookies Aunt Zell was offering for dessert. "How *could* he be so mean as to prosecute Kyle?"

Aunt Zell passed the plate to me. "Well, Kyle did sort of shoot that Wentworth boy," she said, trying to be fair.

(Which was putting it as tactfully as possible, since Miss Eula's grandson had done a lot more than "sort of" shoot Hux Wentworth. Kyle Benson had actually emptied all nine rounds of a 9mm automatic into Hux's back while Hux lay wounded on the floor.)

"But it was self-defense," Miss Eula insisted, as Kyle himself had insisted ever since it happened last fall. "Are you supposed to let yourself be beaten to a bloody pulp before you can defend yourself? You're a judge, Deborah. Is that really what the law says?"

"Not exactly," I answered, speaking around one of Aunt Zell's lemon crisps. As a district court judge who will never hear a murder case of any sort, I could take the academic view. "You can use force to defend yourself, but the third element of self-defense, the one that says you can use deadly force, means that you have to be afraid for your life. Doug Woodall's saying that once Wentworth was down and wounded, Kyle and Brinley could have escaped without killing him. Their lives were no longer in danger, and Kyle shouldn't have kept shooting."

Actually, considering how many bullet holes they found in Hux Wentworth's back and considering the previous history between those two, Miss Eula's grandson was lucky that our DA hadn't asked the grand jury to hand down an indictment for second-degree murder rather than voluntary manslaughter.

And despite Miss Eula's huffing, Doug had considerately waited till after Kyle graduated from Carolina this past June instead of pushing to calendar the case months earlier.

Now it was July, and the whole Benson clan was camped out in the courtroom while the prosecution and defense went through the tedious and time-consuming process of picking a jury.

Miss Eula is their matriarch, and she's also the oldest living member of Bethel Baptist Church out in the country where Mother and Aunt Zell often visited when they were growing up. Mindful of her advanced age and the thirty-minute drive to and from Dobbs, Aunt Zell had invited Miss Eula to come for lunch every day and then to lie down for a little rest afterward before going back over to the courtroom.

Miss Eula's will is strong, but her body's frail, so she'd made only token demurrals before accepting, although she still blamed Doug Woodall for all the inconvenience. "See if any of us ever contribute to his campaign again," she said darkly.

Poor Doug. He was between a rock and a hard place on this one.

Elections are usually a cakewalk for our district attorney, but this time around, he has serious opposition and he's been accused of going easy on people of substance (which the Bensons are) and of not going after a killer as vigorously when the victim is of a lesser social class (which Hux Wentworth certainly was).

While it's true that Doug doesn't exactly bust his budget when one migrant worker kills another over a bottle of Richard's Wild Irish Rose and then flees the state, he does care when residents get themselves killed, even when that resident is somebody as sorry and no good as Hux Wentworth.

The Wentworths were always a violent family, root and stock. Hux's brother is sitting in State Prison right now for murder, and Hux himself had served a short term up in Raleigh for armed robbery. But he was big and handsome and could turn on a rough sort of charm when he chose to.

Having danced with the devil a time or three myself, I can understand how a nice girl like Brinley Davis could let herself be blindsided by a bad boy "misunderstood" by everyone else. Unfortunately, she had to learn by experience that if you're gonna pick up trash, you're gonna get your hands dirty before you can turn it loose.

The Third Element

Hux Wentworth wasn't a piece of mud to be scraped off the heel of a summer sandal. He was bubble gum, twice as messy, twice as sticky, and when Brinley tried to tell him that she was interested in someone else—Kyle Benson, in this case, Hux's first reaction was to threaten to beat the living-you-know-what out of Kyle. Since Kyle is built like a wiry tennis player and Hux had the bulk of a linebacker, it was lucky that Kyle was back in Chapel Hill by the time Brinley told him this, or it might be Hux standing trial for Kyle's death instead of the other way around.

Actually, if you could believe Brinley and Kyle, that's nearly the way it was.

I had heard their story from Miss Eula. I'd heard it from Sheriff's Deputy Dwight Bryant, who was first detective on the scene. I'd also heard it from just about anybody else who could get me to stand still long enough to speculate about Kyle's guilt or innocence with them, including Portland Brewer, my cousin-by-marriage and Kyle's attorney. At this point, everybody in the whole damn county had heard it. The main acts were not in dispute:

a) Brinley Davis had told Hux Wentworth she didn't want to see him again.

b) Hux Wentworth said he'd kill Kyle Benson and Brinley, too, if she tried to go out with Kyle.

c) At fall break, Brinley stayed home while her parents drove out to the mountains to see the leaves. (Portland's eyebrows had arched slyly when she told me, "Brinley said she'd seen leaves before.") Her parents probably hadn't even cleared the Dobbs town limits before Brinley called Kyle and told him she was nervous about being all alone in that big house. (So okay, little Brinley's not a pure-as-the-driven-snow-princess. Who is, these days?)

d) Brinley and Kyle were snuggled on a couch in the den watching a video when Hux crashed through the French doors.

Literally. Without even trying the knob.

Unfortunately for him, French doors are built more sturdily than he realized, and while he stood there, momentarily dazed and bleeding from a dozen superficial cuts, Brinley and Kyle took off like a pair of terrified rabbits.

According to Dwight, Hux left a trail of blood and glass as he tracked the two through the house, up the broad staircase, along the hall, to the master bedroom, where Brinley remembered that her daddy kept a loaded automatic pistol in the nightstand. She hastily dug it out of the drawer, thrust it into Kyle's hands, then dragged him into her parents' bathroom, locking the door behind them.

That door was even stronger than the French doors, but Hux kicked it open with a mighty roar.

At this point, depending on who's telling it, the tale splits. According to Brinley and Kyle, they were in fear of their lives.

"Shoot, Kyle, shoot!" Brinley screamed, whereupon Kyle Benson emptied the gun, all nine slugs, into Hux Wentworth.

Seven of those slugs hit him in the back—as he was trying to flee, said our district attorney—and it was on the basis of those seven extra shots, two of them fired while Hux was lying facedown on the bathroom tiles, that Kyle had been charged with voluntary manslaughter.

Now it was going to be up to twelve citizens of Colleton County to decide.

"So how did your jury shape up?" I asked Portland when we met for an early supper two evenings later at a local steak and ale place that overlooks the river. With her husband out of town and my guy a hundred miles away, we were both at loose ends.

"Who knows?" She shrugged wearily. Jury selection had finished that morning, and opening arguments had begun that afternoon with nothing more than a lunch break.

Ned O'Donnell, the superior court judge who was hearing this case, runs a tight ship. He is very solicitous of jurors and keeps things moving so they aren't inconvenienced a minute longer than necessary.

Voir dire (questioning prospective jurors) is always tiring, and Portland looked drained as she ticked the results off on her fingers.

"We wound up with five middle-aged white women—schoolteacher, beautician, social worker, file clerk, and day care worker, and one elderly black woman who used to keep house for the governor's great-aunt. Judge O'Donnell offered to let her off because of her age, but she said she wanted to do her civic duty. Two black men—an orderly from the hospital and a retired postal worker, and four white men—two farmers, a Sheetrocker, and a driver for Ferncliff Sausage who has tattoos from his wrists to his shoulders."

"Like Hux Wentworth?" I asked, drizzling a little olive oil over my salad of mixed summer greens.

"Exactly like." Portland nodded. "But he didn't give me any grounds to challenge for cause, and I didn't want to use up my last peremptory challenge in case the next person was worse."

"Maybe he'll scare some of the women enough to let them sympathize with Kyle," I said, offering what comfort I could.

She laughed and took a sip of her beer. "Want to split a steak?"

"Sure," I said. We've been splitting food since grade school.

"Another beer for y'all?" asked the waitress even though our glasses were still more than half full. We shook our heads and she went off with our order.

We spoke of this and that, but Portland kept circling back to Doug Woodall's eloquent opening argument.

"Oh, Doug," I said dismissively. "He has to put on a strong case, but you're not really worried, are you?"

"I don't know, Deborah, and that's a fact. We've got a great expert witness, an ME who can explain those shots in the back—"

"He can?"

"She."

"Uh-oh. Mistake right there," I warned. "A woman disputing the word of a male expert in front of a Colleton County jury?"

"Don't try to teach your grandma how to suck eggs," Portland said smugly. "The state's ME is a woman, too."

She held up her hand to illustrate Wentworth's torso and her expert witness's interpretation of the angles of penetration.

"The first slug hit him in the hand. The next one in the shoulder. The force of the first two bullets spun him around"—she twisted her hand and slowly bent it back—"so that the next seven caught him across the back as he was going down. Kyle didn't shoot him on the floor, it's just that the angle changed as Hux was falling away from them."

"Okay," I conceded, playing devil's advocate, "but Kyle grew up with guns. He knows what one bullet can do. How you going to explain away nine of them?"

"That's what Doug argued."

"And your response?"

"Yes, ladies and gentlemen of the jury, Kyle Benson did indeed grow up with rifles, shotguns and an old-fashioned revolver, *but*"—she paused dramatically—"he'd never fired an automatic before."

Our steak and two plates arrived, and I divided the filet right down the middle while Portland did the same with our single baked potato. We'd forgone the Texas toast and made the waitress take the sour cream and butter back to the kitchen so that neither of us would yield to temptation in the middle of swimsuit season. The steak was grilled just the way we like it—almost crusty black on the outside, bright red on the inside—and that first bite awakened the carnivore that slumbers deep in my taste buds. Much as I adore fruits and vegetables, every once in a while I take a truly sensuous pleasure in red meat.

"Mmmm!" Portland murmured happily, echoing my own enjoyment.

"You ever fire an automatic?" she asked, unable to keep her mind off the case.

I nodded. From my own days as a trial lawyer, I remembered this obsession to keep going over and over the facts.

"Well, then, you know that once you pull on that trigger, it'll keep firing till you release the pressure. The gun's empty almost as soon as you start. And don't forget our ear witnesses."

"Ah, yes, the McCormacks."

I've met them and wasn't particularly taken with either. They're from Connecticut. He's upper management in one of the high-tech corporations over in the Research Triangle. Very fond of the sound of his own voice. She's a listener. Reminds me a little of the way Nancy Reagan used to listen adoringly whenever Ronnie spoke.

The McCormacks live next door to the Davises if you can call houses set squarely in the middle of the acre lots and surrounded by lots of mature trees and shrubbery "next door." The McCormacks planned to host a large brunch on their patio the next morning, so they were outside, making last-minute preparations, wiping down the patio furniture, setting up the extra tables on the edge of the back lawn.

When Kyle and Brinley fled her house that night, they had headed straight for the bright lights of the McCormacks' patio.

"Doug's opening statement kept stressing that there was no way Kyle didn't know that those first two shots hit Hux and put him on the floor," Portland told me. "He's going to try to get McCormack to say that Kyle and Brinley were exaggerating their fear, but he can't get around the fact that McCormack heard all the shots and that he's positive there wasn't a break between them."

She gave me an ironic smile. "Unlike Fred Bissell."

I smiled, too, remembering a client my cousin John Claude had defended last year. Mr. Bissell claimed he shot both his wife and the man she was in bed with in the heat of the moment. Unfortunately, three neighbors swore there was a long pause between the first two shots and the last two—one bullet for the wife, three for her lover. He's currently serving a nineteen-to-thirty—not what Portland had in mind for young Kyle Benson.

"What about Mrs. McCormack?" I asked.

Portland shrugged. "She just echoes what her husband says. And you know how Judge O'Donnell feels about superfluous witnesses who don't bring anything new to the table."

Indeed. Doesn't matter if it's prosecution or defense, Ned never hesitates to apologize to the jury for having their time wasted by either side. Doesn't take much to have a jury turn against you.

"What's really worrying me is the way Doug's harping on that old Little League accident," said Portland. "Trying to make it sound as if Kyle and Hux had such a blood feud going that Kyle took this opportunity to deliberately get rid of a lifelong enemy. Hell! They were kids. Kyle barely remembers it."

"He might not," I said reluctantly, "but from what I hear, Hux Wentworth did."

My nephew Reese had been playing the night it happened and half my family were there to cheer him on. It was his and Hux's last year of Little League and Kyle's first. Kyle was small, but he had an arm and the beginning of a good fastball. His team was so far behind, the coach decided to put him in for a little seasoning, and Kyle was told to go out and pitch as hard as he could.

First up was Hux Wentworth, who had a tendency to crowd the plate. Kyle's first pitch was over Hux's head. His second was dead on the money. It would have been a called strike except that it slammed into Hux's hand gripping the bat directly over the inside corner of the plate. Broke the index and middle fingers of his right hand.

Outraged, Hux had stormed the pitcher's mound. It took both coaches, the umpire and my nephew Reese to stop him, and in the melee, the fingers were so badly hurt that by the time Hux's mother figured her home remedies weren't working and carried him to a doctor, there was irreparable nerve damage.

According to Reese, Hux forever after blamed Kyle for ruining his potential baseball career. The hand still functioned well enough for most things, but Hux could no longer control his slider, his "money pitch," as he called it.

"Did he really have that much potential?" I'd asked Reese back when the shooting occurred last fall and that old Little League story had resurfaced.

"Nah," Reese had said scornfully. "His slider that he kept bitching about? It was an okay pitch, but it was all he had, and I guess it got to seem like more the older we got. It was like, here was Kyle with his rich family, that new car they gave him, finishing college and all, and that pissed Hux big time 'cause he won't be going nowhere. Didn't even finish high school. Like he'd've had all that stuff, too, if Kyle didn't break his fingers? Yeah. Right."

This from my nephew, who barely scraped through high school himself, drives a pickup and seems perfectly content to go on working off my brother's electrician's license for the rest of his life.

"And then when Brinley Davis dumped him, I heard Hux was like, 'He took my slider and now he's taking my girl? I'll cut off his effing balls.' And I guess he would've if Kyle didn't shoot him. They say he had a knife with him that night."

"No knife," Portland said regretfully, when I repeated Reese's words. "And Doug's subpoenaed Brinley has a hostile witness. Going to try to make her admit that she'd told Kyle that Hux was bearing a grudge and that Kyle was taking it seriously."

"Hard to prove a negative," I said, quoting one of our law professors at Carolina.

Even though we're practically the same age, Portland kept her life on track back then and graduated from law school three years ahead of me. Despite the time difference, we'd taken courses from many of the same professors.

"Dr. Gaustaad." She pinched her nose to imitate his distinctive pedantic twang. " 'Never ask a question you don't know the answer to.' "

I pinched my own nose and chanted, " 'Always interview your witnesses at least three times.' "

We were laughing so hard I almost choked on my last swallow of steak. The waitress came by and tried to offer us dessert, but we were good and ordered cups of plain black coffee.

"Did you?" I asked.

"Did I what?" Portland asked, looking wistful as the dessert cart, with its generous portions of bourbon-pecan pie and double chocolate brownies, rolled away from us.

"Interview all your witnesses at least three times?"

"Sure."

"Really?"

"Well, all but Bill McCormack," she admitted. "He's so full of himself. I interviewed him twice and read the transcript of the deposition Doug Woodall's staff took, and he didn't change a word of his story."

"All the same," I said, "if Doug's going to try to show Kyle's state of mind with McCormack's testimony . . ."

With her very short, very curly black hair, Portland always reminds me of Julia Lee's poodle. At the moment, she was looking like a rather worried poodle.

Here in July, it wasn't quite dark outside at this hour, but it would have been pitch-black in October.

"You interviewed him in the daylight, right?" I said.

She nodded.

"Why don't you go back and interview him now, when it's dark? Get him to take you out on the patio, turn on the lights and re-create the scene. Maybe it'll spark just that one detail that'll make a difference."

"On the other hand," Portland said dubiously, "it might spark a detail I don't want to hear."

"Better to hear it tonight than on the witness stand next week," I told her.

Reluctantly, she reached for her cell phone.

"Come with me?"

The McCormack home was just as I'd expected from meeting the owners: pretentiously tasteful fieldstone, modern without being modernistic, landscaped for ostentatious privacy.

"I understand your reasoning," said Bill McCormack after Portland reintroduced us all around, "but I've already told you and the D.A. both what happened that night, and walking through it again isn't going to change anything."

Nevertheless, he led us through the house, into the "great" room, and out a set of sliding glass doors onto a broad flagstone patio. Concealed floodlights washed the area in brilliant light.

While Portland went over the events of that October evening once more with McCormack, I engaged his wife in conversation. She seemed a bit surprised that I wanted to talk to her when her husband was holding forth, but I was curious about an exotic-looking stand of daylilies beside the patio, and it turned out that they were hybrids she had bred herself.

"A hobby of mine," she said shyly. "I'm trying to breed a pure red with the stamina of those old orange ditch lilies but with a longer bloom time."

She flipped another switch to illumine a border of

more lilies at the far edge of the closely clipped grass. "I have sixteen different varieties here. They start blooming in May and go till frost."

"Really?" As a new homeowner still fumbling along with no clear idea of how I wanted my yard to look, I was intrigued by an ever-blooming border that wouldn't take much care.

"Yes, I was so worried when Brinley and her friend came running through it last fall. It was the first year my Alyson Ripley lily had bloomed, and I was afraid they'd trample it to pieces."

"The Davis house is over there?" For some reason, I'd thought it was on the opposite side.

"Beyond the crepe myrtles," said Mrs. McCormack with a nod. "They always lose their leaves early and that's how Brinley saw our lights so easily." She shook her head. "Such a terrible experience. They were so scared they didn't look where they were going. Right through my lilies. And the way they kept looking back over their shoulders, I thought I was going to see a pack of dogs at their heels and my border would be wrecked for sure."

"That's my Frances," McCormack said genially as he and Portland came up behind us. "More worried about a few flowers than a man getting shot next door."

He gestured toward the trees. "But this is the way they came all right. First we heard the shots all bunched together, and then while we were trying to decide if we'd really heard shots, they came running through here, across her flower bed and up to where we were standing on the patio. The girl was screaming blue murder, and he was yelling, 'Call 9-1-1.' You don't have to worry about my story, Ms. Brewer," he said magisterially. "I'm quite sure they weren't acting."

"See?" said Portland when we were back in her car and driving away. "What did I tell you? Daylight, moonlight, his story doesn't change."

I couldn't believe what I was hearing. "You're not still going to call *him* as your witness, are you?"

"I don't have to. Doug'll do it."

"But didn't you hear what Mrs. McCormack said?" I demanded.

"About her flower bed getting trampled?"

"What are the three essential elements of justifiable homicide?" I asked, pinching my nose à la Professor Gaustaad.

She stuck out her tongue but decided to humor me. "First, that the defendant must be free from fault, must not have said or done anything for the purpose of provoking the victim."

"Was Kyle at fault? Did he provoke? No," I said, answering my own rhetorical questions. "He was an invited guest in the Davis home, minding his own business when Hux Wentworth burst through the door. The second element?"

"There must be no convenient mode of escape by retreat or by declining combat," Portland parroted as she put on her turn signal to make a left back to the steak house and my own car. "And he did try to retreat, but Hux followed and broke through a second locked door."

"And the third element, if you please, Ms. Brewer?"

"There must be a present impending peril, either real or apparent, so as to create in the defendant a reasonable belief of existing necessity. Well, that's exactly what Kyle believed, but how do we prove it?" Portland said with exasperation. "How's Mrs. McCormack's lily bed going to convince a jury he really truly believed it?"

"Okay, look," I told her, spelling it out. "Hux Wentworth is built like Man Mountain, right? He crashes through a glass door, like it was paper. He's bleeding all over, yet he barely notices his cuts. He chases them through the house and crashes through the bathroom door without even breaking a sweat. Kyle pulls the trigger on an unfamiliar gun, and as soon as Hux goes down, he and Brinley are out of there. You heard McCormack. They were still trying to figure out what the shots were when those two kids ran into his yard. *And they were looking back over their shoulders.* Why were they looking back, Por?"

"My God," she exclaimed as she pulled into the steak house parking lot and stopped beside my car.

"Did they really think Hux could still be chasing them after all that?"

"Why not?" I said. "He'd come through glass, he'd come through solid oak—In their state of panic, why wouldn't they think he could come through bullets?"

Three days later, I adjourned my own court early so I could hear Portland's closing argument.

"In their state of panic," Portland said, "Why wouldn't they think he could come through bullets, too? You have heard Mrs. McCormick state that when they first stumbled into her yard, only moments after the sound of gunshots died away, they kept glancing back over their shoulders. Why? Would you look back if you knew your attacker was lying dead? No, ladies and gentlemen of the jury. They looked back because they were afraid that Hux Wentworth was still coming after them, and they were terrified that he would catch them."

Doug Woodall made a game attempt to persuade the jury that Kyle and Brinley were playacting, but it didn't work. They were only out long enough to pick a foreman before returning with a not-guilty verdict. Ten minutes max.

Ned O'Donnell thanked the jury and then thanked both sides for an expeditious trial. "Not a single superfluous witness," he said approvingly.

Smugly I waited for Portland to finish hugging Kyle and to come thank me, but as soon as we were alone, she said, "I'm writing Professor Gaustaad to thank him for advising at least three interviews."

"Gaustaad?" I was indignant. "Hey, *I* was the one that made you go back a third time."

"I know." She grinned. "I'm going to thank him for hammering it into your head."

Sarah Shankman

Sarah Shankman is the author of ten novels, seven in the highly acclaimed Samantha Adams comic-mystery series. Atlanta-born, Sam's adventures take her on a tour throughout the South: Tupelo, Mississippi; Hot Springs, Arkansas; Atlanta; New Orleans; and to Atlantic City, where she covers Miss Georgia in the Miss America pageant.

Ms. Shankman, like Julie Smith, whose story follows, was born just south of the Mason-Dixon line in Maryland, but growing up in West Monroe, Louisiana—in the no-dancing, no-drinking, no-fun part of the state—gave her credentials as a "real" Southerner. Though she's lived much of her adult life in either Manhattan or Northern California, with frequent stopovers in Santa Fe, it's Southern voices she hears most clearly when she sits down to her computer. And she's never made any attempt to lose her Southern accent, in writing or in speech.

In "Just in Case," a visit is paid to the small town where Ms. Shankman was raised and where, indeed, her mother kept a Colt revolver beneath the counter of her corner grocery store.

Just in Case

For almost twenty years, as long as she'd had the grocery store, Momma had kept her gun right there on a shelf beneath the cash register. The old Colt revolver, a smaller version of the ones cowboys drew from their hips in the Saturday Westerns, was at the ready, just in case.

"In case of what?" I asked again and again with a child's insistence.

The gun nestled beside a small square cigar box, the repository for each and every silver dollar that came sliding across the smooth wooden counter. When the box was full, Momma and I would, with great ceremony, take it to the bank, where the heavy coins were translated into numbers carefully inscribed in purple ink in my savings book. Both the cigar box and the Colt were off-limits to my small hands—and loaded.

"In case of trouble," Momma said.

Before Daddy and I had come to town, Momma, who was my stepmother actually, had run the tiny corner grocery store in West Cypress, Louisiana—a burg in the northeastern corner of the state—all alone. She'd worked twelve hours every day but Sunday through the bone-hard years of the thirties and early forties. She'd opened for business early and never closed until after dark.

Then Daddy had climbed onto a Greyhound bus in New York City—Momma's letters in his pocket, me, a baby squalling on his hip—and made the long trip south. My own mother dead since I was two weeks old, he was in need of another, and Momma's hands itched for a baby girl. The two of them had reached a tentative understanding via the U.S. mail, and three days after Daddy stepped off that Greyhound into the heart of Dixie, the deal was sealed.

Daddy wasn't great shakes in the store. He was shy. He was a Yankee. He stuttered. But even so, he provided relief for Momma, giving her time to rest a bit when she wasn't looking after me.

They'd quickly fallen into a pattern: she'd open in the mornings, then Daddy would take over for the long middle stretch of the day. Come early evening, she'd close up, maybe keeping the door open a bit later in the summer when the days were longer, selling an after-supper ice-cream cone or two while she caught up on paperwork.

One such evening the summer I was nine found Momma sitting on the high metal stool behind the cash register, toting up bills. Daddy had gone downtown to play dominoes with his cronies. It was getting on toward eight, dusk falling, and the store was dim, but Momma hadn't switched on a light yet, saving the electricity. I was doing some accounting too, emptying the cigar box of my silver dollars, stacking them in tens. Then I asked Momma about the Colt for the millionth-and-first time.

"No, there never has been any trouble. Not yet." She answered slowly, as if she didn't really mean it.

"But there could be?"

Momma shook her head. "You can never be too careful in this world."

At that a cold hand gripped my guts, and I wished I hadn't asked the question. Momma's dark outlook weighed heavily on me. I was an only child. I didn't want to be careful. I didn't want to worry. I slipped out from behind the counter and twirled down the center aisle, then on through the front door, outside, into the world.

I stepped over a couple of crispy red worms that hadn't made it across the burning desert of concrete earlier in the day. Then I looked to the right.

If the trouble were coming, it'd surely be from that direction. Not because it was north—though it was—but because that way lay the quarters. Colored quarters. That's what everybody called the neighborhood that began just on the other side of the drainage ditch that marked our modern property line.

"You have to watch them, the colored," Momma warned. "They'll steal you blind."

Why, I wondered, would people steal if they could just walk in our store without a dime and ask for what they wanted? A box of cornmeal, three yards of checkered gingham, two scoops of strawberry ice cream from the icebox so deep I couldn't reach the bottom. Momma or Daddy would write up the purchases in the credit book with their name penciled on the top, and they'd pay when they could.

"Who stole?" I asked Momma. *"When? What'd they take?"*

Her mouth grew tight. *"Don't dispute my word, Emma. I know what I'm talking about."*

Out on the sidewalk the light grew softer, fading. The kerosene tank, with its sharp smell, made popping noises as it cooled. There was something about this time of day that made me wish I had a sister. Or a brother, an older brother. Someone to play with after all the other kids had gone home to supper. But I didn't, and Momma said I wasn't going to either. This world, she said, was such a terrible place that she didn't want to bring another child into it. That's why she'd wanted me, she said, because I was already here.

What was so terrible about the world, I wondered. Then I made a quick run through the hopscotch grid I'd chalked on the sidewalk in front of the store. One, two, three boxes on a single foot. Both feet for the double box. A fourth single. I was about to twirl myself midair for the last double, the trickiest maneuver of the game, trying not to step on the lines, when I spied two little colored boys lollygagging down the road in my direction.

I'd seen these children countless times before, though I didn't know their names. One boy was near my age, the other a year older. I knew that they lived in the very first house—small, unpainted, sagging porch—on the other side of the drainage ditch. Sometimes when I played with my friends among the blackberry brambles and paths that lined the ditch, I saw the boys, but we never talked. They went to the colored school, and we lived in different worlds on either side of that narrow strip of water.

" 'Scuse me," they said shyly as they passed by me, climbed the step, and slipped inside the store.

I stepped up and watched through the screen door as they headed for the big square red Co-cola box filled with not-quite-freezing water, but cold enough to make my fingers ache when I fished for a soda. Momma left off toting up bills to keep an eye on them.

Would she pull out the Colt and shoot them if they tried to steal something? I wondered. No, surely not. She'd just holler at them. Momma's voice, even when there was no reason to be upset that I could see, always reminded me of a fire bell.

She was still watching the boys who hadn't made their choices yet. She stood and crossed the center aisle, hovering over them. "What do you want?" she asked. "Don't keep that box open all night."

The boys murmured words I couldn't hear, and Momma reached in and fiddled out two wet bottles. One orange NeHi. One Delaware Punch. She didn't mind the icy plunge. Momma was tough. She was always talking about how she'd had to learn to be, growing up on a farm. *Life's no tea party, Emma. The sooner you learn that, the better.* The boys unknotted

224

their coins, twisted into the corner of a handkerchief, and handed them over. Momma counted them, a couple of times, then her eyes followed the boys all the way out the door, past me.

It must be exhausting, I thought, being Momma. Always expecting trouble, ready to jump on it before it jumped on her. Just watching her made me tired—and uneasy too. *Trouble*, her posture said, her fingers scrabbling, poking, never soothing. *Trouble everywhere, just biding its time.*

Like the mahogany-colored water bug with great ugly pincers scuttling across the other end of the step I'd been standing on, peering into the store. I'd seen these bugs stomped flat, their insides, like soft white cheese, revealed. I didn't know which was worse, a live water bug or a squashed one, but I did know I didn't want this one running across my toes, bare in my sandals. I jumped down. You can have the step, Mr. Water Bug.

Then down the street cruised a big green Buick, two-tone, light green and dark, with heavy rounded chrome bumpers, a parade of tiny portholes down its sides. I'd spent many hours out here in front of the store, watching cars, and the Buick was my favorite. When I was grown, I was determined to have one of my own.

I told Momma that, and she shook her head. "Why are you always wanting things that cost so much? You have to learn to save, Emma."

I *was* saving. The bank had piles of silver dollars

I'd handed over. Silver dollars with *my* name on them.

"Hey, girl."

I turned to my left, startled. I hadn't heard anyone coming. But there looking down at me were a pair of blue eyes pale and cool as the ice floating in the Co-cola box. Above them, a hank of long dirty-blond hair. The young man looked to be about the age of Momma's nephew A.J., eighteen, nineteen, somewhere in there. But I'd never seen this young man before.

"What're you doing?" he asked.

"Nothing." I climbed up backward, onto the step again.

"Are you going in the store?"

"In a little while," I said, "when Momma's ready to close up."

"Ooooooooh." He dragged the word out long. "I see, it's your momma's store. And you're out here holding down the fort."

I didn't know exactly what he meant by that, but I knew that he was teasing because of that long *Oh* and the way he grinned. He had a mouthful of long white teeth.

The young man kept right on grinning as lightning bugs began to flirt behind his blue-jeaned legs. He wore a blue-and-white-striped short-sleeved shirt, the bottoms of the sleeves rolled to show large round muscles poised to jump like frogs beneath his freckled skin. There was an air of excitement about this young man. Much like my black-eyed stepcousin, A.J., he made something expand within my chest. Every time I saw A. J., when we went to visit his family's farm, I felt crazy, like I wanted to jump out of the hayloft. I would float for a while, I thought, if I leaped high and wide—and then I'd land in A.J.'s arms.

Now I jumped flat-footed, back down the short step onto the sidewalk. "I'm not holding down any fort or anything else," I said. Then I twirled in a circle as if I were wearing my tap-dancing costume with the silver top and short skirt of scarlet net instead of faded blue shorts and a yellow blouse.

The young man's grin grew wider. "She sells Cocolas, this momma of yours?"

"She sure does," I said, proudly. "Ice cold."

"Then, if you'll excuse me, I think I'll buy me one." He opened the screen, then paused and looked back at me, holding it wide, like a gentleman. "Sure you won't change your mind about coming in?"

I already had.

Momma had switched on the light above the counter, its pull chain hanging down above her head. Dull red and blue coin wrappers were spread out on the smooth wooden countertop before her, the change from the register piled in short silver and copper towers. She'd looked up at the chiming of the brass bell on the door. The single lightbulb reflected off her rimless glasses. "Hey," she said to the young man, "can I help you?"

"Sure can," he said. "This little girl of yours says you sell the coldest Co-colas in the neighborhood."

I hadn't said that, but I was flattered by his exaggeration.

"Well, I don't know about that." Momma smiled at me.

"Mind if I help myself?" The young man reached in the icebox, pulled one out, popped the cap, and sucked half of it down in one greedy swig, his Adam's apple bobbing. He wiped his mouth with the back of his hand. "This sure is a nice place you got yourself here."

Momma and I both craned around the little store. Six hundred square feet jammed with rows of canned goods, a long meat counter, the cold boxes for milk, soft drinks, ice cream. Bolts of fabric. Sacks of flour. A handful of fresh fruits and vegetables in bins in front beneath the two plate-glass windows. SEVENTH STREET GROCERY painted on each in careful gold outlined in black.

"Why, thank you," Momma said.

"I *love* the store," I said.

And why not? It was like having a real playhouse with real people who gave me real money I rang up on the old cash register with its elaborate scrollwork and keys with numbers printed deep into the ivory. I loved sitting on the high metal stool behind the register, where Momma was perched now. I especially loved the glass-topped candy counter at her left hand. Hershey bars with almonds were my favorite. Then there were Necco wafers, the black ones tasting of licorice, Tootsie Pops, Almond Joys.

"I always wanted to have me a store," the young man said, taking a measured sip of Co-cola, slowing down now.

"Oh no, you don't," said Momma. "It's awfully hard work. It might look easy, but it's not."

"I ain't afraid of work."

"Of course not," Momma said. Then, "What do you do?"

We waited for an answer. *Rodeo rider,* I thought. Now that I'd had time for a closer look, he resembled a man I'd seen the summer before holding on for dear life to a bucking bronco.

But the young man didn't say. He cocked his head toward the door in the back of the store, which led to our four-room apartment and asked, "You and the little girl live back there?"

Before Momma could answer, I jumped in. "We do. Me and Momma and my daddy. But Daddy's not here. If you want to see him, you'll have to go downtown to the Trenton Street Bar, where he's playing dominoes."

Momma's hand snaked across the counter and gave me a sharp poke in the shoulder. I turned and stared at her. *What?*

"You don't say." There was the young man's grin again, those crooked white teeth.

"What did you say you do?" Momma asked,

something funny in her voice. A note I'd never heard before.

"Meee-eee?" He drew the word out longer than that *Oh* earlier, longer than you'd think a person could, punctuating it with a laugh.

Then, all in one movement, as if performing a bit of choreography learned in dancing school, the young man swigged the Co-cola dry, slammed the bottle down on the counter a lot harder than was polite, wheeled and kicked the front door shut, then stretched one hand long and locked the bolt.

When he turned back around to face us, that same hand held a shiny pistol.

"What I do mostly is rob banks," he said, his voice gruff now. "Except when the banks are closed, and I need some quick cash, then I lower myself to knocking off little old grocery stores." He laughed, a nervous crazy sound, for just a bit. Then, deadly serious, he said, "I'll shoot you, ma'am if I have to. If you don't empty that cash register into a paper bag."

I couldn't see Momma's face because the moment the man had kicked the door shut, Momma had pushed me to the floor. *Scoot!* she'd hissed, and scoot I had. Now I was on the far side of a row of canned goods—tomatoes, green beans, spinach, creamed corn—crawling like a snake on my belly. I didn't have to see her, however, to know that Momma's mouth was real tight when she said, "If you think I'm going to give up my cash, you're going to have to go ahead and shoot me. I work too hard for my money to be handing it over to you."

I hoped the robber didn't plan on arguing with her. There was no point once Momma's mouth tightened. Forget changing her mind. When Momma got mad, she didn't even blink, her eyes boring into you like her fingers, poking, prying.

Suddenly, the young man remembered me. "Where's that little girl?!" he shouted.

"I don't know," Momma said.

"Don't be smart with me, lady!"

I scootched another foot, two, three, feet dust in my nose, splinters in my elbows. All I needed was about six feet more, and I'd have it. I'd fling myself out that door and run for help. I could do it, I knew I could. I wasn't the tiniest bit scared. Things that went *Boo!* in the night were frightening. Bad dreams. The things that lived under my bed. The thought of all three of us, as Momma often warned, starving to death. But for some reason this dream-boat bronco-rider, bank-robber-turned-corner-grocery desperado didn't frighten me one bit.

Though I was sure as heck *startled* when he fired that shiny pistol. *Kapow!* it went, and I lurched sideways, lifting a foot right off the floor. At the same time, Momma screamed, "Nooooo!"

And then I was spattered with wet. I'm hit! I thought. He's shot through the shelves and got me! I looked down for the blood, only to find something yellow and sticky and . . . sweet. To my left a blue can of Dole's pineapple juice spurted like a nicked aorta.

"Emma!" Momma shrieked, and I scrambled up and ran around the corner of the shelves waving my hands to show her that I was okay.

"Oh, my God!" she screamed again, seeing the wet stain on my shirt.

The desperado whirled, pointing his gun straight at me. Keeping my distance from him, I said, "I'm okay, Momma. It's pineapple juice, not blood."

"Shut up!" he snapped. "You both shut up."

But Momma wouldn't. "I'll give you the money! Don't shoot again! Don't hurt my daughter!"

He was looking back and forth between the two of us. "Get over here," he snarled at me, waggling his gun.

I was about to do as he said when at the corner of my eye, on the other side of the plate glass, there appeared the two little boys who had been in earlier for cold drinks. They'd probably forgotten something, their momma had to send them back to the store.

I don't know what I'm going to do with the two of you. You'd lose your heads if they weren't screwed on. Now, get back over there to Miss Rosalie's before she closes, and bring me my . . .

There was no telling how long they'd been standing there, but their eyes, wide as could be, said that they'd heard the shot. They seemed frozen, wanting ever so bad to run, but unable.

Help, I mouthed, *Help*. Without making a sound. Then I turned back to Momma, to the young man, to his shiny gun.

And to Momma's.

For while the desperado had turned, concentrating on me, she'd reached beneath the counter, run her fingers across my cigar box of silver dollars, and pulled out her Colt. Now she was pointing it straight at the young man with the ice-blue eyes.

"You hurt my daughter," she snapped, "and I'll kill you." Motioning, as she spoke, with her free hand for me to join her behind the counter.

I folded myself into her skirt as if I were three years old rather than a big girl.

"Come on, lady," the young man wheedled. "You don't want to be doing this. Just give me the money, and I'll go."

"I can't do that," Momma said.

He couldn't believe it. "Are you crazy?"

Momma shook her head silently. No. The two of them stood there, locked in a battle of wills and nerves, their guns pointed at each other. Both of them breathing hard like they'd been running a race. I could smell Momma's sweat, metallic, like hot pennies.

"Why don't you just go on?" Momma said to the young man. "Git."

She might have convinced him. I thought I could see him wavering. Until, that is, that last word. With *git* she'd gone one step too far, crossed into the territory of insult.

"Git?" the desperado screamed. "Who the hell do you think you're talking to here? I'm a *man*, you understand? I *had* me a job at a tire company in Jonesboro. Worked ten hours a day. Hot, dirty, nigger work, but I was glad to have it. Had me a little house, a car, a wife. . . ." He shook his head. "Then I got laid off."

"Doesn't mean you can't get another job," said Momma, who'd chopped cotton since she was six, cleaned tables in the cafeteria of the normal school where she'd studied, had worked her whole life through. *Loved* work, truth be told.

"I tried," the young man whined, his mouth turning down at the corners. "There ain't no more jobs in Jonesboro. I come over here, thinking my luck'd be better. But it ain't."

"You have to keep trying," said Momma. "A man can't be just giving up."

"I ain't a quitter! That's what you think?" The young man's face flushed. "That's what my daddy always said, I was a quitter." Then he grinned sourly, a different grin than I'd seen before. "Guess I showed him, didn't I?"

"I wouldn't know about that," said Momma.

I looked back and forth between them as they spoke. It was a strange sight, this conversation they were having from either side of the cash register, with weapons drawn.

"I sure did show that old man," the young man said. "My daddy. Showed him good." Then he made popping sounds with his mouth, like I did with my friends, when we played shoot 'em up. Punctuating each burst with a flick of his silver revolver. "So you see." He leaned closer to Momma then, as if he were a girlfriend about to share a secret. "I don't have nothing to lose."

Then, in the far distance, I could hear the wail of a siren on the warm night air, and my heart jumped. A police car, I thought. The little boys' momma had called the police. The men in blue were riding to our rescue like Roy Rogers, Gene Autry, or my favorite movie cowboy, Tim Holt.

Our desperado heard the siren too. Those blue eyes cut back and forth. "Okay," he said, his voice toughening. "Hand the money over now."

"You make a move, I'll shoot you," Momma said. "Don't think I won't."

The sirens grew louder. Closer. They were just around the corner now.

The desperado couldn't wait a minute longer. I could almost hear his thoughts: *Fish or cut bait.* He gave Momma one long last look, then whirled and ran for it. For a moment I thought he was going to crash right into the plate-glass door, but he paused long enough to unlock the bolt.

Momma and I both leaned forward to watch him go. Once his feet touched the concrete, his limbs stretched long. The bug light made a halo of his blond hair for just a moment. He could outrun the police, I thought. He would. He'd get away.

But then the police car raced right past us down Seventh Street, its red lights whirling. The dark shapes of the officers inside, urgent with the effort of going fast, faster, didn't even give our desperado a glance.

With their passing, he put on the brakes. Stopped. Turned. Looked back in at us, Momma and me, staring out at him. Those icy eyes twinkled as a grin split his face. Then he threw his head back and looked up as if he were thanking the Lord. Lowering his chin once more, he raised his shiny pistol toward his forehead as if in salute. Then turned it and took aim straight at the two of us, Momma and me, standing there, frozen on the other side of the glass.

I imagined the *snick* of the trigger, though I knew I couldn't hear it through the door.

Braced myself for the blow.

And, *kapow*, he fell.

Momma shot him!

Momma shot him?

But wait! She hadn't moved.

Then from out of the darkness behind the desperado—crumpled on the cement now, his dark blood flowing toward the chalked lines of my hopscotch—stepped a black man in khaki work pants and an undershirt that glowed stark white against his skin. A shotgun dangled from the crook of his left arm.

"I didn't see as I had any other choice," he said

to Momma as she and I joined him, the three of us staring down at the young man dying on the sidewalk. "My boys said, 'Call the cops!' I said, 'You know we don't have no phone.' So I came, fast as I could, with my gun."

"Thank you, Joe," Momma said, stepping toward the man, her hand out as if she were going to shake his. But she didn't, not quite. She stopped just before she touched him. "I surely do appreciate it. I really do."

I was amazed that Momma knew this man and his name. I didn't think that I'd ever seen him before. Or if I had, he hadn't registered. But then, the lives of the people who lived on the other side of the drainage ditch, no more than a hundred yards away, were unknown to me. They lived in a totally different universe.

"I wouldn't been surprised," Joe replied, "you shot him yourself. Nawh, it wouldn't have surprised me at all. You one tough woman, Miss Rosalie. We all know that. Running this store all by your lonesome all those years 'fore Mr. Jake come."

Momma didn't get many compliments, which didn't mean she didn't like it when one came her way. She stood tall and looked proud. "I would have, if I'd had to. I told him that. I told him I'd shoot him if he even thought about hurting Emma. Before I'd give him my money either. I work too hard for it to be giving it to any stickup man."

*   *   *

No stickup man ever came Momma's way again. That night was the only brush she ever had with crime, which didn't mean that she didn't continue to be vigilant. Just in case.

Years passed. The Krogers and Piggly Wigglys and changing times had long put corner grocery stores like ours out of business, but still Momma held on to her Colt, even after she had the old store and the apartment behind it demolished and built a little brick ranch house farther back from the street. She kept the Colt in a dresser drawer, spare bullets rattling around every time she opened and closed it.

"Somebody might break into the house," she said. "Someone from the quarters."

It didn't do any good to remind her that the only person who'd ever bothered her over all those years was blue-eyed and blond-haired. Momma knew what she knew.

When I was emptying out the house after her death a few years ago—at eighty-four of a heart attack while she was hoeing in her garden out behind the house—I thought about that Colt. I hadn't run across it, and I wondered when she had gotten rid of it. How? And why?

Still, I gasped a little, surprised, when I spied the old gun lying beneath her bed among a tangle of hoses and dust bunnies and long-discarded magazines. How many years had it been resting there? Was it loaded? Rusted? Might it go off at a jiggle?

I placed a call to the police station, which was no

longer downtown but farther out where younger people were building houses. No hurry, I said, but in no time at all, a bright and shiny officer appeared, young enough to be the grandson of one of those policemen speeding past our store forty years earlier. I knew he wasn't, though, because there'd been no black police officers back then. Polite, but clearly amused at my concern, he pulled the Colt from its resting place.

"Wow!" he said, holding the pistol up. "This is an old one. A beaut."

It was a beauty, as guns go. Darkened with age but just as I remembered it, long-barreled like pistols in the Westerns I'd grown up on. Heavy. A plate on either side of the grip of some pre-plastic material, crosshatched and scrolled with the word COLT inscribed within a graceful oval.

The handsome young policeman flipped the chamber open. "It's loaded, all right. Your momma was ready. Except . . ." He eyed the revolver closely. "Come on outside. Let me show you something."

We stepped out into the backyard. Along our side of the ditch bloomed an eight-foot-high wall of red roses that Momma had planted before I was born. The young policeman in the crisp navy uniform aimed Momma's Colt toward the ditch and pulled the trigger.

Nothing. The barrel revolved and the trigger clicked, but the Colt didn't fire.

He pulled again, to the same result.

No shot, no bullet, no nothing.

"The firing pin's bent," he said. "It's a good thing your momma never needed to shoot anybody 'cause this gun never would of fired in a million years."

I thanked the young policeman kindly, and after he was gone, packed the Colt in a box of mementos I intended to take back to the big city with me. *Just in case*, I told myself, I might ever forget the long-ago night when that good neighbor, a man named Joe, made a giant step across the line that separated our lives from his for just long enough to save us and then stepped back to the other side again.

Julie Smith

Edgar-winner Julie Smith grew up in Savannah but was born in Maryland, which, though south of the Mason-Dixon line, is considered Yankee land by "real" Southerners. After graduating from Ole Miss—that most Southern of all universities—she moved to New Orleans, where she worked for the *Times-Picayune* and then on to San Francisco and the *Chronicle*. It was The Big Easy, however, which, years later, would become the setting for her award-winning Skip Langdon series.

It is Southerners' penchant for euphemism, Ms. Smith says, that in part led her to become a writer. "To impose order on the treacherous and unruly set of sounds that passes in the South for English." A region of the country where, to paraphrase Roy Blount, "You can't go! I absolutely forbid you to go. I will kill myself if you don't stay at least another week," actually means, "Get out of my house right now! You've overstayed your welcome by a month of Sundays."

In Ms. Smith's "Let's Go Knock Over Seaside," which owes more to Elmore Leonard than to Tennessee Williams, Roy and Forest have no trouble saying plain out what they want, at least to each other. Getting it is another matter.

Let's Go Knock Over Seaside

They popped him in Alabama that last time, and the first thing Forest did when he got out—after he got drunk and laid—was call his buddy Roy. Roy was out in East Jesus, Florida this time—Forest didn't quite know where, but it didn't make much of a damn. It was somewhere to go.

Roy was so tickled to hear from him, he hollered at the phone like it was Forest himself. "Hey, ol' buddy. Get your ass on over here. Where the hell are you, anyhow?"

"It's where I ain't that I'm callin' about. I *ain't* in jail in Alabama."

"Hey, congratulations, ol' buddy. Where in Alabama ain't you in jail?"

"Mobile."

"Well, that's almost a straight shot—you ever been to the Redneck Riviera?"

"Not in a while." Not in quite a while—so long he'd forgotten what a depressing hole it was. Panama

City, anyhow. Miles and miles and miles of McDonald's and Burger Kings and Taco Bells before you ever even got to the goddamn beach, and once you were there, the whole damn coast was lined with tattered motels looking like they were built twenty or thirty years ago by fly-by-night contractors using substandard materials and hadn't been touched since.

It was ten o'clock in the morning and here he was drinking beer with Roy, who still looked like the Kennedy kid who went down in his own plane. Forest was your average, everyday peckerwood and knew it—beer belly, blondish hair, a face that got red, and a neck that got sweaty. He liked hanging with Roy; it made women friendlier.

They were slugging down Buds in some pathetic bar done up in that unpainted-wood and fake-fishnet style that was so old and tired you couldn't even remember the time before it came in. It smelled of Pine Sol and spilt beer. The bartender was a girl from Waycross, Georgia, who kept stealing looks at Roy. She didn't hardly look old enough to drink herself, and she had her hair bleached out so bad it looked like albino wire. The place didn't even have a jukebox.

Forest said, "*Man*, this place has gone downhill," meaning not the bar, but the whole damn coast.

Roy got it right away, but he begged to disagree. "Mmm-mmm. No. 'S better. Plenty of casinos now.

243

Ever been to Destin? Pretty as ever. And now we got Seaside."

"Seaside? What the hell's Seaside?"

"Oh, Seaside; man, Seaside! Seaside's like *Alice in Wonderland*. One minute you're mindin' your own business, the next minute you're down a rabbit hole. You follow the yellow brick road and like, there it is . . . the Emerald City. Seaside's like . . ." For once Roy seemed at a loss for words. "It's like a mirage." His face took on a dopey look. "Rancho Mirage-O, man."

"Well, now," Forest said. "I wonder if you could be a little more specific."

But he might as well have saved his breath. Roy was on a roll. "What you got here, I mean *right* here, you got this pitiful, fallin' down, tacky, let's-get-drunk-and-pretend, trailer trash vacation hell. Am I right?"

"You couldn't hardly be *more* right."

"And then five minutes down the road, I swear to the good Lord not a second more, you got the Costa Richa."

"Costa Reach-a?"

"Costa Nouveau Riche-a."

"Well, hell." He made it "hail" the way Roy did. "Well, hail. Let's go knock over Seaside."

"Say wha . . . ?" And then Roy got it. And when he got it, he started laughing, right from the bottom of his spectacularly ripped abdomen, the product of two hours a day at the gym, whether in or out of the joint. And the more he laughed, the more he lost control.

He ended up doing a kind of accidental little dance that caused him to spill his beer, and even the bartender, previously his devoted slave, glanced at him crosswise. "Forest, Forest, Forest," he said. "You ain't never gonna change."

"Well, let's go *see* it, anyhow."

They got up and got in the car, and five minutes later, it really wasn't much more than that, they were in the middle of a picture. It was an illustration from a kid's book, a first- or second-grade reader, the kind where a town is a collection of fairy-tale-looking buildings, not just ordinary houses, in colors you couldn't even find in the giant Crayola box. Where nobody litters or tags or keys; where neon hasn't been invented; where the only rodent is a big-eared one somebody's kid got for Easter.

Forest said, "This ain't a town. This is somethin' somebody made up."

"You got somethin' there, bro'. That's exactly what it is. Somebody made it up and then they built it."

The houses weren't even Florida houses. They were Cape Cod houses and Caribbean bungalows and New Orleans town houses, and they were lavender and raspberry and lemon and lime and mango, like flavors off a yuppie-scum dessert menu. Forest couldn't even imagine how much each one was worth, let alone how much you'd have to be worth to buy one.

It pissed him off. "What a goddamn waste." Even he was surprised by the sound of his voice.

"You hungry?" Roy said. "There's restaurants here. I remember you get kind of mean when you're hungry."

He *was* hungry and he did feel mean. What he was mad about, there was all this money here, but there really wasn't. These fucking architectural gems were beach shacks, for Christ's sake. Who kept their furs and jewels at their beach house? Sure, there might be a little cash, a few TVs, some CD players, but nothing worth risking your ass for. That was what pissed him off. That it was just what Roy had said back at the bar . . . a mirage.

They found a restaurant with a view from here to Uruguay and scanned the menu. "Nothing fried," Roy observed, which meant it had to be unique among Gulf Coast restaurants. The only one of its kind within a hundred miles.

"Yeah," said Forest, "but you could drown in balsamic vinaigrette." They ordered hamburgers.

It was still kind of early for lunch, and they more or less had the place to themselves, so Forest said what was on his mind. "There was this poem I learned in high school . . . 'water water everywhere and not a drop to drink.' You know? Can't be done. To make it worth your while, you'd have to get the whole damn town in one place—like at a funeral, maybe, and then you could hit 'em all. Wham, bam, thank you, ma'am." By now, he was working on his second beer, and he was feeling a little better.

Roy nodded. "I like it. Yeah. We punch some fat polluter's ticket for him, do the world a favor, and the whole place is ours."

"Hey, I got it—I got it, I got it. We don't steal nothin' see? All we do, we look at everybody's papers, see where they all live, and then we go knock over their real pads, where they keep the good stuff."

They'd been getting louder and louder, really starting to enjoy themselves, because they both knew it was a game—they weren't going to do any of this stuff, just have fun talking about it. But now a gang of teenage girls came in, and Forest lowered his voice. "And here's the beauty part. The cops can't even call it a 'rash of burglaries,' they can't even connect 'em, because they're all in different places. What do you think, huh? Is it the crime of the century or what?"

The jailbait all wore cutoffs or khakis and they all had their sleeveless white shirts tied at the waist, and they all had shiny blonde hair and perfect white teeth and Anglo-Saxon features (or else cosmetically straightened noses), and they all looked like the kind of babe you'd meet at a ski lodge, Forest thought, although he'd never actually been to one. The thing was, they were kind of whispering among themselves and sneaking glances at Forest and Roy. Or maybe just at Roy.

One of them caught Forest looking, and smiled and

came over. She leaned over the table at Roy like she was about to start licking his ear, and she said, real polite, "Excuse me, but aren't you *in* something?"

Forest like to died. He was pretty sure Roy was going to go, "Say wha . . . ? again, and he was really going to enjoy it, but Roy surprised the shit out of him. He said, "You mean like *Melrose Place* or *E.R.?*" and smiled like this sort of thing happened all the time.

"You might have seen me on one of those, or maybe *Ally McBeal* but, no, I don't really have a series right now. My friend here, though?" He gestured graciously at Forest. "He's Elvis."

Everyone got a good laugh out of that, even Forest, and when the baby babe had gone back to her friends, he said, "Hey, bro', forget about a funeral. How about a wedding? On the beach, say. I do the town, so to speak, while you're gettin' hitched. Yeah. Yeah, I think it could work." Forest scratched his chin, pretending he was serious.

Roy headed for the car. "When hell freezes over, good buddy. Don't even joke about it."

"Let's walk on the beach."

"You're not exactly dressed for it."

Just because Forest was the only man in Florida dressed in jeans instead of shorts. "So I'll roll up my pants."

Forest had just spent several long months in the company of hard, hostile, foul-smelling, foul-mouthed males, and the closeness of all that sweet, soft, jailbait pussy had given him an urgent need for fresh air.

"Come on, Roy."

Roy came on, but kind of slowly and reluctantly, like a kid following Mama. Forest thought the hell with it, and walked on ahead, just wanting to smell the air and fill his lungs with it. Pretty soon he forgot about Roy altogether and did roll his pants up, waded and everything. He was having a fine old time when Roy called to him. "Hey, Forest."

Forest was really getting off on being alone. He hollered, "What the fuck is it?" before he turned around and saw that Roy had a lady with him. Not one of the Buffy clones, but a real grown-up, nice-looking lady. Not a broad, not a bitch. But definitely a babe.

" 'Scuse *me*," he said, abashed. God*damn* Roy. He probably didn't even want her. The man got laid twice a week whether he needed it or not, for the simple reason that if the urge came upon him, there was always ready ass. So far as Forest could see, he never screwed the same broad twice, mostly didn't bother to get their names, and couldn't care less if he never got laid again. Or maybe it just seemed like that because of the way he had to beat them off with a stick. He didn't even have a listed phone number— too many women calling.

"Hey, Forest, I got somebody I want you to meet. This is—uh—"

"Heidi Van Eyck," the woman said, and she had

a slight accent, kind of British. An aristocrat, this one. Probably owned one of these Easter egg playhouses. Her and her husband.

"Forest, uh . . ." He damn near forgot his name. "McElroy."

She laughed at that, as if it were simply chahming, my deah, to forget your own name. And then she started asking him questions, looking at him with these great big pale blue eyes, set like robins' eggs in a round, beautiful face. He didn't have the least idea how it happened, but all of a sudden he noticed they were sitting at the edge of the water, she in a bathing suit with one of those sarong things wrapped around it, he in his rolled-up damp jeans. And Roy was nowhere in sight. Just wasn't there.

Well, that wasn't unusual for him. He'd probably had his weekly poon quota and anyhow wanted to be nice to Forest. But what about Heidi? She'd started out with Roy and ended up with Forest; she couldn't be happy about it.

And sure enough, here it came, in that funny accent: "Your friend is very handsome."

Forest nodded.

"But a little arrogant, perhaps? I prefer someone more . . . real." And with that, swear to God, she grabbed his knee, just for a minute.

It should have made him feel good, but somehow the idea of *her*, this ice-cream confection, touching *him*, this scruffy old felon, seemed almost obscene to him—seemed to widen rather than close the Grand

250

Canyon yawning between her life and his. Something came over him, he didn't know what, and he just blurted, like some ghetto kid on the TV news, some nine-year-old, "What's it like to be rich?"

Hearing the yearning in his voice, the rawness of which even he, its owner, couldn't miss, he could have died.

"Rich? You think I'm rich?" Her laugh was like the sound a wave makes, ebbing over rocks. "If I ever get there, I'll tell you."

Forest was mortified. He could feel blood and more blood rushing to his face, until he figured his nose was probably tumescent. "Don't you live here?"

"Do you know what an *au pair* is?"

He hadn't the least idea, but he nodded. She pointed vaguely at a strawberry house—or maybe at the one next door. "I came here four years ago to take care of the children. Now I'm a friend of the family, sort of. I visit, I help out; I still baby-sit."

"Baby-sit? You're a *baby-sitter*?"

She nodded. "Yes. From Holland."

Forest was laughing his head off. He was starting to enjoy this. "I thought you were Miss Gotrocks."

"Miss who?"

"Oh, nothin'. Just somethin' we say."

"Would you like to know what it's like to *work* for rich people?"

"Yeah. Sure." Forest started thinking about it. Sleeping under their down comforters. Padding around in their carpeted bathrooms. Might be real nice, he thought.

"I get to look at their things," she said. Almost as if she'd read his mind.

"What things?"

"Oh, their juicers and their cappuccino makers and—you know—their cars—oh, and their clothes. But they mostly wear shorts around here. Except Karla Handshaw, of course. She's what they call tacky—you know that word?"

"Tacky? Yeah, I might have heard it once or twice."

"Karla's from Texas. My friend, Marilyn, the woman I stay with, Marilyn says Karla wears furs in summer, but I think she exaggerates. Karla has amazing jewelry, though."

Forest felt his scalp prickle. "Jewelry?" he said.

"Oh, yes, these enormous rings set with rubies and emeralds *and* diamonds, things the size of drawer knobs. And gold bracelets and the most *ridiculous* sapphire earrings, which she wears with her blue bathing suit."

"That right?" Forest couldn't picture it. "Just little stones stuck in her ears, that what you mean?"

"Oh, no. Dripping! Like waterfalls."

"Must be somethin' to see. Say, is it a bikini or one of those, uh, Miss-America-pageant things?"

"A bikini. Really, the earrings are bigger than *it* is."

Forest about had a fit laughing. "You want to go out sometime?" he asked.

She looked at him quizzically, and for a minute, he thought she was going to refuse. But she surprised him. "How about a picnic? I could make sand-wiches."

"Well, uh, you know, I *am* a little short of cash right now."

"Are you?"

Once again he felt the blood rush to his face. It was embarrassing being broke. What he hated was that she'd seen it—somehow, she'd known.

Roy said, "Man, you better watch out with that foreign pussy. Woman like that, you never know where you stand." They were back in Panama City, having a few more brewskis.

"Roy, shut up. I found our pigeon—woman named Karla Handshaw. Jewelry out the wazoo, beach or no beach."

"Oh, yeah? Miss Dutch Treat tell you about that? We knock over Karla, Heidi never suspects a thing, right?"

But, boy oh boy, did Roy underestimate Heidi. She was two steps ahead of the both of them. She and Forest were eating sandwiches on the beach, roman-tic as hell, when Heidi delicately licked a drip of mayonnaise from her forefinger. "I was thinking about your problem," she said.

"What problem's 'at?"

"Didn't you mention being broke?"

"Yeah." Forest laughed. "Sure wish I had some of Karla Handshaw's jewels. A handful of Karla Handshaw's jewels. Oh, hell, just one or two of 'em wouldn't be *too* bad."

She leaned forward and kissed him. "I wish you did too. You're much nicer than Karla."

There was an edge to what she said, a slight urgency, Forest thought. It alarmed him. "Hey. Karla been mean to you or somethin'?"

"Oh, not really." The slight pink in her cheeks belied it.

He grabbed her arm. "Come on. Tell me."

"It's nothing. Just her personality."

"What?"

She shrugged, surrendering. "She treats me like a servant, that's all."

Forest didn't think so. "Come on. What else?"

"She started a rumor about me. No one believed it, of course. But . . . you know, she's a little overweight . . ."

Forest saw it instantly. "She's mean to you because she's jealous."

She flushed that baby-pink again, and looked down, embarrassed. "I don't know. Maybe she is."

"Well, dammit, let's get back at her!" He spoke at saloon volume, like someone who'd had a few Lone Stars, to make it sound as if he wasn't really serious—testing the waters, kind of.

She laughed that laugh again that sounded like a

wave ebbing over rocks. "Oh, Forest, you're so funny."

"No, I mean it, let's steal her damn jewels."

She looked at him in utter delight, like she couldn't believe anyone could be so crazy, and laughed and laughed and laughed, pure fresh water, crackling its way back to sea over a bed of sun-soaked stones. "I know how to do it! I know exactly how to do it! She told me how herself."

"Well, that was mighty accommodatin' of her. What exactly did she say?"

"She said, 'Who was that hunk I saw you with the other day?' "

Forest was incredulous. "Meanin' me?"

"Meaning Roy."

"Well, don't I feel like an idiot. 'Course she meant Roy." He began to see an advantage. "Roy, yeah. Hey, I got an idea. We get him to plank her and pick up the loot on his way out."

It was like a deep, earthy bubbling, that laugh of hers. He felt soothed when it came out of her, and one thought followed another. "Ah, that's no good. She'd probably miss it right away."

Bubbling again. Waves on rocks. "Oh, Forest, you're as bad as I am. I didn't think anyone was as bad as I am! I'm starting to think you mean it."

"Do *you* mean it?" Thinking she couldn't possibly.

"She told me everything—she told me exactly how to rob her."

He was speechless.

"That jewelry of hers is flashy, but it's ordinary. When I baby-sit for her, oh, and for the other ladies, I look through their catalogues. *You* know—Tiffany's; Nieman Marcus."

"Uh-huh." He wasn't getting it.

"Well, it's all in there. Her stuff."

"Uh-huh, yeah."

"We could have fakes made. I mean, use the pictures and . . ."

"Have *fakes* made. We could have goddam fakes made!" He found the conversation deeply erotic. He launched himself over the cloth they were using for a tablecloth, grabbing for her, but somehow ending up knocking her over, with him on top of her and sand in both their mouths. "Mr. Smooth," he said, embarrassed.

But she put her arms around his neck and looked up at him; even in the dark, he could see the eerie blue of her eyes.

He kissed her gently, his sand mingling with her sand, making mud in their mouths, as earthy and timeless as her laugh. But when he tried to get a hand between her legs, she sat up and shook out her hair, as if she'd just woken up from a nap. "I must go now," she said, and ran, a fairy princess scampering toward a magical town. Just when he was starting to think she was a mirage herself, she turned and hollered, "I'll call you."

She did, too. The next morning she called, and he was so tickled he asked her out for that night. He was just about beside himself to find out if she was serious or not.

And to get into her pants.

Well, she was serious. She brought it up herself. He took her to a place she knew, an Italian joint where they served neither chicken fried steak nor balsamic vinaigrette, and she let him pay for it, which meant she knew he was about to come into some money. By that time, they had more or less made a pact. "Karla told me something else today," she said. "You know what I found in her house? A Houston phone book."

"Uh-huh." He knew it must mean something.

"And I found a place in the Yellow Pages that makes copies of jewelry."

Well, damn. If she had pictures of the jewelry, and she had a place to get copies made, then they had a plan, didn't they? Her voice came from a long way off, maybe out of a tunnel. "Forest, what's wrong?"

He grabbed for her wrist, knocking over a glass of wine in the process. She stared straight into his eyes, and he couldn't tell if she was afraid or not.

"You're serious, ain't you?" he said. And she nodded.

So she *had* to let him pay for dinner. If she hadn't, he would have known she wasn't serious.

They drove to Panama city that night and found Roy and worked out the details. After that, Forest got to kiss her a little, but she drew the line at hooterhands. He kind of liked that about her. She was a lady. He wasn't sure he'd ever met one.

"You mean I got to fuck some fat chick?" Roy had said. "I don't know if I can. My body's a temple of God, man."

"Oh, but think of *her*," Heidi squealed. "It'll be just like church for her." Forest could see Roy was going for it.

Heidi did the hourglass thing with her hands, "Anyway, she's not fat, she's pleasingly plump."

"Hey, ol' son." Roy poked him in the ribs. "What you want to bet she ain't a natural blonde?"

So Forest had to plunk down fifty bucks on a bet he couldn't win, but what the fuck, it was the perfect setup. He didn't have to do a damn thing but sneak in and lift the lovelies.

The next day they got started. Roy went over to Rancho Mirage-o, walked up to Mrs. Karla Handshaw's mango-colored house, rang the bell, and asked her if she needed a handyman.

Heidi started collecting catalogue pictures of Karla's jewelry.

And Forest took over Roy's grunt-work construction job to bankroll the two of them till the moment of truth.

Everything went great. Everything went perfect.

But it was a long damn week. Forest and Heidi had agreed not to see each other for the next week or so, just in case, and that was what was long about it. Forest told Roy he might be falling in love, and

Roy told Forest that was good, that way they could keep the money in the family. So to speak.

Like to scared Forest to death—he figured Roy must be falling for her too, say a thing like that.

He couldn't even see her on the weekend, because that was when she had to go to Houston to order the fakes. But that was okay—he could hang out with Roy. Karla's husband was home, and she didn't want Roy working when he was around. He hadn't planked her yet, but he was planning on it for Monday afternoon.

"I could've," he said. "I'm just makin' her wait. She come up behind me yesterday, while I was under the kitchen sink, fixin' the p-trap, come up, pretends to trip over my feet, falls down on top of me. Falls right in the middle of my back. Hurt! Man, it hurt!

"I couldn't quite decide how to play it, pretend it wasn't nothin' and catch her and kind of roll around with her, or be the wounded soldier in need of nursin'. In the end, there wasn't much choice. Hurt too bad. So 'course she had to rub it, and put ice on it, you know, generally get into the layin' on of hands. You know what I did? I stroked her cheek a little, looked right in her eyes like some Hollywood pansy-ass, but I didn't try to kiss her, didn't feel her up or nothin'. I want her burnin' for me, man! I want her so hot she won't know whether it's me or the second comin' of Rhett Butler."

Forest said, "You goofball. Rhett Butler wasn't a real person."

"That right? Nothin's ever what it seems like, is it?"

Monday night they met at a McDonald's in Panama City—a lot safer than the bar, they figured, and anyway, Forest liked the fries.

Roy was puffed up like one of those color-change lizards—not iguanas, some other kind of thing. "Man, oh, man, is she gone. Man, that babe is *gone*. Hey, we don't even have to rob her—she'd gimme the trinkets just to get me to screw her again. Man, is she *crazy* about me."

"Crazy period, sounds like to me." Forest cut his eyes at Heidi, and she rewarded him with a laugh like the music of the tide ebbing over rocks. He looked at Roy to see what Roy thought, and Roy looked dumbstruck. Shit! Was he going to have to fight his own best friend in the world for this broad?

Just shit.

She said, "Hey, y'all, look at this."

"Y'all? They say y'all in Holland?" Roy was flirting with her, Forest was pretty sure of it.

But she didn't even give him the time of day, just turned to Forest and said, "Want to see what we're getting?" She pulled a file folder out of her backpack, full of fancy store catalogues, with pages turned down and pictures circled in black ink.

There were eight pieces of jewelry in all, and Forest, who was pretty much ready for anything, was flat-out blown away by the price tags.

He passed the pictures on to Roy, which turned

out to be a mistake. "Hey, man! We're talking two hundred grand here!" Roy hollered it, shouted so loud they were dead in the water if the kids behind the counter spoke English. Forest figured they didn't. Nobody in restaurants did anymore.

"Keep it down, man," was all he said. "Let's work out the details."

"Good." Heidi was nodding. "I can pick up the fakes next weekend. What about Monday, a week from today?"

"Hell, yeah, girl. Sooner the better. How long you think Rhett Butler here's gon' hold Miss Scarlett's attention?"

"Don't you worry none, asshole."

That night Heidi let Forest unhook her bra and play with her titties. She had on a sundress kind of thing, and he stuck his hand between her legs and got it damn near up to hell and gone before she brushed it away. It was like high school—kiss on the first date, make out on the second, take her bra off on the third.

Goddam, she turned him on! If that asshole, Roy, would just keep his mitts off.

According to the plan, they didn't see each other again but briefly Sunday night, when Heidi turned over the replicas. In the meantime, that damned Roy saw Karla a *couple* of times. "I gotta keep her happy," he'd say, in that satisfied way of his, and Forest had to give it to him, he did it right. He was giving it to her on the living room floor, just like he said he was gonna be at the time he said he was gonna do it when Forest slipped in the back way. Those fools had turned the AC way the hell up and lit a fire so they could rut like pigs in front of it (and also, so Forest could get in the bedroom where the stuff was.)

Up to a point everything went great—couldn't have been better. Forest found the swag as easy as if Karla had drawn him a map. The fakes turned out to be so exactly perfect Forest wouldn't have known the difference himself. He took the old ones and planted the new ones, easy peasy, nothing to it, all the while reassured by preoccupied sounds from the living room—oh, baby, oh, baby, kind of stuff.

He was just putting the box back in Karla's bureau, with the fakes in it, the real stuff safely in his pocket, when all hell broke loose. Some man hollered "what the hell . . . ?" and it wasn't Roy. Karla screamed, and then yelled, "Ben!," and there were unmistakable scuffling sounds.

Oh, shit, oh, fuck, was about what Forest thought, and he didn't even try to sneak a peek—what he figured, the husband surprised everybody with an unscheduled appearance. But, "hell," he said to himself, "Hail. That doesn't mean all is lost. That is, if I can move fast enough and nobody shoots anybody." He slipped out the back, just like in the original plan, and ran for his car instead of walked, and gunned it, and stopped in front of the Handshaw place, leaning on the horn. And then he did hear a shot, and out tore Roy, naked but holding his clothes over his crotch, shoes God knows where.

Roy jerked open his door. "Drive, my man, drive." Forest checked the house to make sure they weren't being followed, but a good-looking gray-haired dude was just clearing the front steps.

"He said he was gon' hunt me down and kill me if it took him the rest of his life."

Forest said, "What about Heidi?"

"Just drive, bro'. That's what you do best."

He was right. It was. So Forest drove. Drove like the hounds of hell were after him, and didn't stop but once till they got to Miami.

They'd done jobs like this before—well, nothing like this, but there *had* been jobs involving jewelry— and they had a real good man down there.

Forest had the stuff tied up in a bandana, and when he untied it, Mac's face lit up like Christmas. "Wooo. Looks like you boys fell into good company."

Roy and Forest slapped each other's shoulders, grinning like hyenas.

Mac got out his loupe. "Only one thing wrong. This stuff's fake."

Forest said, "Say wha'?"

And Roy jumped to the obvious conclusion. "Goddammit, Forest, you screwed up the switch!"

Forest like to died. "Shit! Fuck! Pussy!" Knowing it had to be true.

"See this little mark here?" Neither one of them

cared, but Mac kept going on about it. "Company in Houston makes these. *Damn* good fakes."

"Forest, I'm gonna kill you, I swear to God . . ."

"The Handshaw Company. Been in business for years."

Only Forest heard him. Roy was still raving. When he had shut up, and gotten the message—Handshaw, as in Karla, was what the message was—he said, "Fuck a duck. Your girlfriend screwed us."

Forest felt his bowels go liquid on him. He guessed it was true, but he couldn't wrap his mind around it. "What for, man? What the hell's this all about?"

"Well, why don't we just call Miss Heidi up and find out?"

And Forest had to admit he didn't have a number for her; in fact, didn't even know where she lived. She'd kind of been a little vague about that.

Well, they got to drinking, the two of them, and when they sobered up about three weeks later, they drove clear back to Seaside to find out what kind of truck had run over them. Karla was their one link to Devil Woman, so Roy bit the bullet and went to find her.

And damned if she didn't fall all over him; flat-out tried to eat him like a box of chocolates, right out on the beach.

Roy was Roy, though. He'd fucked her way more times than his limit, and he wasn't even tempted, far as Forest could see. He said, real hangdog, "Karla, honey, I came to apologize. I hope you fixed things up with your husband."

Karla snorted. "I swear to God I'll never speak to that asshole again for as long as I live. Know what that bastard did to me? Left me for some little foreign slut used to work for the Neilsons." Forest watched as Roy walked off without another word, while she fumbled for a Kleenex.

What they figured, Roy and Forest, Heidi'd been seeing the husband, but he didn't have the balls to leave the missus, so Heidi gave him the little push he needed.

"Knowing all along Karla never had any jewels," Roy ranted, "She just wore whatever she wanted from hubby's store."

"All Heidi had to do was go get matching ones," Forest observed. They were having one or two cocktails, trying to piece things together.

"Yeah—on the weekend. Knowin' he was in Seaside with Karla."

"Human nature sure is fucked up," Forest said. "Using his own company product as bait. How low can you sink, man?"

"Hey, man, how about me? I was the sacrificial lamb out there—no clothes on or nothin'. That asshole could've killed me."

Well, they had a few more cocktails, and damned if Roy didn't hit on the most brilliant plan of his entire life. "Hey, I got it! I got it—I know how to get her back."

Forest thought about it. "Not sure I want her back."

"No man, get revenge. That kind of 'get her back.' All we got to do is tell ol' Ben Handshaw what she did and fuck up her whole life for her. What do you think, man?"

"Wait a minute. I got a better idea. We could blackmail her—just tell her we're *gonna* tell him, collect a little of what's due us."

"Hey, bro', yeah! Let's do it!"

"Okay," said Forest, "Let's do it. First thing tomorrow." But he kind of hoped Roy wouldn't remember. Maybe he did want her back.

Steven Womack

Dead Folks' Blues, the first installment of Steven Womack's best-selling series featuring Nashville P.I. Harry James Denton, won the 1994 Edgar, and each of four following series books has won or been nominated for a major mystery award. Also an assistant professor of screenwriting in Nashville, Mr. Womack has television movie credits for *Proudheart* and *Volcano: Fire on the Mountain.*

"I've watched Nashville grow from a small town in the fifties to a city that buzzes twenty-four hours a day. I've lived in Cleveland, New York City, St. Louis, and New Orleans, and finally came back home, only to discover that it didn't exist anymore. On one hand, this is a really cool place to be. But I can't help but wonder if every city south of the Mason-Dixon line wants to be another Atlanta. . . ."

It's that modern South that Mr. Womack depicts in his redneck comic noir cyber-thriller, "www.deadbitch.com," which has to be the year's best title.

www.deadbitch.com

There are people in this world who just need killing. I mean, some people go through life letting shit happen to them, and others act in such a way as to draw the shit to them. They're the ones that need it.

My wife, Jolene, was one of them. Actually, is . . . She's not dead. Yet.

I wish I could remember the precise moment when I decided to kill Jolene. I think it was about the time Tiny sold me the Amoco station in L.A.—L.A. being Lower Antioch, of course, not the big L.A. out in California. Lower Antioch was that chunk of Antioch—which was itself part of Nashville—south of Blue Hole Road down Antioch Pike as far as the Sam's Wholesale Club, just the other side of Woodbine, which some of the older folks still call Flat Rock. I'd been working there for years—almost twenty of them, in fact—pumping gas, changing oil and batteries and spark plugs, doing any kind of lightweight mechanic shit Tiny needed doing. Then about six months ago, Tiny went to the doctor and found out his blood pressure was something like 800/650 and his cholesterol level was just a few points shy of 750. I'd been wondering what that yellowy-white goop under his skin was and now I knew.

Of course, none of this had anything to do with

Tiny's habit of starting the day with a bag of fried pork rinds crumbled up in yesterday's sausage gravy, washed down with a couple of sixteen-ounce cans of Budweiser and polished off with a pack of unfiltered Camels, all before ten in the morning.

The doctor put the fear of God into Tiny, and he decided to take early retirement. Personally, I'd have waited until I had the heart attack so I could go on disability, but it was his call so I didn't argue with him.

The Amoco station had been in Tiny's family for three generations, but Tiny's only boy, Sonny, was up at Brushy Mountain just starting the ten-to-nineteen he'd got on an armed robbery that went sour. So there wasn't much chance he'd have any immediate interest in or claim on his inheritance. And nobody else wanted the place, even at the price Tiny was asking. It's not exactly prime real estate, being on the downhill side of the railroad tracks between the little Vietnamese tailor shop and Mandy's Tavern, which was where me and Tiny always went after closing the station at six. You know, jam down a few tall cold ones before going home to face the old lady.

Anyway, rumor was the EPA was going to be coming through town the next couple of years making everybody dig up their underground tanks and put in new ones. Whoever bought the station was going to have a hell of an expensive renovation on their hands. Personally, my attitude is screw the EPA; I'll take my chances. They want new tanks put in, let them pay for it. But I didn't tell Tiny that when I offered him ten thousand less for the station than he was asking. He jumped on it immediately, which pissed me off big time because that meant I probably could have knocked off another five.

The bank turned me down on the loan; that little problem I had a few years back was still on my credit report, even though it was Jolene's fault and the judge had cut me loose on it. Personally, I say screw the banks; they only loan you money when you can prove you don't need it anyway.

So Tiny financed the deal, with me paying him off over fifteen years. I gave him my life savings—$2500—as a down payment.

And therein lay the problem. Jolene, you see, had plans for that money. Big plans.

"Damn it, Billy Ray!" she screamed when I told her. "You did *what*?"

I vaguely remember a time when the sound of Jolene's voice didn't make me want to go down to the Humane Shelter, adopt the cutest little puppy dog I could find, and then strangle it on the way home. But that was a long time ago.

"I bought the gas station," I said, my voice low. It didn't do a bit of good to raise your voice to Jolene because she could out-scream anybody this side of the *Jerry Springer Show*.

"*And you give him our life savings?*" she shrieked.

Her voice was so loud I couldn't hear my fishing show.

"Jolene," I said, "I got one nerve left, and you're starting to get on it."

I turned to her as she stood there in the kitchen/dining area of our double-wide with her hands on her hips, locked and loaded in the pissed-off position. I almost laughed. Jolene went to the beauty shop every ten days, just like clockwork. For a week after, she'd wrap her head in toilet paper when she went to bed in an attempt to preserve the do. The last few days before she went in for a tune-up, she just looked like somebody who'd been sleeping in toilet paper. A stray piece was caught on the side of her head, draping over her ear like a wisp of something delicate and lacy.

"*I got one nerve left and y'er gittin' on it,*" she mimicked. I hated it when she did that.

"Baby," she said, her voice shifting gears faster than Jeff Gordon in the Cracker Barrel 500, "I had plans for that money."

I narrowed my eyes. When Jolene adopted that tone of voice, she was up to something.

"What kind of plans?"

She smiled. "Sugar Bear, I was going to buy us a computer."

I reached over and grabbed the remote, then muted my fishing show. This ought to be a good one.

"What'n the hell're you talking about?"

"I saw it on a infomercial last night," she said

brightly. "Make a hunnert thousand a year on the *innernet!*"

"On the *what*?" I asked incredulously.

"On the innernet!"

"Jolene, you can't even spell Internet, let alone get on it. How the hell you going to make a hundred thousand dollars a year with a computer?"

She rolled her lower lip out a fraction of an inch, an attempt at a sexy pout that worked about twenty years ago when she was waiting tables at the Shoney's Big Boy over by the mall. Nowadays, though, it just made her look thick-lipped.

"It's all in that package I ordered," she said, poking the tip of her tongue just past the rolled-out lip. Guess that's supposed to get me all hot and bothered.

"What package?" I asked cautiously.

"It'll be here by second-day air," she said. "It'll have everything in it. All I need to get started. I just have to get a computer, which was what I planned to do with that twenty-five hundred before you went and give it to Tiny."

She turned back to the kitchen, shaking her head. "Damn gas station ain't worth twenty-five hundred," she muttered. "Let alone twenty-five hundred down payment."

I stared at her back, through the thin material of her yellow polyester blouse to the rolls of fat that had appeared above her waistline within six months of the time we got married up in Gatlinburg back in '82. My throat got real dry all of a sudden, and I felt this roiling in my stomach, like something was stirring up whatever it was I ate last.

And then I knew it: Jolene had to die.

Things were mighty cold around the double-wide for a while after that, but about two weeks later, Jolene got her computer and life got back to being as normal as it ever gets around here.

"It's beautiful!" she sighed as I pulled the monitor out of the box, yanking the Styrofoam packing material off. I set it on the kitchen table, and we both stared at it for a moment as if expecting it to come on by itself. She seemed thrilled, but to me it just looked like a damn small TV.

I unpacked the rest of it, set it all up on the kitchen table, then went to gathering up the boxes and packing material to throw out in the Dumpster.

"Wait, Sugar, that's the warranty card," Jolene said, reaching across the table toward me. I stepped back, the card still in my hand, then crumpled it and threw it on the pile.

"Don't fool with no warranty," I said.

She looked at me with this quizzical expression on her face. "Why not?"

"Just don't fool with it."

"All right, Billy Ray, what is it you ain't telling me?"

"Look, Jolene, don't worry about it. I got a deal on it, but there ain't no warranty."

She put her hands on her hips, narrowed her eyes, and gave me a kind of smart-assed sneer.

"How hot is it?" she asked.

"I didn't steal it," I answered.

"If you didn't, who did?"

I took a deep breath and held it for a second, trying to keep from turning red. "Tiny's cousin Buck works the freight dock at the Circuit City over by the mail. He got us a . . . well, an employee discount."

She shook her head, disgusted. "Five-finger discount is more like it," she sighed. "What the hell am I gonna do with you, Billy Ray?"

"You want the damn thing or not?"

She reached down on the table and picked up the owner's manual. "Yeah," she mumbled. "Yeah, I guess so. I just don't know what I'm gonna do with you."

I threw the last of the packing material into the biggest box and hefted it up off the floor.

"You could start by fixing me some dinner," I said.

Jolene tore into that computer like a wild-assed kid into Christmas packages. She set the computer on top of her old sewing machine table in the spare bedroom and nagged the hell out of me until I ran a phone line in there so she could, as she put it, *go own-line to tha' innernet.*

After that, it seemed she was in there twenty-four, seven. I'd try to call her from the gas station, and all I'd ever get was a busy signal. At night, she'd come out to the kitchen, throw some microwaved dinner on a paper plate, then shut herself back in the spare bedroom, which she'd now taken to calling "her office."

It seemed I'd go days at a time without speaking more than a word or two to her; not that I'm complaining, of course. It just seemed kind of odd for her to disappear like that. I had to make my own meals and get my own beer. Wasn't no big deal; I knew where the beer was, and I could boil a hot dog as well as Jolene any day. It was just kind of weird.

Truth was, I appreciated the quiet so much I almost forgot for a while that I'd decided to kill her.

But then it went on for weeks, until it finally started to get to me. I'd get up in the morning, and Jolene'd have the coffee on and ready for me, but I'd have to drink it alone because she'd already be sitting at the computer in her housecoat with toilet paper still wrapped around her head. Sometimes I'd get up in the middle of the night to pee and see light coming out from under the crack of the closed door, and I'd hear the clattering of her fingers tapping the keys. Hell, I didn't even know Jolene could type.

I'd come home for lunch, and she'd still be at the keyboard. "Damn, woman," I said one day. "Don't you ever eat anymore?"

She looked up from the monitor. "Maybe I'm trying to lose weight for you, Billy Ray." Then she looked back down at the computer and was gone.

One afternoon a couple of weeks later, Tiny came

by the station for a visit right at closing time, and we decided to walk over to Mandy's for a couple of beers. It'd been a hot day, and I was glad to get in out of the humidity, even if Mandy's did smell like they'd mopped the floor with a bunch of mildewed towels.

Tiny looked like he'd lost a few pounds, and I noticed he'd switched to filtered cigarettes. Then when we got behind the bar at Mandy's and he ordered a light beer, I knew something was up.

"Yeah," he said, staring down into his beer mug like there was something ugly in it. "Gotta start behaving myself." He lifted the mug up and held it there for a moment. I raised the Budweiser long neck up and tapped his glass.

"Clean living ain't going to kill you, Tiny," I said, toasting him. "You can handle it."

He polished the mug off in one long swallow, then lit a cigarette and motioned for another beer. I sipped my beer slowly; for one thing, I only had a twenty on me and that had to last for beer and smokes the rest of the week. The gas station wasn't doing too well, and cash was a little short. Maybe Jolene's hundred grand a year would start coming in soon.

"So what's going on with the wife and the new computer?" Tiny asked.

"Funny you should say that," I offered. "I was just thinking about her."

Tiny grinned. "She made any money yet?" I'd told

Tiny about Jolene's infomercial and we both got a good laugh out of it.

"Not that I've seen," I said. "Mostly she's just on the goddamn thing day and night. Far as I can tell, she don't even watch her soaps anymore."

Tiny's eyebrows moved a fraction up toward the red-veined, broken, tightly stretched skin of his forehead. "What's she doing?" he asked.

"Hell, I don't know. She types on it all the time."

"You know," Tiny said. "I read a article in *Hustler* about all these horny housewives logging onto the Internet and going to these chat rooms and dirty Web sites."

"Dirty Web sites?" I asked. The bartender, a good ol' boy named One-Eyed Johnny who'd done some time for car theft before he grew up and found Jesus, stepped over to where we sat and leaned against the bar, hiking his hip up onto a wooden stool across from us.

"Hell, yeah," he said, drawing the word *hell* out into about three syllables. He adjusted his eye patch, then crossed his arms and stared at us with his one good eye, which was continually bloodshot even though I never saw him drink a drop. "I read me a article in *Reader's Digest* about summa that shit. You got to be careful with that Internet."

"What the hell's a dirty Web site?" I asked, my curiosity piqued.

"You know," Tiny said. "Porno and shit."

"And them chat rooms are even worse," Johnny offered.

"What'n the hell's a chat room?"

"Well," Johnny explained, "you get on the Internet, and then you type in where you want to go. And when you get there, there's a bunch of other people online who want to go to the same place. And when they get there, they all got like fake names and shit so you can't tell who they really are. And you never know what they look like or where they from. People talk dirty to each other, have what they call 'cybersex.' "

Tiny pointed his index finger at Johnny as if he'd just remembered something important that he couldn't wait to say. "I read you got a bunch of yer homosexuals who go online and pretend to be women, then get all hot and horny with men."

"And some of these women," Johnny said, picking up the thread. "They get online with these men and start talking dirty with 'em, next thing you know they're arranging to meet somewhere at a motel."

"Yep," Tiny said, shaking his head. "You got to be careful with that Internet."

"So let me get this straight," I said, tapping my right index finger on the bar. "You get on the Internet and type in where you want to go. So if I want to see some nekked titties, I just type in 'nekked titties' and there they are?"

One-Eyed Johnny grinned. "Well, it's a little more complicated than that. All these places are on what

you call your World Wide Web, so you've got to
know where on the Web and how to type the ad-
dress. See, like maybe there might be a Web site out
there where you can look at nekked titties. So you'd
type in 'www.nekkedtitties.com.' If that's the name
of the Web site, that is."

"Only a normal woman ain't gonna want to look
at no nekked titties," Tiny added. "A normal woman's going be looking for, like, *www.goodlookingguys
withbigdicksandalotofmoneyandahotcar.com*."

"Jolene better not be doing any of that shit," I said,
tightening my hand around the base of the long neck.
"Or I'm gonna find me a Web site called
'www.deadbitch.com.' "

Tiny and One-Eyed Johnny looked at each other
and started laughing.

"I'm serious as a heart attack here, boys. I catch
her doing that shit, I'll kill her deader'n hell."

Oops, I thought. *Probably shouldn't 'a said that. . . .*

"Don't be talking about killing nobody, Billy Ray,"
One-Eyed Johnny warned. "Not around me anyway.
That ain't God's way."

"Yeah," Tiny added, grinning. "Just slap the dawg
snot out of her. That'll straighten her out."

We ordered more beers and continued our conversation, with Tiny and One-Eyed Johnny continuing
to scare me with tales of the Internet.

"Next thing you know," Tiny said about an hour
later, "she'll be driving off to meet some guy and
leaving yer ass behind."

"That ain't like Jolene," I said, noticing for the first time my words were beginning to slur a bit. I'd only had about six beers. Or was it seven? Hell, must be tired. Maybe I'm just getting old.

"It's like any woman if temptation sets in," Johnny offered as he set another beer on a paper coaster in front of me. "They all the same."

"Not Jolene," I said. "She's different. For one thing, she's too dumb to pull shit like that."

"You can always look for the clues," Tiny said. "There's always clues."

"Like what?" I asked.

Johnny nodded his head as he polished a bar glass with a dingy rag. He had to speak up; some idiot had just punched the volume up on the jukebox. "Like for instance, she suddenly goes out, buys new clothes."

I shrugged. "Jolene ain't a big one for buying clothes. Not unless there's a sale at the Wal-Mart."

"Or changes her hairstyle," Tiny added. "That's a dead giveaway, too."

I thought of Jolene with her head wrapped in toilet paper and grinned. "Naw, ain't gotta worry about that," I said.

"Or loses weight," Johnny interjected. "That's a big one! Woman starts losing weight, a man's gotta ask hisself: *'Who's she losing it for? I been around for years, and she sure as hell ain't losing it for me.'*"

I stared into my reflection on the wall mirror behind the rack of liquor bottles across from us. Suddenly, the room seemed a whole lot quieter.

I stood up, took the twenty out of my billfold, and laid it on the bar.

"Good night boys," I said. "I gotta go home."

Then without saying another word, I turned and walked toward the door. Behind me, I heard Tiny: "What'n the hell's 'a matter with him?"

It was near ten o'clock by the time I walked back to the gas station, got my truck, then drove to the trailer park. Our trailer park's normally pretty quiet; mostly old folks and working people here. Not too many of your Mexicans or your Laotian gang-bangers yet, although they're getting closer by the week. But for now, it's still a nice place to live.

The double-wide was dark as I braked the truck on our short gravel driveway. Normally the lights in the living room would be on, and Jolene'd be watching *M*A*S*H* on channel 58. The kitchen light was off, too. Maybe she's gone to bed.

"Hell," I muttered, "she ain't in bed. She's on the goddamn Internet."

I walked around to the back of the trailer and along the backside. Sure enough, the light to the second bedroom was on. There was just enough of a glow from the window and off the moon for me to sneak along without hitting that pile of used cinder blocks I picked up last year for ten bucks. I tiptoed along the back wall as quietly as I could and eased on up to the window. A tiny crack between the blinds and the window frame was just wide enough for me to see through.

Jolene sat at the sewing machine table, her back to me, tapping away furiously on the keyboard. The light from the monitor made a kind of glow around her head, her bleached-blonde hair all loose and falling down on her shoulders. She looked almost angelic for a moment or two, which surprised me because that's not what Jolene usually looks like.

Then I realized one other thing made her look different: Jolene was wearing a black, slinky kind of lacy nightgown. The material was so filmy I could see the white of her skin through it. I couldn't see below the level of the bed by the window so I couldn't see how long the nightgown was, but I damn sure knew it was new because she hasn't worn anything like that for me in years.

I felt the blood rushing in my head, and my breath seemed to come in short gulps.

"Damn it, Jolene," I whispered. "I been meaning to kill you for weeks now. Tonight just might be the night."

I snaked my way around the other side of the trailer and came up to the front door. I slipped my key in and turned the knob slowly. The trailer floor creaked a lot if you didn't know where to walk; fortunately, this wasn't the first time I was sneaking home later than I'd planned.

I pushed the door open, then stepped onto the sill and took a long step over that place by the front door that was extra loud. I pushed the front door to behind me, then eased along the wall down the hallway to the spare bedroom. The clicking of Jolene's fingers typing stopped for a second, and I thought she'd heard me. I froze, stood as still as I could, and a moment later the typing began again.

My hand seemed cold as I touched the doorknob, and I suddenly couldn't feel the beer anymore. It was like I was stone-cold sober. That bothered me, maybe even scared me a little bit. I figured, though, that the thought of getting ready to commit murder would sober anybody up.

My grip tightened around the knob and I stood there a second holding it still. Jolene never stopped clicking away on those keys. The more I thought of her typing away in that slinky black thing, the madder and more sober I got.

I twisted the knob counterclockwise and then slammed my hip into the door. It flew open with a cracking sound and smashed against the wall. Jolene jumped up out of her chair and nearly fell backward onto the bed.

"Damn you, Billy Ray Warrick!" she screamed, stumbling to keep her footing. "You scared the hell out of me! What're you trying to do, you old fool, give me a heart attack?"

I stared at her for a few moments. The nightgown was floor-length, made like a robe out of a gauzy, thin material that was practically see-through. It was open in the front but tied at the waist with a black satin sash. Her titties pushed against the fabric, and in the dim light, I could see she wasn't wearing any panties.

"Something like that," I whispered.

"What?" she said, standing straight up. She took in a deep breath that forced her titties even tighter against the fabric. She cocked her hands on her hips and glared at me.

"What the hell are you talking about? How many beers you had tonight?" she demanded.

"Not enough," I answered truthfully. I took a step toward her, then turned and looked down at the computer monitor. "Whatcha' doin,' Jolene? You on the Web tonight? You checking out the dirty Web sites? You in a chat room with some hot guy? *Bitch. . . .*"

"Don't speak to me that way, Billy Ray. I've had enough of that." Her voice was low, steady. I couldn't have her talking back to me like that. A man's home is his castle, even if it is a used double-wide with a squeaky subfloor.

"I didn't mean to insult you, Jolene," I said. "Hell, as dumb as you are I oughta compliment you for knowing how to turn the damn thing on."

"You can learn a lot on the Internet," she answered. "I know I have."

"You're learning how to dress better," I said, eyeing her in the nightgown. "I'll give you that much. You play your cards right, I might give you something else tonight, too."

284

Jolene smiled. "What have you got that I could possibly want?"

I grinned back at her. "You might be surprised." We stared at each other for a few moments. Her nipples got erect beneath the sheer, gauzy material, and I suddenly wanted my lips wrapped around them.

"What else you learned on the Internet?" I asked, my voice low.

She motioned to the computer with her head. "Sit down and take a look, Billy Ray. I'm sure you'll be interested."

I turned around. The monitor was filled with cartoon fish swimming across it. "What'n the hell's that?" I said.

"Screen saver," Jolene said. "It comes on when you don't type anything for a while. All you have to do is jiggle the mouse or touch one of the keys. Go on, Sugar Bear. Give it a shot."

I ran my tongue across my lips, which suddenly felt very dry. "I think I got other things on my mind right now."

Jolene smiled sweetly, almost seductively, as she shifted her weight on her feet. She brought her hands to her waist and started to untie the knot on the sash.

"Go on, Sugar Bear, see what your baby's been learning on the Internet," she cooed.

"All right, Jolene," I said, sliding onto the chair while I still faced her. "But then we get down to business, okay?"

"Oh, you're so right, Billy Ray." She undid the

285

knot of the sash, and the belt dropped off her hips, one end in each hand. "We'll get right down to business."

She let go with her left hand and pulled the sash behind her as the robe fell open. Jolene had lost weight, with the folds around her waist smaller and her legs thinner. The triangle of brown hair between her legs was like a frizzy bush, and I wanted to reach out and grab it. To hell with it, I thought, let her wait. Get her good and hot this time.

"You look good, Jolene," I said, knowing she'd welcome the compliment. "I hope you don't lose too much more weight, though. You know what they say, the bigger the cushion . . ."

"The sweeter the pushin'," Jolene said, smiling, as I turned and touched one of the keys.

The swimming fish cartoon disappeared just as I heard a swishing sound behind me. I felt more than saw Jolene moving faster than I'd ever seen her move before, and in a split second there was pressure on my neck, around it, on all sides.

Pressure, incredible pressure . . .

I grabbed at my neck and felt satin: smooth, silky satin that was cool and slick and sexy. I tried to yell at her, but nothing came out except a grunting noise. She was pulling down as well as behind me, and when I tried to stand up, she just relaxed her legs and her weight settled on me, jamming me into the chair, holding me back against it. I felt her titties on the back of my head.

Damn, I thought, this bitch is stronger than she looks. *All right, Jolene, enough playing around here. Let me up and let's go to bed.*

Only nothing came out.

I realized I hadn't taken a breath and tried to, but nothing came in, nothing went out. I felt her weight on me even harder. I lifted my legs to try and push against the desk, and she shoved the chair forward, my legs uselessly scraping the floor.

Okay, this isn't fun anymore, Jolene! Goddamn it, let me up!

Then something happened. I don't know what, but suddenly I was shaking and thrashing around, and all I could feel was her heaviness and this thin, agonizing pressure around my throat. My eyes felt like they were pushing against my eye sockets, and my ears hurt from the pressure. And these little colored sparkles started dancing in the corner of my vision.

Then, down next to my right ear, I felt Jolene's hot breath, and her fevered breathy voice seemed to come from somewhere far away.

"Take a look, Billy Ray," she whispered. "Look, Sugar Bear, see what your baby's been learning on the Internet."

My eyes felt like they were about to pop out. *You crazy bitch, what are you—*

"Go ahead, Sugar Bear, see what Jolene's been learning on the World Wide Web."

I looked over at the monitor as the colored spangles started moving in from my peripheral vision toward the center. They were dancing and sparkling and so pretty, and all of a sudden I felt a sound like running water or wind rushing by, and it was peaceful and sweet.

I strained to focus on the monitor, but I didn't have much left. I'm so tired all of a sudden.

"See Billy Ray?" Jolene's voice rose just above the sound of the wind. "See . . ."

I looked down at the computer monitor and hated it, that stupid little damn thing. My eyes jerked into focus just as the colored glittery lights started to meet in the middle.

A thin white box ran across the top of the screen, and inside the little white box, a row of letters read:

http://www.deadbastard.com